D0238170

Sheila Newberry

Bicycles and Blackberries

ZAFFRE

First published in Great Britain in 2004 by Robert Hale

This paperback edition published in 2016 by

ZAFFRE PUBLISHING
80-81 Wimpole St, London W1G 9RE
www.zaffrebooks.co.uk

Copyright © Sheila Newberry 2004
All rights reserved.
No part of this publication may be reproduced,
stored or transmitted in any form by any means,
electronic, mechanical, photocopying or otherwise, without the
prior written permission of the publisher.

The right of Sheila Newberry to be identified as Author of this
work has been asserted by her in accordance with
the Copyright, Designs and Patents Act, 1988.

This is a work of fiction. Names, places, events and
incidents are either the products of the author's imagination or
used fictitiously. Any resemblance to actual persons, living or dead,
or actual events is purely coincidental.

A CIP catalogue record for this book is available from the British Library.

ISBN: 978-1-785-76161-4

also available as an ebook

1 3 5 7 9 10 8 6 4 2

Typeset by IDSUK (Data Connection) Ltd

Printed and bound by Clays Ltd, St Ives plc

Zaffre Publishing is an imprint of Bonnier Zaffre,
a Bonnier Publishing company
www.bonnierzaffre.co.uk
www.bonnierpublishing.co.uk

For my friend for always, Margaret G, who so enlivened our Salad Days, and 'took me inside the portals of Goodbody's Bank . . .'

RENFREWSHIRE COUNCIL	
198956321	
Bertrams	28/09/2016
	£6.99
JOH	

'The friendly cow all red and white,
I love with all my heart;
She gives me cream with all her might
To eat with apple tart.'

R. L. Stevenson

PART ONE

ONE

'Keep your chin up, Georgia, stand taller than the rest,' Mum repeated for the umpteenth time. 'Then there won't be no chance they'll lose *you*, see.' She straightened her daughter's beret. They'd see Georgia all right, she thought, with that frizzy, flaming hair.

Georgia's round, green eyes were resolutely tearless, but the tip of her nose was a tell-tale pink. Mum tucked a bar of Fry's Chocolate Cream in her pocket. 'Don't eat it all in one go,' she said, giving Georgia a little push. 'Cheers.'

Then she tilted her own chin so Georgia couldn't miss seeing *her*, among the crowd of forlorn, anxiously waving parents on the east-bound platform at Liverpool Street, as the special train steamed grumpily away that morning at the beginning of September 1939.

Georgia, leaning perilously out of the carriage window, indignantly shoved from behind by shorter classmates and admonished by her teacher, spotted her mother's old brown felt hat with the bent orange feather and made out the strident shout: 'Love you, Georgia! Don't get no smuts in your eye! Be good!'

'Why can't I stay here with you?' she'd pleaded earlier, through a mouthful of bread and dripping. Her mother sawed fiercely at yesterday's loaf, spreading marge and slapping on cheese, dipping her knife in the sweet-pickle jar, making sandwiches for the journey. In Georgia's view, all this rush and worry was perplexing.

Her reply still echoed in Georgia's head: 'Because you *can't*. See all them sandbags piling up in the streets? There's going to be a war any minute now, Georgia – ain't our boys already joined up? There'll be air-raids – we had a taste of that last time – London ain't a safe place to be.'

'Why ain't you coming with me, then?' Georgia's teacher frowned on the use of 'ain't' but Georgia employed it to emphasise a point, like Mum.

She sighed. 'Who'd look after your dad, eh? And I've got to be here for when the boys get leave. Reckon I'll have to give up the market, do something more useful – you'll be better off out of it. You ain't going as far as some. Your aunty's lot's off to Wales. Might as well be Russia, if you can't speak the language, she says. You'll be with most of your school pals and your teacher.' She added, unconvincingly: 'At least I won't have to worry about *you*.'

Now, Georgia held tightly to her attaché case, daring Miss to tell her to put it in the luggage-rack. Like new it was, she thought proudly: fake, brown leather, from her mother's second-hand goods stall. Their family usually made do with brown-paper carriers with string handles, which bit into your fingers if the bags were overloaded – as they always were with soggy bathing-costumes, shells, pebbles with a hole in the middle and giant sticks of Brighton rock after Sunday trips to the sea in the summer.

They went by steam train then, too, not by the usual tram or tube train, taking plenty of sandwiches – but you couldn't make sandcastles when you got there because the beach was all stones. Made you wince, walking gingerly over them rocks to the sea, Georgia thought. 'Plenty of water in the old Thames,' Dad reminded Mum. 'Why go further?' He should know, being a lighterman. But her mother got her way and Brighton it was, probably because that's where the two of them met as kids, when she had hit him in the back with a pebble she was aiming at the water. Mum might pretend not to be sentimental, but she was.

Thinking of Dad, Georgia blinked hard. Bit of a musician Old Dad, plenty of entertainment at home with Dad riffling the keys of the piano-accordion, like he did Friday nights at the Prince Albert pub round the corner. They could hear the singing from their house. 'At it again.' Mum would bang the iron down on the ironing-board, so that the flex swung wildly from the light-fixture above. 'No prizes for guessing what his favourite song is, eh?' That's how Georgia got her name, of course. She could just hear his deep voice, gravelly from too many fags and all that fog on the river.

'Do come and sit down, Georgia,' Miss Stedman entreated now. 'You're supposed to be setting a good example to the younger ones; aren't you the biggest of my Big Girls? After all, you are almost eleven years old.'

You're big and ugly enough, Georgia told herself silently. That's what you always tell me, Mum, when you want me to do something. I know you're only joking, but I *mustn't never forget that*.

'Stillbrook Stashun!' was the shout: then Georgia was busy helping Miss to herd the suddenly revitalised evacuees well away from the line, as the train departed, enveloping them in billowing smoke. They stood back, coughing and spluttering, rocking the tubs of bright geraniums, while the two women they'd seen from the train wheeling their bikes onto the platform, greeted them. 'Here you all are, then!' They were to escort them to the village hut for refreshments and relocation.

Down the long, winding road they marched, mostly quiet and solemn-faced again, as they had been throughout the journey: Georgia had failed in her attempts to get a nice sing-song going. Walking under a cloudless sky towards the yet unseen village, mostly overdressed for a sunny afternoon – for it made sense to wear winter-warmers to lighten the load of the parcel or bag each had to carry – they were a straggling crocodile. Sometimes the path petered out, but there was only the odd bike wobbling on the road as the rider stared at them curiously.

Bringing up the rear with Miss Stedman, Georgia observed: 'Where's all the bloomin' buses, Miss?' Blithely ignoring her teacher's sigh, she added: 'Not even a bloomin' horse and cart, eh?'

'Flowers bloom, Georgia, not horses and buses,' Miss Stedman said.

'But a'jectives are the *colour* words, Miss – ain't bloomin' an a'jective?'

'I don't really care. Not today. Must you keep asking questions, Georgia?'

'No, Miss.' Be respectful, Mum had warned her daughter. No lip.

Two boys ahead of them were darting at the brambles, plucking at the berries.

'Oh dear, did they ought to – are they ripe?'

Miss Stedman looked as if she'd never sampled a blackberry in her life. Come to that, Georgia considered, she probably didn't eat much at all. Skinny she was, in Mum's opinion. Dad grinned when he heard that and said, 'All she needs is a spot of your steak and kidney, Nell, and a glass of stout, to fatten her up. Got a pretty face, that's a start.'

Miss Stedman wore a beige, belted coat with a mock-fur collar. She must feel real uncomfortable, Georgia thought, but teachers had to look smart. Even middle-aged ones like Miss Stedman, who must be over thirty.

'They won't hurt 'em,' she reassured her teacher cheerfully. She couldn't keep quiet for long. 'It's other berries you got to watch out for. You should know, Miss. Showed us that picture of woody nightshade, didn't you, in bot'ny last term? Drop down stone dead you will, if you try that . . .' She clapped her free hand to her narrow chest, rolled-up her eyes and made a gagging sound to illustrate the point. Miss Stedman chose to ignore the dramatics.

They were approaching civilization: cottages with flaking pink walls, poky windows winking in the sun, balding thatch; marigolds as bright as Georgia's hair in the gardens, and spiky lavender hedges. Barking dogs leapt up at gates and mothers in cross-over pinnies held up infants to watch their progress.

Here at last were the crossroads, the Jubilee seat at its crux, with the oak planted to commemorate King George V and Queen Mary's twenty-five years on the throne providing shade for weary walkers, and a stop and turning-place for the weekly bus to the nearest town.

The children scrambled to sit on the bench, to examine the carved hearts and initials embellishing the wood, despite it being so recent a landmark. Georgia reminded them sternly: 'Just you keep them penknives in your pockets!'

Like Miss, she mentally ticked off an imaginary list. Name-tags, gas-masks, parcels . . . But she balked at wiping the noses of the younger ones with her pristine hanky, which she'd dabbed with Mum's Californian Poppy.

'This way,' one of the welcome ladies smiled. 'Past the shops and school, past the church, turn up the High Road and there'll be a nice cup of tea waiting for you in the hut.' She balanced a couple of bundles on her bike seat.

Georgia considered, *she* looks all right. Wonder if she'll take one of us home? Mum's voice echoed in her head: 'Pick someone with a bit of flesh on her bones – likely to feed you on good country grub, Georgia . . .' They talk funny round here, she thought, but nice, all soft and slow. *Don't let go, Georgia, don't start snivelling now. Just think about getting back home as soon as you can.*

Naturally, the pretty little girls were chosen first. Georgia accepted that with equanimity. She was plain and unprepossessing and she knew it. Also, ginger hair was supposed to go with a fiery temper. Well, she could stamp her foot on occasion, but she wasn't that *bad*, Georgia thought. Boys were selected not for good looks but for wiry frames, by farming families perhaps hoping for a willing pair of extra hands. 'Like animals, d'you boy?' was the laconic query.

A flicker of interest, and the lads were off to what they hoped were good homes. Time would tell.

Georgia sipped her second cup of tea. Plenty of sugar, but the milk was too creamy for her taste. They used skimmed at home because it was cheaper. Hard pastry but plenty of jam in the tarts. She became aware that a tall lady, who'd just come in, was eyeing her from across the room. The tea-urn belched forth a constant stream of boiling water into huge brown-betty teapots, but now there were empty chairs along the trestle-tables down the centre of the room. The chiming of the church clock startled her. Five o'clock. Mum would be peeling spuds and aiming them at the saucepan so they splashed in the water. She'd still be wearing her hat: 'Ain't had a moment to take it off!' she'd sigh to Dad. Georgia's tummy rumbled. It wanted comfort food, lots of it. Hot spuds with a dab of real butter; meat and gravy. A chunk of bread to wipe the plate clean. She always apologised to their dog at home, waiting for scraps, but Dusty was well named: he could dislodge the lid of any dustbin down their alley.

She couldn't help it. Thinking of Mum, Dad and the dog. She put out her tongue and captured a rogue tear, rolling down her cheek.

'Hello, will you come over to the committee table with me?' the tall lady asked. 'I'd prefer an older evacuee as I'm out at work all day. I'm Phoebe Bliss, and you are?'

'Georgia Smith,' she replied. 'Mum don't like it short-ened to Georgie.' Make that clear, right away, Mum had insisted.

'I wouldn't dream of doing so, it's a good name,' the lady said. 'I'm sorry I've left it so late, but I had to get changed after work.'

Georgia considered Miss Phoebe Bliss. She wore a smart pink-linen dress. Her thick, black hair was shoul-der length and severely centre-parted – coo, that comb mustn't half have scraped her scalp, Georgia winced. Miss Bliss had dark eyes and startlingly red lips. When she held out her hand, Georgia was instantly reminded of a picture in the *Mirror* of Mrs Simpson, who'd run away with the Prince of Wales – only then he'd been King Edward VIII, just for a short while, of course. What was it the newsboy had shouted in the street two or three years ago? 'Read all about Mrs Simpson's trossacks!' When she'd asked Mum what he was on about, Mum said she guessed he meant troo-soo, you know, spelt French, *trousseau* – fancy undies. Miss Bliss was better look-ing than Mrs S, it was the hair-do made Georgia recall that. Bet she's wearing a silk petticoat though, Georgia thought, with a grin.

Miss Bliss probably wasn't what Mum had in mind for a guardian, nothing motherly about her. Just one question needed: 'Are you a good cook?'

'I should hope so: it's how I make my living. Satisfied? Will I do?'

'You'll do, don't worry, you won't have to put up with me for long,' Georgia said, confidently. Miss Stedman ticked her list. 'Got rid of me at last, Miss, eh?'

Eva Stedman managed a weak smile in return. 'You've been a great help today, Georgia, thank you. Mind you write to your parents tonight: you brought that stamped envelope with you, I hope?' Georgia nodded. 'If you want me you'll find me at the post office in the street. I'm billeted with the postmistress. School as usual next Monday.' She turned to Miss Bliss. 'Georgia is among the brightest of my pupils: she will sit her scholarship next spring, and I have high hopes she will succeed. Please make sure she does her homework each evening.'

Miss looks tired, Georgia thought sympathetically, but she didn't need to say the bit about homework. She could do with a spot of lipstick, like Miss Bliss. Make all the difference to her face, that would.

'Bye for now, Miss,' she said cheerfully. 'Keep your chin up.'

TWO

Another march, downhill, past imposing houses, glimpsed behind huge hedges.

'The cricket field,' Miss Bliss indicated. 'You can spend summer Saturday afternoons under the sycamores with a good book, listening to the crack of bat on ball. As a young man, my father played for the village team. The bank here was covered with snowdrops in spring. Not far now, Georgia. Weary? You must be.'

' 'Course not,' Georgia said. She squared her drooping shoulders. She saw Miss Bliss glancing at her case, but she wasn't about to hand that over.

They crossed the road at the bottom of the hill, turned left. She realised they were completing the triangle from the Jubilee seat. There were railed-in gullies, with water puddling through, on either side of this street. 'The water is much deeper in the winter – best to keep out of them,' Miss Bliss warned.

'Wouldn't mind a paddle right now, though,' Georgia said. 'My feet ain't half sore after that long route march and all.' That was quite an admission for her.

'See the scum, and the colour of the water? All sorts drains in there . . .'

'You don't have to spell it out, Miss. I can use my imagination.' And my nose, she thought. The gullies had a definite whiff.

'Glad to hear it, Georgia.'

Long Lane (more a beaten track) ran alongside the extensive grounds of an aloof, red-brick house. Fronting the road was an octagonal, single-storey cottage.

'Recently, my brother and his wife moved into the gatehouse from the main house, which was requisitioned. Don't ask me why, because I don't know! Lawrence is a professor of music. Since Grandpa died, he doesn't need to work – unlike me – he can spend all his time composing . . .

'I was born *there*,' Phoebe added, in a matter-of-fact way about the house. 'My grandfather had Red House built before he was married, but he and Grandma didn't settle there until he'd retired from his mountaineering. He wrote books about his exploits, then. After my father was killed in the Great War, my mother, my brother and I lived with my grandparents . . . We turn off here, this is Little

Lane; what else? See that pair of cottages ahead? Mine is the one on the left. A Mr Diamond Jubilee Hardy – how about that for a name? – lives next door.'

'He's a bit older than the Jubilee seat then, that was only a silver,' Georgia reckoned. She did a bit of mental arithmetic. 'Forty-one?' she guessed.

'About that.' Miss Bliss was amused. 'He's known as Jube, in the village. Perhaps I'd better say we're not exactly the best of pals, but he's a good sort.'

'At school with him, were you, Miss?' The path had dwindled to rough grass now, taking the shine off her best shoes.

'Now you're trying to guess *my* age! Call me Phoebe, then I won't feel as old as you think I am. Here we are. Stand back, the dog will come rushing out.'

'Oh good, you've got a dog.' Georgia was pleased. She looked at the pitted walls as Phoebe inserted a large rusty key in the lock of the front door. 'What made all them holes, Phoebe?'

'Masonry bees; don't worry, they won't bother with you. They lay their eggs in the holes they bore. House is all abuzz at times.'

'Got stung on the bum once: sat on a wasp in the park. Didn't half hurt.'

The door swung open and a small, scruffy, sandy-coloured dog launched itself at Georgia. She set down her case, and the next minute the dog was in her arms, licking her neck enthusiastically. 'Reckon you're called Sandy, eh?'

'You reckon right,' Phoebe said. 'Well, let him go and come in, Georgia. There's the kitchen, there's the stairs, and your room's the first one you come to. No bathroom, just the scullery, but no shortage of hot water – the stove's always on the go. Plenty of wood-gathering needed; you can help with that. Go hunting, sack on back, in the plantation – as the locals call it; copse at the back, to you. When you've had a wash, explore the garden if you like. Privy next to the back door, by the way. I'll rustle up supper. All right?'

'All right,' Georgia agreed. She'd write to Mum tonight to tell her so. Miss Bliss was chatty, unlike Miss Stedman, and she liked that.

There was a lengthy, narrow stretch of ground at the back of the cottage, with a leafy tree. Under its shade was a sagging deckchair. The grass was overgrown and starred with daisies. There was a little shed at the end. Sandy came bounding up with half a rubber ball in his mouth, then dropped it hopefully at Georgia's feet.

'You can't hurt anything,' Phoebe said from the open doorway. 'Jube grumbles and says the weed seeds blow onto his vegetable patch. But I haven't been here long.

I'll get around to the garden next spring, I hope. See his cow in the field beyond? Makes me think of that Rudyard Kipling poem – *The friendly cow all red and white, I love with all my heart; She gives me cream with all her might, To eat with apple tart . . .* He's got bees next door, too; see the hives?'

'I like the poem, we read it last term. 'Scuse me saying it, but it's by Robert Louis Stevenson, ain't it? What's the tree, Phoebe?'

'It's a cherry tree. Birds had most of the fruit this summer. Jube said I should have put a piece of net curtain over the fruit.'

'Can't he hear you?' Georgia mouthed, with a nod at next door.

'Don't care if he can,' was the quick reply. 'He thinks he knows it all.'

I must tell Mum I reckon I'm going to like it here, Georgia thought, with the proviso: for a month or two anyway . . . She scooped up the poor excuse for a ball, threw it as far as she could and Sandy bounded after it. Made a friend, she thought. Dusty would sulk under the table if he knew.

A rather distracted, 'Hello, you're here, then,' from the postmistress to Eva, when the billeting officer introduced the two women, before leaving them to get properly acquainted.

The living-room, crowded with gloomy old furniture, was off the shop. A one-eared cat sat on the table, already laid for supper, grooming itself unconcernedly, its tail flicking the butter dish, which made Eva blanch.

'Just let me close the shop,' plump little Miss Gathercole said. 'Sit down and make yourself at home.' Her bunions were throbbing painfully after a long day on her feet and there could be no plummeting down on the twanging settee, with her guest to feed and water.

'Phew! That's wholly hot!' she sighed on her return, dabbing at her glistening brow. 'Hungry, Miss Stedman? Want a wash and brush up 'fore supper?'

Eva murmured a vague reply.

'Take your coat off, dear; hang it on the scullery door. I made a peg spare for you, see? The bedrooms are one 'top the other. Turn the corner by the first one, that's mine, and go up the next flight of stairs; they're steep, mind, so hang onto the rope along the wall,' she warned Eva. 'It was my brother's room: he never left it for more'n fifteen years; lost his legs, poor soul, in the War. There was just the two of us; our parents died afore their time, you see.'

Like Georgia, Eva made a swift, silent calculation. She had an awful urge to laugh at the relieved thought that the room should be well aired by now.

'I'll get on with the cooking, then,' Miss Gathercole said brightly, opening the door to the staircase invitingly. 'Take your time, I'll give you a call.'

Eva heaved her case onto the bed. It was stifling with the door closed and the one, small window under the eaves firmly shut, too. She gave a little shudder of distaste on discovering the bedside table was in reality a mahogany commode, disguised with a faded, still-beringed curtain and stood close by the iron-framed single bed. Wondering where she could stow her possessions, she opened a cupboard door to discover, with relief, empty-shelves above and hanging-space below for clothes.

She stooped to peer out of the window once she had forced it open: the street, so bustling earlier, was deserted. Everyone had gone home to tea, including the evacuees. There was a definite aroma of onions being frizzled and blackened, wafting upwards from the kitchen. She felt quite nauseous. Last night, she thought, she'd eaten lobster with green salad tossed in vinaigrette. A farewell dinner, if a solitary one, in an anonymous hotel in West London, but then, she hadn't really believed he would come. She'd told her landlady, whose interest in her affairs was irksome, she was at the school making last-minute preparations for today's exodus . . . She'd alighted from the taxi a street away from her lodgings.

Perhaps, she sighed audibly now, it was a blessing in disguise, shunted here, away from temptation.

She became suddenly aware of the squeaking, protesting sound of wheels that needed a touch with the oilcan. A person with a bulging sack fastened over one shoulder, was riding past on the opposite side of the street on an ancient, black bike. At first sight the long, wild haystack of hair, yellowed by the sun, was misleading; then, as he glanced up at her, sensing her presence, she saw he possessed an equally untidy, blond beard. He raised his hand in a sketchy salute. Eva stepped back, jerking the curtains firmly over the glass. 'The Wild Man of Borneo, I presume,' she said aloud.

She bolted the bedroom door, then she pulled off her sensible brown dress in a sudden, fierce gesture and kicked her court shoes under the bed. She rummaged in her bag. Yes, here it was, with the book of matches embossed with the name of the hotel, which she supposed she had taken as a souvenir. She lit the rather limp cigarette. She needed fortifying after all she'd been through today, she thought, lying back on the bed, resting her head on the flock pillows. She smiled ruefully. She knew exactly what Georgia, her fellow pupils and everyone else come to that, thought of her: prim Miss Stedman, never been kissed . . . She glanced down at the sensuous, peachy satin-slip she wore. It had been a present from *him*, on her last birthday. I'm liberated at last, she told herself: I don't have to abide by society's rules, its expectations. Who'd have thought I'd find romance at the Albert Hall? Swept away on a tide of music, of emotion; the fresh smell of cologne and hair pomade from the well-dressed man on my left.

The catch in her throat, her suddenly watering eyes, made her rouse herself. She disposed of the stub in the commode, rinsed her face and hands, cleaned her teeth. The water in the jug on the washstand was soft, refreshingly cold.

She smoothed out the dress over her slender hips once more, tidied her rumpled hair, powdered her nose.

'Supper's ready!' came the call.

Georgia looked slyly at her reflection in the long mirror. She'd undressed down to her interlock vest and fleecy-lined, navy blue knickers. Mum made her wear both, winter and summer. Come next month, she'd add a liberty bodice, exchange short socks for long ones. Her undergarments doubled as nightwear. Got no bumps yet, she thought wistfully. 'Your mum's got a figure like Mae West; if she fell in she'd float down the river,' Dad said once approvingly, and Mum had made a face and went, 'Oh, you!' Skinny Lizzy, her cheeky brothers dubbed her. Were they still at Aldershot, drilling and all? She missed the boys, who were seven and eight years older than her, and their teasing. Slipped her a sixpence each, they did, from their wage packets each Friday. Mum made her save half her pocket money. She knew very well that she was the family favourite, being the only girl, coming along when her parents thought they were past it.

The sausages and mash had gone down a real treat. Phoebe heaped on a pile of golden fried-onion strips. 'Onions burst out of the soil here,' she'd told Georgia. 'Not in my garden, though. Still, Jube keeps me supplied; he doesn't ask if I want anything, just leaves a trugful on my front step.'

She could hear voices now, outside in the garden. Curious, she darted to the open window and peeped round the lace curtain. Phoebe was hanging out some bits of washing; funny time to be doing that, Georgia thought. It was near enough eight o'clock. She watched white overalls being pegged to the line. Of course, hadn't Phoebe told her she was a cook? Sandy dashed about, shaking his ball with much pretend growling, and a large man was chopping energetically at the hedge between the two gardens. Bit late for that too, wasn't it?

Goliath! Georgia fancied. She was a regular at Sunday school, at Mum's insistence. She enjoyed the parables best, because they were stories. This was actually Miss Stedman's Wild Man of Borneo, but, of course, she didn't know that.

What was he saying to Phoebe? She strained her ears.

'Got a 'vacuee, then?'

'I have. You're making a mess my side, Jube, with your twigs and leaves.'

'Surprised you can see 'em, in that rough grass. I'll come round and tidy up.'

'No thank you.'

'Like that, is it, you ain't forgiven me for what I said that time, eh?'

'You said no one would believe I was once a scarlet woman. D'you expect me to?' Phoebe glanced up, saw Georgia. 'Shut up!' she hissed.

'Oh, Phoebe, you know I was joking.'

She picked up the empty laundry basket. 'Good night, Jube,' she said firmly. Georgia sat up in bed, notepad balanced on her knees. She licked her pencil. She didn't have to cogitate, words always spilled out, even if her spelling was erratic.

Dear Mum and Dad,

Had a good jurney. Only one of the kids was sick. Luckily I had eaten all my sandwidges in one go, so my paper bag came in very handy. Miss was flapping, so I had to deal with it.

Now I know what the country looks like. Plenty of shops, that's something, but not a Woolies in sight. Plenty of fresh air, too.

I am biletted in a cottage, see the address above, up the end of a little lane, off a long winding lane. I am with a single lady, Miss Bliss, who says I can call her Feebee – but I don't think that's how you spell it. She's about Miss S's age, but she's a lot more lively. You will like her. She will write to you soon and tell you how I am getting on. If I am behaving myself, I suppose.

Anyway, it is nice here, and I am not crying my eyes out. I promised, didn't I?

Going to school Monday to see what's what.

Lots of love to you both and to the boys when you write, and to Dusty. (Don't let him out if there is bombs about, will you?)

Georgia xxx

P.S. There is a dog here called Sandy. And a man next door called Diamond Jubilee. What about that? He likes F. a lot. Oh, and a cherry tree in the garden.

P.P.S. What does a scarlet woman mean?

P.P.P.S. I miss you! I WILL BE HOME SOON! You can count on it.

THREE

'Lovely egg,' Georgia said appreciatively, dipping in her toast and causing the yellow yolk to run down the side of the eggcup.

'Not too small, I hope?' Phoebe asked. 'It's a pullet's egg: Jube left half-a-dozen on my step, earlier on.'

'Peace offering?' Georgia asked.

Phoebe looked hard at her. 'Heard us having words last night, did you? You don't want to take notice of that, nothing unusual.'

Georgia nodded. 'I reckon you like each other really, though,' she observed, buttering a second round of toast.

'Of course we do,' Phoebe agreed ruefully. 'And you won't get any more out of me than that,' she added firmly. 'Eat up. You'll have to come to work with me today. Can you ride a bike?'

'Sort of . . . Got any roller skates?'

'You'd be more in danger on those with all the rutted lanes hereabouts than you would wobbling on a bike. Glad you're wearing dungarees, I'll find you some clips.

You've egg on your chin, by the way; use the napkin, that's what it's for.'

'Seven o'clock, blimey, is that all it is?' Georgia exclaimed, as the clock on the kitchen dresser whirred, then delivered the chimes in a fit of coughing.

'I'm on breakfast duty this morning.'

'Where d'you work?'

'Didn't I say? At the Union.'

'What's that? Cook's Union?' Georgia guessed.

'No! It used to be the workhouse; it's on Middle Moor. Still a few old people there, but not segregated, thank the Lord, as they used to be –'

'Segregated,' Georgia interrupted. 'Parted, ain't that it?'

'Yes. It was barbaric, parting couples who'd been married nearly half-a-century, sometimes. Still, now they're looked after properly and so are the incurables. I don't have to explain that to you, I imagine?'

'Nope. Want me to wash-up?'

'Would you? Thank you, Georgia. You're well trained.'

'You can thank my mum for that,' Georgia told her. 'She says I might get married one day and then I'll be washing-up for ever and ever. Heaven forbid . . .'

They cycled for a good quarter of an hour alongside Middle Moor, which was purple with heather. No shops here, no habitation, until Georgia sighted a large, forbidding building. They dismounted, wheeled their steeds up the gravel, propped them against the massive stone pillars of the porch.

'Reckon only Samson could move *them*,' Georgia said with awe.

The heavy door swung open and a lanky, fair-haired girl glanced at them indifferently, then stood aside to let them pass.

'This is Georgia Smith, May. Georgia, this is May Moon, who lives here.'

Georgia liked the name, but wasn't sure about the girl. 'How d'you do,' she said politely.

May Moon didn't deign to answer, merely waited for them to go along the corridor before she closed the door, then she followed them, keeping her distance.

Underground, the basement kitchen, Georgia thought, with huge saucepans, steamers, colanders, mincing machines, whisks, ladles, a dustbin sized bread-bin, more bins for flour and sugar. And *mice*, I bet, Georgia grimaced to herself.

May Moon took-up position at one end of the table, where a youngish woman, with a dreamy expression, added green ribbons of peel to a heap on a tin plate. The girl chopped the apples into pieces, which she dropped into a bowl.

'You don't have to, of course, but if you'd like to help, I'm sure May and Helga would be grateful. Helga doesn't speak, Georgia, but she can communicate with May. I must stir the porridge, it's been standing overnight,' Phoebe said.

'I don't think May wants me to help,' Georgia whispered back. Helga looked up. The smile that illuminated her pale face was directed at Georgia. She's not deaf as well, then, Georgia realised.

'Nonsense! May, find Georgia an apron, give her some of those apples and a knife; then you'll be ready for the pastry when I've knocked it up, eh? Windfalls, Georgia, so watch out for bruises and the odd maggot.'

'Maggots, ugh!' Georgia exclaimed. Mum always complained when she sent the peas flying in all directions when she found something wriggly in a pod.

'We have to rely on local generosity quite a lot, so windfalls it is,' Phoebe reproved her mildly. 'Don't sample any: they're as sour as old Harry, because they're not really ripe yet. But in a pie, with sugar, they're fine.'

Nearly an hour later, they were still slicing. Georgia was sucking a finger when Phoebe, in her white overall and hair-confining cap, arrived back with the porridge bowls, plates and tin mugs to wash-up.

'Bleedin' knife slipped; last apple, too,' Georgia sighed.

'If you must swear,' Phoebe told her, 'say "bloody" –'

'Oh!' Georgia was shocked. Mum said *that* was swearing.

'All right now?' Phoebe asked.

'Stopped, *blooding*, if that's what you mean.'

'Good. But maybe you'd better wipe, rather than wash?'

'What did your last slave die of?' Georgia cheeked her with a grin.

'A surfeit of washing-up, I reckon,' Phoebe returned, grinning herself.

There was an unexpected nudge from May Moon. She held out a torn strip of clean rag. 'I'll tie your finger up, shall I? Helga has to wash all them tea cloths; she don't want your blood all over 'em . . .'

Georgia and Phoebe ate their dinner on their own in the kitchen: mince, carrots and onions, with boiled potatoes, followed by apple-pie and custard. The residents, of course, had been fed first. Matron, with her booming voice and imposing stature, presided over the long table. Some of the more severely handicapped residents were spoonfed, Phoebe explained, which was a job patiently tackled by the younger ones like May Moon.

'Why is she here?' Georgia wondered.

'I'm not sure. But don't ever tell her you're sorry for her, will you? She firmly intends to leave here as soon as she can; she'll make something of herself, I'm positive of that. May Moon attends the village school. She's about your age. A strange girl, but very determined. I admire her spirit.'

'And Helga, is that really her name?'

'She was named after my Norwegian grandmother, who was a welfare visitor here around thirty-five years ago. Helga's mother died soon after her birth.'

'Why doesn't she talk?' Georgia persisted. She couldn't help feeling curious, thinking: I bet that's not the whole story . . .

'I suppose because she doesn't choose to do so.'

Georgia pushed her plate away. 'I'm so full, I could burst! You know,' she added, 'this ain't the sort of place I'd expect you to work. You're rather . . .'

'Posh?' Phoebe supplied, laughing. 'It's not unlike the spartan boarding-school I went to! I trained as a chef and I worked abroad for years in small hotels. I wasn't studious, serious, like my brother. Maybe I disappointed my mother, although Grandpa put in a good word on my behalf, and said, "Well, she's *athletic*: we've climbed a few distant hills together and skied down some in our time."

'Eventually, I decided to come home. It's a challenge to serve up good food here. In fact, I'm grateful to Matron for giving me a chance, taking me on, when . . . Come on, let's sit outside while the residents have their nap, before it's time to prepare the Spare Penny – which is what the locals call the house – supper.'

'Why?' Georgia enquired.

'Well, local lore has it that when tramps came here asking for a bed for the night, they first buried any pennies they'd earned that day in the bank outside the house. It was just called the Union, then. They had to prove they were destitute and homeless, you see. Sometimes they were so drunk they couldn't remember where they'd hidden their treasure. It's true that the gardener very occasionally comes across a copper or two, but that's all.'

Eva had spent most of that day in her room. Yesterday had sapped her strength, she thought: the onions for supper proved the last straw, she had a gippy tummy. If there were any problems with the evacuees, well, they knew where she was.

That wretched commode was the only suitable writing surface. She opened her stationery wallet; selected deckle-edged paper, thick and watermarked; uncapped her slim Waterman ladies' fountain pen. Her writing was small, exquisitely neat, with exact loops. The gold nib moved surely along the paper.

Darling – here I am, in a real backwater. I went to our hotel the night before I left. I raised my glass to you, to us, to the past, to the future, to the unknown. I'm afraid, so afraid, what this might be – I wonder if I will ever see you again . . . Now you have my new address, I hope you will write, when and if you can. I will never forget you, but I am not foolish enough to think it will be the same for you. I believe you did love me, just a little, for that time, didn't you?

If only . . . I adore you. Eva.

She recapped the pen, folded the paper, ran her thumb nail along the crease. The letter would go to a box number in London. She closed her eyes. You fool, Eva, you fool, falling for the oldest ploy ever.

Jube was lifting sugar beet on a local farm. Sweat poured off his bared torso, reddened – because of his fair skin – rather than tanned by the merciless sun. More the day for plunging into the sea, always gaspingly cold here on the east coast, he thought with sudden longing. Not more than five miles away, along Middle Moor road. Not the safest place to send all these evacuees, if the war began at sea . . .

Blast that wretched woman. He couldn't get her out of his mind. That summer she left school. Seventeen, with a long black plait hanging over one shoulder, glistening like the tarred rope which restrained his father's fishing boat on the beach. He could picture her clearly: leaning against the haystack, in her blue shorts and brief top revealing her shoulders and midriff. 'Scratch my back, Jube,' she'd requested. 'The stooks make me itch like mad.'

Of course, he knew she was really asking to be kissed. He being older she thought he was experienced; that was a laugh. He'd always been shy with the girls. His clumsiness gave him away. Disappointed, she gave him a shove. 'Your lips are all wet, Jube! You're not trying to take advantage of me, are you?' Then she'd laughed, to hide her own uncertainty.

He'd stomped off that day. Soon after, she left the village.

He jabbed at a beet, split it with the tines of the fork. He'd like to do that to that foreign fellow who'd hurt her. What had happened to Phoebe Bliss over these past fifteen years? Her estranged brother Lawrence and his wife Beryl had been living in their grandfather's house since he died in 1932. She hadn't come home for the funeral. Her inheritance was the cottages they lived in: he guessed she'd inherited him too, as the sitting tenant, when she finally returned last summer.

There was a muffled roar of thunder, then great drops of rain began to fall. Jube looked up. Black clouds, war clouds were massing. Strangers already here. That cheeky-faced, red-haired girl next door, and, at Miss Gathercole's, a pale young woman had looked down at him from the window.

The storm was over before Phoebe and Georgia left the Union and rode home.

'Sunday tomorrow, thank goodness, my day off. Fancy a lie-in?' asked Phoebe, as they put their bikes away in the garden shed.

'Wouldn't say no,' Georgia yawned. 'I get a lot of reading in on Sunday mornings as I'm not allowed to disturb Mum and Dad. Got to wait for the call, and the eggs and bacon,' she hinted.

'Plenty of books here, mostly from my childhood. Help yourself. Just put them back when you've finished with them.'

There was a tall aluminum jug on the step, with a flip-up lid. 'From the evening milking; Jube never forgets. Glass of milk to take up to bed with you?'

Georgia nodded. 'Thanks. Mind if I go straight up?'

'You do that. I won't be long. Just want to listen to the news . . .'

Georgia closed the book. *What Katy Did.* She'd read it before, but she'd been drawn to select it. 'What Georgia did next,' she said aloud. Suddenly she was blubbing, and she pulled the sheet over her head. Are you missing me, Mum and Dad? 'Cause I'm missing you, can't keep my chin up, Mum, not in bed . . .

Phoebe, in pyjamas and dressing-gown, patted her lap. Sandy leapt up. She stroked him absently. No good news, just the measured tones of the announcer. Where was Karl now? Would she ever get over him?

That awful row she'd had with her brother and sister-in-law. She'd not met Beryl before she returned to Suffolk, and their dislike was immediate, mutual. She guessed that Lawrence's wife feared she would encroach on their comfortable life, ask for money. That made her angry, say things she regretted later. If only her mother had been there, but she'd moved away, to live with her widowed sister. There had been no reply to her letter: *Dear Mother, I'm home.*

'Leave Mother in peace,' that's what Lawrence had said bitterly. 'Apparently she decided that she'd had enough of *both* of us . . .'

Phoebe sighed, indicated to the dog that he should jump down. 'Come on, old boy, let's take a turn round the garden.'

Jube was in his scullery. He watched as she walked up to the boundary hedge and back. We're both lonely, he thought, but she doesn't want *me.*

FOUR

Phoebe and Georgia went for a long walk across the fields, the Sunday that war was declared. Phoebe observed the slight tremble of Georgia's bottom lip, then the resolute squaring of her shoulders. Georgia, she thought, wants her mum, at a time like this. She switched off the wireless.

'Well, this is it, I suppose,' she said aloud. 'However, it's a nice day, Georgia, and the plan was to pick all the blackberries we can this afternoon, then bottle 'em up for winter, eh? The nation's in for a fight, and it may go on some time, but I don't think anything much will happen today.'

She didn't mention going to church and saying a fervent prayer or two, and Georgia didn't like to say. Anyway, she thought, the service will have started, and I expect the news was given out there. Bet Mum's getting on with the dinner at home, war or no war, and Dad's off to the pub . . .

They ducked under the wire fence, with their empty baskets and walking-sticks. 'Oo-er,' Georgia exclaimed, coming face to face with the cow.

'You can stroke her, look, she's very friendly, though she's not too keen on Sandy. Well, he will leap about like that.'

'C'mon Sandy, let's see if I can wear you out, eh?' Georgia ran ahead toward the perimeter of the field. The grass was rough and full of thistles: she soon had to stop and look where she was going, because her socks were snagged on the prickles. She was glad she'd put on her plimsolls and not her sandals, or her toes would have been stabbed.

Phoebe followed at a more leisurely pace. She looked younger today, Georgia thought, without lipstick, and she'd braided her hair so it wouldn't get caught up in the brambles. She had on a pair of patched slacks and what she said were her climbing boots, though there were no hills round here.

'It's a blackberry jungle, Georgia, you need to cover your limbs or you'll get all scratched,' she'd advised. So Georgia wore dungarees instead of shorts.

The berries were ripe and luscious. The layers piled in their baskets; their hands and mouths were streaked and stained purple. The sticks were really useful, for hooking down brambles. The heat made them perspire and very thirsty. When they'd picked enough, they walked back to a shady tree and drank tepid water from the bottle which Phoebe carried in her haversack.

'That's better,' Georgia said thankfully, wiping her mouth on her sleeve.

The unexpected noise startled them. 'Siren,' Phoebe said. She looked up apprehensively at the sky. 'Can't hear anything else, can you?'

Georgia shook her head. She supposed Phoebe meant enemy aircraft. The blaring faded. 'Got to take cover, ain't we? We didn't bring our gas masks.'

'Who'd have thought . . . well, we'd better make for home, and the cellar . . .'

As they approached the wire, they saw Jube on the other side. He yelled at them: '*Get down in the ditch!* What d'you think you're doing, out in the open?'

Some of the blackberries spilled as they obeyed meekly, and Sandy jumped down after them. Within seconds, Jube joined them. The drainage trench was dry; not very deep, but wide.

Before long, came the welcome notes of the all clear, and Sandy was the first out, under the wire and streaking down his own garden.

'I came to tell you, you had a visitor,' Jube said, 'then I heard the warning, so I put the cow in the shed first. The lady went back down the lane a fair while before. I hope she's all right.'

'Who was it, Jube?' asked Phoebe. Georgia had gone ahead to fill Sandy's water bowl.

'Miss Stedman. Your girl's teacher, she said. She's been doing the rounds to see if all the children are settled, like, and not too alarmed by the news.'

They were home now, looking down the lane. No one in sight. 'Thankfully, it was a false alarm,' Phoebe said.

'Hope so. I should go and see to the cow.' He'd carried the baskets for them. 'Here, still a good few berries left.'

'Thanks, Jube. We'll do a couple of jars for you.'

'I like your hair like that, reminds me of the old days,' he said unexpectedly.

'It's a mess.' Like my life since then, she thought. *Your girl*, that was a funny thing to say. Although I hadn't thought of it like that, I suppose I *am* Georgia's foster parent, but not for long I hope, for *her* sake. She's putting a brave face on it, but I know she wants to go home.

Eva had actually reached the gatehouse when the ear-splitting noise commenced. She halted, wondering what she should do. It would be a fair old dash to the post office. Then her arm was seized, she was shepherded through the gate, the open door, urged along a narrow hall then down a flight of stone steps, into a dank cavern lit by a candle stuck in the neck of a wine bottle in a niche in the wall.

'Sorry about grabbing you like that, but I spotted you coming down the lane. I told my wife to make for the cellar and I'd bring you to join us,' the man said. 'Here, take this stool. I'm Lawrence Bliss; this is my wife Beryl.'

'Good afternoon,' she said formally, from the shadows. 'And you are?'

'Eva Stedman. I am the teacher in charge of the evacuees from London.'

Eva's eyes were adjusting to the gloom now. Mr Bliss leaned against the wall, next to his wife. He was tall, with black hair turning grey and his face was oddly familiar. 'Oh, you must be related to Miss Bliss, who has one of the evacuees. It was Miss Bliss I was calling on, but she was out.'

'Yes, indeed. I am her brother,' Lawrence said evenly.

'We, too, have been evacuated,' Beryl said. 'We have been ousted from our home, Red House, for the duration.' Her indignation was palpable.

'We must regard it as a necessary sacrifice,' her husband reminded her. 'Surely you prefer it to my being called up?'

Eva felt uncomfortable. They are at war with each other, she guessed.

'You wouldn't make the grade physically, and anyway you are too old. My husband is almost forty, Miss Stedman.'

'Oh . . .' Eva was really embarrassed now. She was saved by the welcome sound of the all clear, which meant any danger was past.

She rose immediately. 'I must go, Miss Gathercole may be worrying about me. Thank you for your kindness, I do appreciate it.'

'I'll see you out,' Lawrence said.

'Thank you.' She held out her hand. 'I am glad to have met you, Mrs Bliss.'

'You must come again,' Beryl said unexpectedly. 'Goodbye for now, Miss Stedman.' Out of the shadows she was revealed as almost as tall as her husband, but rakishly thin, with silvery blonde hair in a severe Eton crop. She ascended the cellar steps first, entering a room immediately opposite and closing the door.

Eva and Lawrence stood for a moment at the gate. 'I met Miss Bliss's neighbour,' she said, she didn't know why.

'That rough-looking chap? Don't be alarmed, he's harmless enough. Jube Hardy. Worked on most of the local farms here since he left school. A protective element for my sister, I feel. It's rather isolated where she lives.'

'It's good she has you not too far away.' Eva latched the gate.

'Perhaps I should say my sister and I are not on speaking terms, but that doesn't mean,' he paused, 'I am not concerned for her welfare.'

It seemed to Eva that he glanced apprehensively over his shoulder. She thought, he's a nice man, but he's obviously afraid of his wife.

Next day, the evacuees joined the local children in the village school. It was deemed to be less of a risk, in the event of real raids, to be under the same roof. But all was quiet, rural life followed the normal pattern, even though the two groups viewed each other suspiciously.

The younger children retained their own teachers, but the rising eleven to fourteen-year-olds, a smaller group, were accommodated together in the head's study. She would take them for maths; Eva for the rest of the curriculum. All were taught at the same level, regardless of ability.

The children sat at two long tables brought from the hut. There was little elbow room. Georgia found herself sitting in the back row next to May Moon, and squashed against the wall. May gave her a cool glance, then appropriated the inkpot. Georgia sharpened her pencil, then wondered how to dispose of the little pile of cedar shavings. She missed her old school desk.

The headmistress appeared austere. Her narrowed eyes flickered from face to face. She wore a rather dusty gown. No mortarboard, though, Georgia mused.

'You!' Miss Worley's voice boomed. 'Yes, *you!*' she repeated, as Georgia realised she was addressing her. 'Stand up. Repeat ten times, *I must pay attention in class.*' She chalked these words on a swinging blackboard.

As Georgia unhappily obeyed, she was aware of the muffled counting.

'Sit down!' May hissed. Then she nudged her, 'Don't let 'em see you care.'

Keep yer chin up, Georgia. I am, Mum, I am.

She was relieved when Miss Stedman arrived to take the first lesson. She looked hot and bothered, being fifteen minutes late. There was a muttered conversation between her and Miss Worley. Straining her ears, Georgia caught, 'A telephone call; I'd just left. Miss Gathercole called me back.'

'The register,' Miss Worley indicated. Then, 'Who is that girl?' She's looking at *me*, Georgia realised. She lowered her own gaze, fiddled with her books.

'Georgia Smith.'

'I shall remember that,' the headmistress said. There was a concerted hasty-rising as she considered the class for a long moment, then left the room.

'Oh dear . . .' Miss Stedman waved to the children to sit. 'Please put your hand up and respond when I call your name. Betty Barber –'

'Here, Miss.'

'Kenneth Button?' This was a new name to Eva.

'Absent, Miss,' May Moon said loud and clear. 'Kenny's in hospital with a stranger-lated hernia.' There was a smothered snigger from the class.

'Oh dear,' Eva repeated faintly.

'A quick word, Georgia, please,' she requested at break-time, when the children filed out. 'What was all that about, earlier?'

'Her saying she'd remember my name, you mean?'

'Exactly that. Were you playing up?'

'No, Miss, honest. She said I wasn't paying attention –'

'Not *she*, Georgia: Miss Worley. Is this true?'

'Miss Worley made me stand up and say so, ten times. But my eyes just glazed over for a second, like. You know . . .'

Eva did know. But she couldn't express disapproval. 'Try and be less conspicuous; keep your head down,' she urged, 'until things are more settled.'

'Bit difficult to keep your head down and your chin up,' Georgia said, but she smiled at her teacher. Reckon you and me are on the same side, she thought.

'An official-looking letter,' Eva's former landlady had said on the telephone, obviously intrigued. 'That's why I thought I'd better phone you, in case it was an emergency, like. Shall I open it, my dear, and read it to you?'

'That's not necessary,' Eva replied. 'Kindly forward it to me please.'

I hope she won't be tempted to steam it open, she thought, but no, she may be curious, but she's very correct. From him, it must be. It must mean he's going away, or already gone, as he intimated. It might be the last time I hear from him.

She glanced out of the study window. She saw that Georgia and May Moon were deep in conversation. That's good, she thought. She's found a friend. I hope I will be as fortunate.

'Old Worley's not as bad as she seems,' May told Georgia. 'Her father's bedridden, and she has to keep popping in and out next door, the schoolhouse, to see he's all right, you see. She's due to retire, but they say she'll have to carry on, now, all the young men being called up and that.'

'I didn't like what she said. It sounded om—ominous.'

'Better to be remembered than not, isn't it? She's put me forward for the scholarship, anyway, and Miss Bliss says you'll be sitting for that, too. We got something else in common, eh, as well as being regarded with suspicion here.'

'You're a bit sharp, but I like you,' Georgia said, and she smiled.

'Same here. You heard what I said about Kenny Button?'

'Hernia, wasn't it?' She guessed *stranger-lated* was an exaggeration.

'Well, he delivers the groceries from his dad's shop to Spare Penny, and round the village too, and he knows *everything* that's going on round and about. He's my mate, 'cause he sticks up for me if kids go on about where I come from.'

'Can't wait to meet *him*,' Georgia said.

FIVE

Georgia cashed the postal order at Miss Gathercole's. Good old Mum, she'd sent two-and-sixpence as promised. *Have a little treat. Got the pictures near you?*

May nudged her. It was Friday, after school. 'What you going to spend that on?' They wheeled their bikes along the street before riding up Middle Moor, where Georgia would wait for Phoebe to finish work.

'Fancy going to the pictures with me tomorrow? I'll pay,' she offered.

'What, catch the bus to town? There's only one cinema, by the railway, but it'd have to be a matinée 'cause I help out Saturday mornings as you know.'

'That's all right. I'll give you a hand and then we can get off quicker. That's if Phoebe says I can go.'

'Oh, she will. You're lucky, being put with Miss Bliss. Don't treat you like a kid, does she?'

'Oh, I'm always being told I'm old for my age.'

'Same with me. But you're lucky, you've got a mum and dad. The only person who really cares for me . . .'

She hesitated.

'Is Helga. But you look after her more'n she looks after you.'

'Now, perhaps. When I was a baby she was my nurse-maid. She'll be upset when I leave Spare Penny, but when I get a home of my own, I'll send for her.'

The Regal Cinema hardly lived up to its name with its tin roof and stark interior. They were in the third row from the front, in tip-up red plush seats, which looked as if the moths had had a field-day, with ashtrays bulging with sticky, squashed Eldorado ice-cream cartons and toffee wrappers. There were the sour odours wafting through the constantly swinging doors of the WCs, either side of the stage, conflicting with the cheap disinfectant liberally employed by the management. There were other cloying scents like face-powder and hair unguents used by the clientele, together with sucked oranges and cough candy sweets. Georgia and May were soon oblivi-ous to all that, for they were absorbed in a roistering western, where the arrival of a steam train was boosted by the authen-tic sound effects from the railway just yards away. As the real express thundered past, the cinema building shook, adding to the excitement.

Lights up, and the hazy beam from the film projec-tor above switched-off. The interval. A hefty girl in a cerise outfit walked up the aisle, tray slung round her neck: 'Choc ices, vanilla cups?' There was a mad scramble to join the queue.

Georgia and May were still scraping the waxed cups with the little wooden spoons when the lights dimmed. The main feature film was about to begin.

They met at the station. Eva had been sitting in the waiting-room for some time, flicking the pages of a magazine, but alert for the arrival of the London train.

She moved up, allowed him to settle beside her, to place his rolled umbrella and the leather case with brass locks between them. He removed his hat, smoothed his hair, then finally asked, 'How are you?'

She gazed at the starched white cuffs protruding from the sleeves of his dark suit, at the chunky gold cufflinks. His hands were long-fingered, with manicured nails. He was fastidious. She liked that.

Eva sighed. 'We can't talk here,' she said softly. A woman with two quarrelsome children in tow opened the door. Eva looked up, met the curious gaze. She rose, caught the door before it closed. 'Thank you.' She guessed he would follow her in a few minutes.

She walked away from the station and paused by the cinema hoarding. *It Happened One Night*, with Clark Gable. How appropriate, she thought wryly. She'd seen this in 1934 with him; not the premiere, of course, he couldn't risk that with the press around. It had been their first night together, too.

They went through the swing-doors. 'Big picture's started, but you haven't missed much,' the cashier said, clipping their tickets.

'Anonymity in a crowd,' he murmured in Eva's ear, as they slipped into seats at the far end of the back row, where the view of the screen was partially obscured by a pillar. The case, the umbrella, again precluded close contact, but she was vibrantly aware of his presence.

'Why did you come?' she whispered, after a while.

'I wanted to see you, just once more.'

'This is goodbye, then?'

'You mustn't think that.'

'What, then?'

'Eva, this is difficult for me.'

'What about me?'

'I know, I do know . . .'

'Can't stand the soppy bits,' Georgia squirmed in her seat. She didn't mean the comedy, but the flirting and sparring between the two main characters, played by Gable and Claudette Colbert. She knew there would be the inevitable, embarrassing love-scene after much misunderstanding. The final kiss was always in close-up, and it was a relief when The End flashed onscreen.

'Have a Pontefract cake,' May offered. It was the last one, but she didn't say. She'd blown her Saturday sixpence in one go, this afternoon. She, too, would rather have been watching Laurel and Hardy. Now *they* were really funny.

Later, blinking in the late afternoon sunlight, they sauntered to the bus-stop.

'Thanks for treating me,' May said, meaning it.

'Thank you for coming,' Georgia responded politely. They watched the crowd emerging from the Regal dispersing, hurrying home for tea, no doubt.

Unexpectedly, they saw someone they knew. Miss Stedman, in a pretty blue crepe dress with a navy jacket, her hair all combed loose and pink lipstick. She was walking beside a distinguished-looking man, with a pencil moustache like Clark Gable's, but they weren't talking, so maybe they weren't together after all, Georgia conjectured. Then the man's hand was on Miss Stedman's elbow and he was guiding her across the road to the big hotel which dominated the main street.

'She didn't see us,' May hissed to Georgia, for there were others behind them now, waiting for the bus.

'Good. I can't smile 'cause I've got black teeth from the liquorice!'

'Shouldn't say nothing.'

'I won't,' Georgia agreed. She knew what May meant.

Eva toyed with the cream slice on her plate, cut it into smaller pieces. The tea was strong, in shallow cups, poured from a silver teapot. They were not the only ones in the hotel dining-room, but the tables were a discreet distance apart.

After a while he said, 'Shall I book a room here? We only have tonight.'

'I said I was meeting my brother, who is expecting to be called-up at any minute. I said I would be back this evening, but –'

'You can telephone. You are fortunate to be billeted where you are, Eva.'

No privacy in the post office, she thought. 'Is there any point?' she blurted.

'I believe there is. There will be more regrets, for both of us, if we don't seize this chance.'

Deceit, more lies, she thought. But how can I help myself?

Georgia parted from her friend at the Jubilee seat, where they had left their bikes. 'Come straight home,' Phoebe had said. 'I'll be there, with supper on the table.'

She pedalled energetically, and soon arrived at the cottage. The door was ajar. 'Hello, I'm back!' she called unnecessarily, for Sandy bounded to greet her.

'Enjoyed yourself?' Phoebe asked. 'We've an unexpected visitor.'

'*Mum!*' Georgia cried joyfully, knocking her mother's hat askew as she flung her arms around her.

'I couldn't wait no longer to see you,' her mother smiled. 'When him next door said he was going to see his boys, and would I like a lift, I asked Dad did he mind, he said no, so I hopped on the back of Mr P's motor bike and clung on tight!'

'Mum!' Georgia cried proudly. 'You could've fallen off!'

'Laddered me stockings, that's all, dearie. Didn't even lose me hat.'

'Fortunately, I was here when your mum arrived,' Phoebe said. 'Mind, I'd have tidied up a bit if I knew you were coming. We've had a good old natter, Georgia, and I think your mum approves of me and my abode.'

'It's very nice here, but I still want to come home,' Georgia said frankly.

'Dearie, it's early days. Things'll hot up, won't they, Miss Bliss? You stay here for a bit, there's a good girl. I shan't worry now I know what's what.'

'When have you got to go back?'

'Want to get rid of me already d'you?' Mum teased. 'My chauffeur's calling for me after dinner tomorrow. I'm sleeping in your bed, and you'll be on a camp-bed alongside. All right?'

'Oh, Mum I do love you!' Georgia hugged her again.

'That's just what I needed to hear,' Mum said, wiping away a stray tear.

'Ready for the fish pie?' Phoebe asked. 'Local codling courtesy of Jube . . .'

When they were in bed, later, because the walls were only lathe and plaster, Mum whispered, 'You struck lucky, coming here, Georgia.' She groped for Georgia's hand. 'Your little bed all right?'

'Bit narrow,' Georgia admitted. 'But the cushions help. I wish you could stay longer, Mum.'

'You'll have a good laugh, seeing me perched on that pillion tomorrow. I have to watch out me skirt don't catch on the wheels. What I do for love of you! Still, you are my daughter.'

'Your *only* daughter! You know, Phoebe sees the funny side of things too . . .'

'You spell it with a Ph, not an F, Georgia.'

'I found that out after I sent my first letter. I'll be home for Christmas, won't I?'

'Dearie, how can I say? It's not just you away, look at our boys, they got marching and drills and that, and an old sergeant major shouting at 'em: don't you think they're homesick, too?'

Phoebe was on night patrol in the garden, torch beam directed at the ground, as the new regulations decreed. Sandy darted to the hedge, gave a gruff bark. 'Jube, is that you?'

'Who else would it be? Can't I take a breath of air, too?'

'Shush ... Georgia's mum is here. They're already in bed.'

'Come through the gate, inside mine for a bit. We need to patch up our differences, don't we? Have a glass of my elderflower.'

'Think that will help me sleep? Obliterate all the regrets?'

'Can't promise that. What d'you say?'

She sighed. 'Just let me put Sandy in the scullery.'

'We're on the same side, you know,' he said. And she knew he wasn't referring to the war. 'You can tell me things, and it won't go further.'

'You're a good friend, Jube,' she admitted, 'but –'

'No buts. Don't keep things bottled up.'

'Or they might explode, eh? Like your home-brewing does on occasion?'

'Maybe. But it's cordial, tonight ...' And a shoulder to cry on, he thought.

Eva was sobbing softly, and he looked at her anxiously. 'Don't want you all red-eyed at the breakfast-table, darling.'

He had come prepared, unlike herself, but the hotel provided the softest of bath towels, soap and other toiletries. He'd already bathed, and she was about to follow suit. She watched as he took the new shirt from his case, unwrapped it from the cellophane, removed the pins. Clark Gable daringly bared his chest too, in the film, defying the censors, she recalled with a sudden, involuntary smile.

'That's better,' he observed. The cufflinks were in place, his tie neatly knotted. He stood by the mirror, combing his thick hair. His reflection showed a somewhat lined face, a suspicion of jowls.

He was already in his late thirties when we met, she realised with a start. He's fourteen years older than me. I don't know anything about his wife, his family. I know he has an important position in Whitehall, that's all. He's afraid of scandal, of being found out.

He turned, crossed over to the bed where she was still reclining. He bent to kiss her bare shoulder. His face was smooth; he smelled of the astringent he had used after shaving. 'Time to get up, Eva. I've a train to catch in an hour.'

She trembled, reached out to pull him close. He disengaged himself smartly.

'Eva, please. I did tell you –' His voice had an edge to it.

'That last night is exactly that? Our last time together?'

'No, I didn't say that.'

'And you didn't say you loved me, not even *then*; in fact, you never have . . . Go now, have your breakfast. I won't join you, that would be ever so indiscreet.'

'No need for sarcasm.' She'd wounded his pride.
'*Goodbye*,' she said.

Tucked in her handbag, she discovered later, was an envelope. It contained several, neatly folded five-pound notes wrapped in a double-sheet of notepaper. She did not count them. There was a cryptic, typed message. Unsigned, as always. He must have used his secretary's machine, she thought. She'd never received a letter in his handwriting: this was all part of the secrecy of their *affaire*.

TAKE CARE! WOULD YOU
PLEASE BUY YOURSELF A
LITTLE GIFT FROM ME?

'Money can't buy love,' she said bitterly, aloud. Then she wept again.

SIX

The class stood to attention. Miss Worley had an announcement to make. She looked at the expectant faces, her gaze lingering for a moment on Georgia.

'Our eminent local musician, Mr Bliss, has very kindly offered to take a class in pianoforte, on Friday afternoons in the hut. Only those pupils with aptitude and willingness to practise will be acceptable. Who has a piano at home? Hands up.'

'*Or I'll shoot*,' Georgia whispered in May's ear. May waved her hand: there was a piano in the Union. They played Chopsticks when Matron wasn't around.

Georgia raised her arm, too. Phoebe possessed a small upright piano, which was dusted regularly rather than played.

There were hesitant takers. 'I could play my nan's, Miss.' 'Dad says we're not to bash about on the iv'ries, but if I learned to play properly . . .'

Then there came the realisation that it would be an escape from school, something different, hopefully enjoyable. Six of the children were selected for a trial period, including Georgia, May and Kenny Button, who was tall and skinny, with untidy black hair, and back at school, if temporarily parted from his bike. 'Any silly behaviour,' Miss Worley warned, 'and this privilege will be withdrawn. Miss Stedman will accompany you. I will take the rest for singing here, as usual.'

As she swept out, Georgia nudged May again. 'Now's my chance to prove to Dad I *am* musical. He won't let any of us touch his precious accordion. And at least we'll miss "What shall we do with the drunken sailor?" with Miss Worley.'

'Did you see Miss blushing? I think she fancies being Mr Bliss's assistant!'

'She fancies *him*, more like! Like Miss W does the drunken sailor!'

Lawrence Bliss, seated at the hut piano, apprehensively awaited his first pupil. Eva, supposedly in charge, was distracted by the presence of his wife and what she was saying, about their home, Red House, being invaded by the British Army.

'Great boots stamping all over the parquet floors indoors, and vehicles tearing up the turf outdoors. Thank goodness we took the silver with us, and Grandpa's precious books. The colonel has commandeered my bedroom, no doubt. We were given no advance warning . . .' She was obviously upset.

'Oh dear,' Eva murmured. She looked at her watch. 'Excuse me, Mrs Bliss, but we must begin. We only have an hour.' She called out to Georgia, 'Ready?'

'Yes, Miss.' She sat down beside Mr Bliss. 'Aren't you going to crack your knuckles?' she queried, disappointed. Instead, he extracted a pill from a little tin which he replaced in his breast-pocket. He's either got nervous indigestion, she conjectured, or he's covering up for smoking, like Dad. I can smell peppermint.

'Not today. Middle C,' he indicated – but she saw that he was smiling.

'I know all the keys, though I can't make head nor tail of 'em on paper.'

'That's a good start,' he said kindly. 'Let's try some scales . . .'

'Same as singing, then?'

'You've got the idea. Right hand first, that's it.'

He's nice, can't think why Phoebe doesn't get on with him, she thought.

By the end of the session, it was also the end of the school day: home time.

Eva and Lawrence replaced the chairs on their neat stacks, while Beryl yawned and patted her mouth with red-tipped fingers. 'Would you care to join us at the gatehouse for tea, Miss Stedman?' she asked, when all was tidy.

Eva hesitated. 'I have my school books,' she began.

'We'll walk back past the post office. You can deposit them with Miss Gathercole; let her know you will be back later. All right?'

'Thank you, Mrs Bliss. Tea would be most welcome.'

'Beryl, please.' she said graciously. 'And I shall call you Eva.'

Georgia and May followed Kenny out of the hut. 'Want to come to my place for five minutes?' Kenny asked. 'Mum'll have the kettle on.'

'Tea would be most welcome, wouldn't it, May?' Georgia grinned. They'd listened in to the interchange between Miss Stedman and Mrs Bliss, of course.

They went down the step into the shop, jangling the bell. Almost everything was sold here: from paraffin to pies. Kenny's dad was making up the weekend orders on the long counter. You could see where Kenny got his height from, but his dad was burly and balding. 'We'll need you behind here, when I go out on deliveries,' he reminded his son gruffly, adding, 'I'll fetch the stool for you. Got to take it easy for a few days, eh?' He smiled at the girls. 'Hello! Go straight through; here, take a bag of the new broken biscuits, plenty of custard creams.'

Kenny's mum made good, strong tea and was generous with the sugar lumps. 'Make the most of it before we get food rationing, as they say. How'd you all get on with the music lesson?' She had thick black hair and dark eyes like Kenny's.

'Not too bad,' Kenny said off-handedly.

'Don't be modest,' Georgia said. 'Mr Bliss said "you've obviously played before, you've got a good ear".' Both Kenny's prominent ears reddened.

His mum beamed. 'I tried to teach him myself but he got fed up with practising. Maybe he'll persevere this time. I had lessons in Red House with old Mrs Bliss, at his age. So did Kenny's dad, Bob, and Helga from the Union; the three of us were best pals at school in those days –'

'Like Kenny, May and me!' Georgia exclaimed.

'Yes! Mrs B took a special interest in Helga: said she was musically gifted. She talked then. In fact, she worked part-time in the shop after we married, when Bob and I took over from his parents, then she suddenly clammed-up . . .'

'I've never heard her play the piano,' May said, astonished.

'Well, she gave that up around the same time. Old Mrs Bliss was quite upset. But I keep my hand in, now and then, like at Christmas. More tea, girls?'

'Thanks, but we'd better go or Phoebe will wonder where we are,' Georgia answered for them both.

'Take a couple of biscuits with you, then, to keep you going.'

The biscuits weren't broken at the gatehouse, but crumbly and rather stale, Eva discovered. Tea was served in delicate cups, rimmed with gold, with a slice of lemon instead of milk. Lawrence made his excuses and retired to his study. 'A commission to complete: I'm sure you have plenty to talk about together.'

It was a one-sided conversation. Eva was relieved, however, not to be questioned about herself, but to listen to Beryl and nod occasionally.

'After my husband's grandparents died, when he inherited Red House and his mother moved away, he had the daunting task of sorting through all the effects. His sister did not trouble herself to return at that point. Eventually he realised that he would need professional help, especially with his grandfather's books and papers: he advertised in *The Times*, I applied for the position and was accepted. I am a qualified librarian and secretary and I had worked in big houses on such projects before. This was seven years ago.' She took a sip of tea.

They obviously haven't been married long then: Eva was surprised.

Beryl continued, 'It soon became obvious that Lawrence, absorbed as he is in his music, was not equipped to run the house on a day-to-day basis. This had always been left to his formidable grandmother, assisted by his mother. I don't blame Lucy for seizing the chance to lead her own life, at last. I suspect it was she who suggested to her son that he invite me to stay on permanently, as his wife.' She looked at Eva. 'You understand, ours is a marriage of mutual convenience.'

Eva did understand. Convenience, yes, but irritation and intolerance on Beryl's side. She felt sorry for Lawrence. He'd been patient with the children this afternoon. She'd noted the peppermint on his breath, too. Maybe he'd escaped to have an illicit smoke. He deserved better, she thought. Grandmother Helga was not the only formidable one. Beryl was obviously frustrated, with her work in the big house truncated and living here, taking on for the first time the role of housewife, for there were no servants, no gardeners at the gatehouse.

'I really must go, thank you so much for the tea,' she began.

'You will come again? I feel we can be good friends, Eva.'

'Yes, of course I'll come,' she was forced to say, aware that they had some things in common. Not being loved, for one, she thought wryly.

Georgia's imagination was working overtime, as she and May made their way to Spare Penny. May seemed to be concentrating on her pedalling, as Georgia said, 'Don't you ever wonder, May, what happened, what made Helga decide she wasn't going to talk any more?'

To her amazement, May shouted, 'Why don't you mind your own business, Georgia Smith?' Then she shot-off

ahead on her rusty old bike, her bony knees and legs working like pistons, leaving Georgia behind.

Shocked by this outburst, Georgia didn't attempt to
catch her up. She had to complete the journey, of course,
as Phoebe was expecting her. Hot tears blurred her eyes.
What could she say, to make things right? What would be
Mum's advice? *Keep quiet for a bit, don't make things worse
by going on about it.*

'Aren't you going to tell me what's wrong?' Phoebe asked, as
she stirred Oxo cubes in the jug of hot water. It was chilly
in the evenings now, the plantation wood pile was in need
of replenishment, and this was a satisfying supper drink.

Georgia accepted her steaming mug. 'Nothing really . . .'

'Oh come on, I couldn't help seeing that you and May
had obviously fallen out. I imagined you'd had a nice afternoon, with the music lesson.'

'We did. Though I don't think your – Mr Bliss thought
he'd discovered any real talent. But it was fun, anyway.'

'Good. So why the sour faces?'

'May thought I was being nosy.'

'Were you?'

'I suppose so. I only asked about Helga not talking,
because Kenny's mum – we had a cup of tea at the shop
after the piano-playing – said they'd been good pals when
they were girls and she spoke all right, then. May bit my
head off.'

'She's very protective of her friend.'

'I thought she was *my* friend, too.'

'I expect she'll get over it.'

'Before my birthday on Sunday, I was going to ask if she can come to tea?'

'Of course she can.'

'She won't want to now . . . I wish Mum and Dad could be here. I wish . . .'

'You wish you could go home. I do know the feeling: I never quite lost it, when I was living abroad all those years.'

'Couldn't you afford to come back?'

'It wasn't that . . . You'll have some pleasant surprises on Sunday, I reckon. I've put aside some intriguing parcels from the postman. Anyone else you'd like to share the cake with? Pals from your old school?'

'Not really. The ones I liked best went back to London after the first week. Miss Stedman's been real nice to me. And I'd like Kenny, only he's May's friend, of course, and Jube, we ought to ask him.' *Your* friend, she thought.

'I agree. He's promised some cream to go with the jelly and fruit. There you are, then, it'll be a party, won't it? Just the right number in a little house.'

Along with *The Coot Club* by Arthur Ransome, which Mum wrote was set on the Norfolk Broads – 'you might visit one of these days, as it's up your way, I reckon' – there was a red velvet dress – 'It didn't get as far as the stall! Only worn once, hope it don't clash with your hair!' – and a pair of pink-striped flannel pyjamas with a waist cord, because Mum guessed it was colder here than in London, as well as a harmonica from Dad, 'which you can play along with the piano'.

'Don't know about that,' Georgia grinned, but she had a go, there and then on her birthday morning, perched on the end of Phoebe's bed, managing a breathy version of 'Happy Birthday To You', which made Sandy bark.

The boys had sent postal orders and identical cards, even though they weren't together when they bought them. There was even a shiny card with a dog on the front, signed 'Dusty'. The smug card-dog had a big bow round his neck. 'If that was Dusty, he'd worry that off and shake it to bits,' Georgia said.

She wiggled her bare toes in Sandy's fur: he'd crept upstairs to see what all the fun was about. He was a comfort on a Missing-Mum-and-Dad day.

The birthday cake oozed bramble jelly and cream. Kenny brought a box of little candles from the shop and stuck them on the top. 'Eleven – that's lucky, one left. You're older than me, it's not my birthday until the end of October. Where's May? Thought she'd be coming.' He passed over a small box of chocolates and a card.

Georgia was saved from explanations by a knock on the door. Miss Stedman and May had arrived together. 'Happy birthday, Georgia. You look very nice in that dress,' Miss Stedman approved.

'Let me take your coat,' Phoebe said. 'Then we'll go in the parlour.'

Georgia looked at May, waiting for her to speak first. 'Here you are,' May said ungraciously. She thrust a small parcel in Georgia's hand. 'I wasn't going to come, but Helga said I must.' Belatedly she realised what she had revealed.

'You should have brought her, too,' Georgia told May impulsively. Then, 'Oh, let's forget we had words, May, and enjoy the party, eh?'

May nodded. 'All right. Kenny here?'

'He's helping in the kitchen, putting sausage rolls on a plate and that.'

'Let's go and see if there's any odd ones spare, then!'

Jube came along after his chores, and Georgia, opening the door to him and taking the can of milk, looked at him and exclaimed, 'You've had your hair cut!'

'Met old Bert in the pub at lunchtime, his day for the barbering. He had his scissors out before I could think twice. Mind, he charged half a crown, saying it needed shears and I said, "no army short-cuts for me, Bert, just trim the thatch".'

'It's only yellow on the tips now,' Georgia told him frankly.

'Think Phoebe'll approve? She's been on at me to get it done for ages.'

'She does,' said Phoebe, coming up behind them. 'I'd have charged you five bob! Just in time for tea, Jube. Thanks for the milk, did you –?'

'Did I bring a present? Of course I did. Happy birthday, Georgia.'

'Thanks.' She unwrapped the pink comb with the long handle and admired the enamelled roses. 'It's pretty, Jube.' She wanted to tell them that they sounded rather like Mum and Dad just now, but wasn't sure they'd be pleased.

After Georgia cut the cake and got jam on Phoebe's best tablecloth, she persuaded Kenny to play 'The Bluebells of Scotland' on the piano, while she accompanied him on the mouth-organ. Jube had the fire roaring up the parlour chimney, and Eva gratefully stretched out her cold hands to the blaze. Georgia noted with surprise that Jube was paying her teacher quite a bit of attention. Maybe she'd been wrong about him and Phoebe, she thought. May was still rather off-hand with her, despite her warm thanks for the bottle of scent.

It was dark outside: time to pull the curtains, time for the guests to disperse. 'I'll walk you all home,' Jube offered. 'You'll come along, eh, Kenny?'

The birthday was drawing to a close. The pink pyjamas were warming on a stone hot-water bottle in Georgia's bed. She tucked the harmonica under her pillow; draped the red velvet dress on the back of her chair.

Phoebe looked in as she settled under the covers. 'Good night, Georgia. We had a lovely party, didn't we? Sorry I didn't quite get your present finished, just the buttons to sew on; I might tackle that tonight.'

'I don't mind, really. It's a nice pattern, that cardigan. I can't knit –'

'I'll teach you, shall I?'

'Yes, please. I could knit comforts for the boys, then . . .' She yawned, feigning sleepiness. She wanted to think of her family at this moment.

Jube was back. He tapped on the scullery door. 'All safely delivered. 'Night, Phoebe, if you can hear me.'

She opened the door. 'Come in, Jube. You must be cold. You've kept my fire going and neglected your own, I reckon. I'll make some cocoa.'

'Got nothing to hurry back for, no one waiting up,' he said laconically.

They didn't talk much. She finished her work, folded the jacket. Then, 'I was thinking, how, if I'd followed a conventional path in life, I might have had a daughter the same age as Georgia.'

'You're doing a good job with that girl.'

'I'm glad you approve. But it makes me realise.' She hesitated.

'What you've missed? I keep thinking that, lately.'

'Is that why you made a pass at Eva? Smartened yourself up?'

'Ah, I knew you noticed. Look, nothing's changed in one respect.' He stretched out one huge hand and, with it, covered both of hers, clasped in her lap. 'Look at me, Phoebe. I'm lonely, so are you –'

'I'm alone, for now, there's a difference.'

'You're still hankering after that foreign feller?'

She sighed. 'I'm afraid so. We were together a long time. I don't want to talk about it.'

'Well, he's not here now and I am. I care for you.'

'I know you do. That helps, believe me, Jube.'

'I'd best go,' he said.

They stood for a moment by the door, then she wrapped her arms round him and hugged him fiercely. 'You don't know how much I miss –'

'Believe me, I do.' His lips brushed the top of her head. 'Goodnight.'

SEVEN

The newspapers referred to it as the Phoney War, for all the action seemed remote, with the Channel between Britain and Europe. Some rationing of essential foods began in November, and, as Button's was the main grocery store in the village, everyone registered there. Not that there was a shortage of staple products in Suffolk. Jube's own modest needs had to be accounted for, but still his neighbours did not go short of eggs, milk and homegrown vegetables. Meat was not yet officially rationed, but anyway they ate the cheaper cuts, as they did at home, Phoebe disguising the meat with rich gravy and dumplings, just like Georgia's mother.

You say you want to come home for Christmas, but it's bread and scrape here, duckie. Grub is in short supply, rationed or not. Dad misses his crispy bacon for breakfast, but he says at least the beer's still flowing down the pub. Not that he gets much time for that, now he's a warden. At the moment he's mainly looking out for chinks in the blackout and them showing a light where they shouldn't. But there's a lot more to it than that, of course. Learning what to do if the worst comes to the worst. I hope to visit you soon, bearing gifts, as they say, but Mr P is filling sandbags at weekends. The kids who are still around help. School has only just opened again in the mornings. The bags are piled up round every door. The old place don't look the same. It will be nippy this time of year on the bike, so I am taking in a pair of your father's old trousers. He don't know yet. Still, he always says I wear the trousers, don't he? Heard from the boys, they send their love, but are not ones for letter writing, like you and me . . .

There was a much diminished congregation in the church for Midnight Mass on Christmas Eve, but this was one service that Phoebe said she wouldn't miss. It was rather exciting, Georgia thought, stumbling along the lanes in the dark, with flurries of snow, which had threatened to lay all week, dampening and chilling them despite both being wound round with winter woollies. They groped their way along the aisle bordered by flickering candles, while Mr Bliss played the organ and Kenny pumped the bellows. Some of the evacuees had returned to London, and most would not come back, but Phoebe consoled Georgia and said her parents were wise to say she should stay put. Miss Stedman spotted them and sat with them instead of going to the front pew to join Miss Worley.

'Are you all right for lunch tomorrow?' Phoebe whispered to Eva.

'Yes, Miss Gathercole insists I join her and her cousin from Ipswich. She was widowed recently and has had to give up her paper shop.'

At the end of the service, after they sang 'Hark The Herald Angels' with gusto, there was a potentially awkward moment – especially following the lyrics 'peace on earth and mercy mild'. As the rector bade them all a happy Christmas, despite the strife, they spotted Beryl Bliss in a sleek fur coat with matching hat, standing aloof in the porch, waiting while Lawrence collected his music.

Phoebe cleared her throat. 'Merry Christmas,' she managed. 'To you both.'

Lawrence Bliss came up behind them. 'Thank you, Phoebe. It will soon be a new year. Time for a change of heart?' he asked diffidently.

She turned, reluctant to include her sister-in-law. 'I hope so, Lawrence.'

'You must join us on Boxing Day, Eva,' Beryl said, deliberately loudly.

Kenny gave Georgia's arm a nudge, in passing. 'See you after Christmas,' he whispered. 'Have a good time! The shop's closed for two days, thank goodness. Dad's made me a new sledge, for deliveries as well as fun. Hope the snow lasts!'

'It's bloomin' cold! Never like this in London, with the houses all around.'

'Oh, you'll get used to it,' he said.

Early on Christmas morning, after Georgia had opened the contents of her stocking, they cycled up to Spare Penny. She enjoyed helping May and Helga prepare the sprouts: twisting them off the thick stalks; cutting a cross on the root end. May wore the pixie hood Georgia had knitted. It was chilly in the cavernous kitchen, despite the huge stove. Poor May had chilblains on her ears as well as her toes.

'Phoebe had to finish it off,' Georgia admitted. 'Sorry about the colour.'

'It's warm, that's what matters. Fawn goes with anything. Helga likes her mitts, don't you?' Helga nodded, smiling. They poked out of her apron pocket.

'This packet is for you and Phoebe. Helga and me baked them last night.'

Georgia took a sly peep. Star-shaped shortbread biscuits, dusted sparingly with icing sugar. 'Mmm ...' she murmured. 'Thank you.' She gave Helga a warm hug. She didn't presume to repeat this with May.

The goose had been cooking overnight; at 11.30 all was ready, amid much happy anticipation.

'Are you sure you won't stay?' asked Matron, beaming at them.

'Thank you, but no,' Phoebe answered. 'Jube's busy our end, stoking the fires and basting the capon, which is his contribution to the feast as he's eating with us. We prepared the vegetables last night. Also, Georgia must be longing to take a proper look at all her presents. I'll be back to work the day after tomorrow. She'll come with me, weather permitting. Is that all right? She likes to help.'

'She's a good-hearted girl, and young May will be glad of the company. They get on well, don't they? There's no one here her age. May's not so much of a little old woman, as they say, since Georgia came to your house. We'll save you both a nice slice of cake: you surpassed yourself with that, this year.'

'Drop of Stone's ginger wine, courtesy of Button's, that'll warm us up,' Phoebe encouraged Georgia, as they rode carefully home along the rimed road. The sky looked very grey and threatening: obviously there was more snow to come.

There was a big cardboard box and a tall bulging sack on the front step. On the mat was a Christmas card, which

Phoebe opened immediately. She smiled at Georgia, 'From my brother. We'll have a look at the surprises later.'

'I'm glad you've made up,' Georgia said, happy for Phoebe. She couldn't imagine not talking to her brothers when they were all at home.

'Ah, but the card just says to you and me, from *Lawrence*.'

'Expect he did it behind old Beryl's back,' Georgia guessed.

'I ought to reprimand you for calling her that, but, I'm sure that's true!'

'Must have been delivered while I was seeing to the cow – the dog was with me,' Jube said, lugging the stuff in. 'Time for me to carve up, eh?'

'You're growing your beard again,' Georgia told him, shaking her head.

'Best way to keep warm when the east wind bites,' he returned, grinning.

'True,' Phoebe said. 'As long as you don't expect to kiss me under the mistletoe you've hung over my chair, until *after* you've shaved.'

Georgia looked hopefully from one to the other. Jube had the red face, not Phoebe. 'Mum won't kiss Dad with a whiskery chin either!' she remarked.

She missed the decorations they always put up at home: sticky loops of paper chains; lights like Chinese lanterns on the tree, which was a puny specimen from the market transformed with tinsel and funny animal shapes fashioned from twisted pipe-cleaners, with a Mum-made crepe-paper fairy on the pinnacle. Still, there were sprigs of berried holly tied with red ribbon, here, and the table was set with blue and white china, polished silver cutlery and fine glasses for the celebration meal.

'Just to remind me of the old days,' Phoebe said softly.

That evening it snowed in earnest. It was bitterly cold the following morning. Jube looked like an iceman, heaving a load of wood into the kitchen: 'Keep the home fires burning.' Pails of water were lined up under the sink, in case the pump froze. 'Thanks, Jube,' Phoebe was grateful. 'What would we do without you?'

'I'm laid-off the farm until it improves, so call on me whenever you like.'

Sandy leapfrogged in the garden, where the snow had piled up. 'I don't think he minds it, though,' Georgia observed. 'Wonder if it's snowing in London?'

There'll be that sour, sooty aroma from chimneys belching smoke from fires banked more with slack than coal, she recalled sharply, and snow soon turns to yellowy slush there. Round here the trees are magical with white-laced branches, and there's wood smoke for breathing in, especially if it's pine.

'Says so, on the wireless. It's going to be a long, hard winter, they tell us. It's the same in Europe. I hope our troops are equipped for it. We'd better knit balaclavas for your brothers next, eh? By the way, I looked in the box and sack after Jube went home last night. Now, how d'you think we'll get to work tomorrow?'

'I suppose we'll have to walk.' Georgia shivered at the thought.

'There could be drifts. The wind sees to that. See.' Phoebe removed the cushions, lifted the lid of the long window-seat in the living-room. 'Skis! Boots, varying sizes; poles, the lot. I thought my sister-in-law would have thrown out my Norwegian things long ago! The boots need a good dose of dubbin, though.'

'I didn't know you could ski in this country,' Georgia exclaimed.

'Oh, you can – I've skied in Scotland, in conditions resembling Norway, which is where I learned. Grandpa took Lawrence and me there for the first time in 1920. I was taught by my cousin Nils, who is two years older than me. Lawrence wasn't too keen, winter sports and mountaineering were never his forte. He didn't accompany us again; he was too involved with his music.'

'Are you going to teach *me*?' Georgia asked, excited.

'That's the idea. You can only come with me tomorrow if you can keep your balance. No hills to swoop up and down! We'll practise along the lanes today. Try on the middle-sized boots: your toes should be near the top, but definitely not squashed, and your heels and ankles firmly supported. All right?'

'Yes thanks.' She yanked at the laces. 'Norway isn't in the war, is it?'

'Not yet. It's a neutral country, but well-fortified against any sudden attack by sea. They have the reassurance of British ships in the vicinity and can expect their full support, in the event of trouble. You see, at present the Germans draw their main iron-ore supplies from Sweden, also neutral, via the port of Narvik in Norway and there is a very real danger that they will decide to invade Norway and Denmark. Oslo still has an ambassador in Berlin, though.'

'You never talk to me as if I'm too young to understand, I like that.'

'That's good! It was my grandpa's way, too. I'll show you snaps of our Norwegian trips. It's a beautiful country. We explored the fjords by boat, climbed lesser mountains, saw icy glaciers shimmering in the midnight sun, spectacular water cascades and vast forests of giant spruces.' Phoebe's voice was dreamy.

'Is that where you were when you lived abroad?'

'No, but we – I visited Nils several times over the years. Well, go and tell Jube we need him, his tin of polish and plenty of elbow grease!'

Skiing wasn't as easy as Georgia imagined. 'Done the splits a few times! Phoebe said you have to watch your shins,' she said ruefully to Kenny, when she met him along Long Lane, dragging the sledge, with a can of precious paraffin for the lamps and the primus stoves that took the edge off the chill in the cottage bedrooms.

'Saw Mr Bliss shovelling snow off his front path: they were expecting Miss Stedman, he said. Next door the soldiers were out in the grounds. I couldn't see much through all that barbed wire barricade, though I heard a lot of cranking-up of the lorries. They need to keep the engines turning over, I reckon, in case we get invaded here on the coast, even though it's more likely to happen in the south.'

'We ain't going to be invaded at all!' Georgia said firmly. 'My dad said so. They wouldn't have let me come here if it wasn't safe. Phoebe says us kids ought to keep away from Red House and the army and not annoy them. You'll get caught one day, Kenny, nosing about.'

'Be prepared. That's what *my* dad says. He thinks it's strange we never see the soldiers in the village. They must be up to *something*. Where's Phoebe?'

'She left me to my practising – said be careful – went back to boil the spuds. I'll clump along behind you now – it's easier than gliding.'

Eva wasn't looking forward to lunch at the gatehouse. She still felt bloated after her Christmas dinner. Miss Gathercole had done her best, but the roast pork was fatty, the vegetables overcooked, the pudding too rich, and her cousin Doris never stopped talking. They'd pulled a cracker or two, washed-up, and then Eva had escaped to her room on the pretence that she, like the two stout ladies on the twanging settee, needed a lengthy snooze. Would she fare any better today?

'Hello, good to see you,' Lawrence said. 'You can walk along the path without fear now.' He looked younger in a thick, navy roll-neck jumper and corduroy trousers. He opened the gate, offering his arm to escort her to the door, which opened immediately for Beryl had obviously been watching out for her.

She wished she'd worn something more sophisticated than her pleated skirt and cream blouse when she saw Beryl in a light wool Chanel costume, with braided jacket. She recognised the perfume – No. 5, Chanel's own – because she had an empty but still fragrant bottle herself, tucked away among her underwear. *He* had given it to her, of course.

Unexpectedly, Lawrence's hand lingered on her shoulder for a moment as he took her coat. Startled, she realised it was a deliberate gesture.

'It's cold in the hall, come in by the fire,' Beryl said, and Eva knew she had observed her confusion. 'Call us when lunch is ready,' she added dismissively to Lawrence, with an unnerving smile directed at Eva. She's playing a game, Eva thought, and I must watch my step . . .

Fortunately, Eva was not expected to over-indulge. Thinly sliced ham with mashed potato, mustard and red cabbage, followed by mincepies and a small jug of cream. The wine with the meal was good, and the black coffee later, piping hot. She didn't feel the need to unfasten the top button of her waistband surreptitiously, like yesterday. She worried she'd put on weight since arriving here. She didn't realise that it suited her to be rounder, fuller in the face, not so sallow.

Lawrence joined them in the sitting-room, proffering a selection of games.

'I'll lean back and close my eyes,' Beryl resolved. 'You two play.'

Draughts, they decided. A quiet game, where you concentrated on the board. There had been a disquieting moment when she glanced up once, and noticed for the first time that, like his sister, he had a full, sensuous mouth. It implied a warm impulsiveness, well concealed. They were evenly matched and, to Eva's surprise, it seemed no time at all before Lawrence rose to draw the blinds and switch on the light. They had electricity here, fronting the main road, unlike the isolated cottages. Red House, of course, had its own generator, courtesy of the army.

Beryl stretched, yawned, opened her eyes. 'I expect you'd like to get back, before it's too dark, Eva. Lawrence will walk you home.'

'Oh,' Eva said involuntarily. She'd imagined that the invitation included tea. Had Beryl really been asleep, or hoping to eavesdrop on some flirting?

'You'll excuse me if I don't see you out.' Beryl yawned again.

There was no one else about, just the beam from the torch lighting their way across the road and past shadowy houses with blanked windows.

They paused outside the deserted school playground, before walking on to the post office. 'Thank you for a pleasant afternoon, a nice lunch,' she said.

'Thank you for coming,' he replied. Without warning, his arms went round her, he bent to kiss her cold cheek, then, lingeringly, her lips. She was right about all that pent-up feeling. 'Why so passive?' he whispered after a while.

'It's not right, you know that . . .' Her back was pressed against the railing. Now she put both gloved hands against his chest, pushed him away.

'I'm unloved, you know, but not I hope unlovable,' he said wryly. 'It was only a kiss, after all.'

'You're a married man; I know that one kiss is never enough –'

'I can guess the rest, Eva. I'm sorry if you've been hurt. Forget this happened, eh?'

'I can't! Don't you understand? I find you attractive – that's dangerous. Goodnight!' And she hurried off, leaving him standing there.

'I'm so thankful you're back,' Doris babbled. 'Lena came over funny after we'd had our dinner. I couldn't get a word out of her, she went all limp. So, I phoned Mr Button at the shop, and he called the doctor out. Had a slight stroke she has. I shall stay on until she's better and look after things here – I've nothing really to hurry back home for, now my poor Alfred's gone. I'm afraid you may have to look out for a new billet, two nights on the sofa's enough for me.'

Just when I have decided to stay on, Eva thought. I can't go back to London now. 'I'm so sorry,' she said, meaning it, because she got on well with kindly, cheery Miss Gathercole. 'You mustn't worry about me. I'll speak to Miss Worley, my headmistress, about it as soon as I can. I'm sure she'll help.'

EIGHT

Next day, Eva called at the schoolhouse and explained the situation briefly, aware that the older woman was regarding her thoughtfully. They were in the sitting-room, dusty and musty, fireless, obviously not often used.

'We have a spare room here,' Miss Worley said at last, 'where I keep my overflow of books. But if you help me box these up, I see no reason why you should not join us, on a temporary basis initially, because who can say how long it will take Miss Gathercole to recover from her stroke of bad luck?' A fleeting smile, then, 'I've been expecting you to speak to me, on another matter.'

'I'm not sure what you mean?' Eva said warily.

'I thought you would decide to return to London, now that most of your charges have done so, especially as the education hierarchy here has decided to postpone next term's scholarship examinations, due to all the upheaval.'

'You don't really need my services now, is that it?'

'Oh, but I do. You are a dedicated teacher. I can trust you to take the reins when my father needs extra care, as he does from time to time. I was hoping you would stay on permanently. Your future in London would appear to be uncertain, a part-time position at best. I also understand that the majority of senior schools are now located many miles away, unfortunately for Georgia and her like.'

'I really *would* like to stay, but –'

'Good. I have to say I am aware of your present predicament.'

For a long moment Eva was unsure how to reply. Then, 'I thought it wouldn't be . . . obvious, for another couple of months . . .' she admitted painfully. 'When the school board are informed, I will have to leave anyway.'

'It is a rule I cannot agree with. They will not learn of this from me. There is a precedent, set by a young teacher at this school with a fiancé in France during the Great War. There was talk of course, but so much of the same was going on, people were kind and the situation accepted. It helped that her parents were much respected. She carried on teaching until just before her baby was born, after which the child was fostered by a friend and she resumed her duties.'

'What happened to her? To her lover, and her child?'

'She is still here, Eva, if I may call you that. The young man was posted "Missing, Believed Killed in Action". Their son was well brought up by his new family, who moved away after the war. His mother learned lately that he, in turn, is doing his bit in France. He is very much in my thoughts . . .' Perhaps the little slip was deliberate, but not to be commented on.

Miss Worley withdrew a small box from a desk drawer. 'Would you care to borrow this? *She* wore it for a time. Folk can make what they like of it.'

Eva slipped the wedding ring on her finger. It was a trifle loose. She said simply, 'Thank you. I shall never forget your kindness.'

'I gather that the man concerned is not prepared to do the decent thing?'

'He doesn't know; he is older than me, married,' she stated baldly.

'Ah. You can expect no support from him, then?'

'Our relationship is over . . . Unlike your . . . friend, I have no family. My father, well, I never knew him. My mother died while I was at college.'

'Is money a problem, then?'

Eva shook her head. 'I have enough to get through, and there is my salary, of course.' She thought, I have fifty pounds: his conscience money.

'We'll get by,' Miss Worley said briskly.

The 'we' was heartening; her handshake firm.

There were ice-slides in the playground; it was almost as cold in school as it was outside. There was a tortoise stove in each room, but fuel had to be carefully conserved. The children kept on their coats but gloves were necessarily removed when it was time to write with numbed hands. The snow was no longer a source of excitement but of endurance, as January ended and February 1940 began.

This war appeared to be a waiting game. When the thaw began, surely things would accelerate? Lord Gort's British Expeditionary Force still surrounded Arras, but in France neither the Germans nor French made more than cautious moves toward the other. The Maginot Line seemed invincible.

There was as yet no real war in the air. The RAF dropped more propaganda literature than bombs over enemy territory. It was generally assumed that the navy would play the more vital role, as in the First World War. The British public were heartened to have the charismatic Winston Churchill back in office, as First Lord of the Admiralty in Chamberlain's new Coalition Cabinet.

Yet there had already been great naval losses. The liner *Athenia* had been torpedoed off the coast of Ireland on the very day war broke out. Five hundred lives were lost on HMS *Courageous* the day after Germany invaded Poland, and in October 1939 there had been the further devastating loss of 800 from the *Royal Oak*, sunk at Scapa Flow. In December came the great Battle of the River Plate when the 'phantom' German warship the *Admiral Graf Spee*, which in varying forms of clever disguise had sunk a number of

British ships, was fiercely engaged by the cruisers *Achilles*, *Ajax* and *Exeter*. Unable to escape, the *Graf Spee* finally scuttled herself in the harbour at Montevideo. Her commander, Captain Hans Lansdorf, a gallant veteran of the Great War and a gentleman of the old school, shot himself the next day in Buenos Aires, while the rest of his crew were interned.

On 16th February, the *Altmark*, a German store ship that had fuelled the *Graf Spee*, was located lurking in a fjord in Norway. There were many British naval prisoners aboard, who had been transferred earlier from the *Graf Spee*, which was responsible for sinking their vessels as well as for picking up the survivors. There was public euphoria when a force from HMS *Cossack* daringly boarded her. The former captives were now on their way home, having also endured the necessary bombardment by the RAF.

'I can't believe Norway will be neutral for much longer,' Phoebe observed.

Georgia wrote to her parents:

It is very, very, very cold in the country!! But the roads are kept salted so walking's not too bad, but no need to ski, blow it! You said last time you saw me, Mum, that I had rosy cheeks. Well, I am all **BLUE** now! I wish Phoebe would let me have

Sandy on my bed at nights to help keep me warm! How is my dear old Dusty getting on? I expect the dustbin lids are frozen tight! I know you can't come in this weather, but please do as soon as you can. I am saving up my pocket money for the train to come home next holidays. You can't stop me!

What do you think? Miss Stedman is having a BABY! They haven't told us kids but we're not daft. She has got a ring so she must have got married secretly. There is just her and me now from home. I don't mean to grumble, sorry, because Phoebe is so kind to me, and I have my best friend May, and Kenny Button too. Still, I miss you both and the boys and Dusty, more than I can say.

All my love, Georgia. xxxx

PS I am keeping my chin up, but it's a bit wobbly.

The Friday music lessons continued. From the time Miss Stedman began wearing baggy clothes, Georgia noted that Beryl Bliss avoided speaking to her teacher, but watched her husband like a hawk.

'She cut her dead, as they say – did you see? Miss looked for a minute or two like blubbing,' she said to May.

'At least old Beryl needn't worry about Mr B and Miss now,' May thought.

'He still likes her, I can tell. Anyway, she's better off being friends with Phoebe, isn't she? When she's round ours, I'm allowed to call her Eva. It must be very dull at Miss Worley's. She only listens to the news, then switches off. Fancy missing Arthur Askey and Stinker Murdoch! Laugh a minute, Jube says.'

'Shush! Kenny's about to play.'

But Georgia was in full flow. 'He's doing better than us, well, me anyway. You practise, don't you?'

'Helga sees to that,' May said. 'But I'll never perform at the Albert Hall.'

'Girls,' Mrs Bliss's voice cut in. 'I am going home. It is *freezing* in this place. You children will have to help my husband pack up afterwards.'

'Now we can all relax,' Georgia said brightly, as the hut door closed.

After Kenny had done his bit, Mr Bliss cut the lesson short and advised them all to 'Run along. It looks as though there's more snow on the way. May should get back before dark, anyway. Miss Stedman and I can tidy up here.'

'They want to talk, I reckon,' Georgia said, as they braved the elements.

'Eva,' Lawrence said diffidently, 'I am concerned about you. Is there anything I can do to help? You can confide in me.'

'I don't think that would be fair; Beryl –'

'Is bigoted as always. I imagine you are relieved to escape her company. I really must apologise again for my unwanted attentions at Christmas, I had no idea, of course. Just tell me' – he indicated the ring, as she stacked the music – 'I am right in thinking there has been no marriage in haste?'

She nodded. 'Please don't ask me any more. And I don't want you to say sorry. I . . . suppose I *wanted* you to kiss me.'

'Please allow me continue to be your friend, Eva.'

'It's not possible, is it? You must realise that.'

'Well, if things change – unlikely as it seems now . . . I'm glad you and Phoebe are close, anyway. She also went through a very difficult time.'

'She doesn't talk about it.'

'No, but she was exploited too, that much I gathered. She's a strong woman, like my late grandmother. I imagine you are the same.'

'Thank you, Lawrence,' she said. She wished that was true. Then she caught her breath. Was that fleeting sensation the first discernible movement of the baby? She was apprehensive rather than thrilled.

'Are you all right?' he asked anxiously. 'Have you seen a doctor yet?'

'I shall soon. I'm keeping well, Lawrence, honestly. I have to say the food is more wholesome at the schoolhouse. Miss Worley sees to that. Three ration books mean more variety than two. And Jube,' she paused, 'well, he helps us out. As you once said, he keeps an eye on Phoebe – and now, me.'

'As I shall, too.'

On a sudden impulse, taking him by surprise, she came close, looked up at him. 'I appreciate that promise. I just wish things were not so complicated.'

Phoebe had left work after lunch because of the threatening weather. She walked down to the shop later on, intending to collect Georgia, too. Kenny and May arrived shortly after her. Kenny said she'd just missed Georgia, who was already on her way home. 'Dad's offered to see May gets back safely,' he said.

Approaching the hut, Phoebe observed the light. She decided to say hello to Eva. About to enter, she caught sight of two people locked in a silent embrace.

She closed the door carefully, hurried away. *Lawrence and Eva!* She had an overwhelming feeling of sadness for them both.

In March, Georgia's parents caved in. Her mother travelled by train to Suffolk one weekend. 'Mum! Why ever didn't you tell us you were coming? May and me would've met you at the station!' Georgia welcomed her indoors and hugged her tight.

'Spur of the moment, dearie, guessed I'd be welcome anyway! Cor, me feet aren't half throbbing, couldn't half do with a cup of tea! Hello, Phoebe, nice to see you, and you, May – spending the day with Georgia? Why don't you two take the dog for a little walk, so I can have a talk with Phoebe first,' she said to Georgia, after the rapturous welcome. 'Don't worry, I'm staying tonight. Tell you all when you get back. Quarter of an hour will do.'

The tea in the pot was still hot from after lunch, so she was soon revived.

'We miss her a lot,' she told Phoebe. 'And things being quietish on the home front, Albie and I was talking about her coming home, for a while, anyway, see what happens, eh? I thought, Georgia's growing up fast, there's things I ain't told her yet and should; a girl needs her mum at a time like that, don't she? Of course, I know you'd be good about it, as you have been all along, but –'

'I understand,' Phoebe reassured her. 'I've loved having her here, Nell. But I guessed this was coming. Yes, let's wait and see if things hot up, and you know I'll always welcome her back here, if need be.'

As Georgia and May arrived back, they saw Eva approaching.

'Guess what, Eva,' Georgia cried, 'Mum's here, and she's been having a private yarn with Phoebe – sounds mysterious, but *hopeful*, maybe!'

'Maybe I shouldn't intrude,' Eva began, when the door opened and Nell stood there beaming.

'No, join us, Miss Stedman, do – I was intending to see you, anyway!'

'Everyone calls me Eva here in the country, especially your irreverent daughter, so I hope you will, too!'

'And I'm Nell, of course. D'you know I've been calling 'em Mr and Mrs P next door for over twenty years, and things really are changing, 'cause now I have to think before I say Phyllis and Bert!'

'But don't call her Nellie, 'cause that rhymes with –' Georgia interrupted.

'Jelly!' Nell put in smartly, but everyone laughed.

It turned into a bit of a party, the farewell sort, with Jube being invited over to hear the news and bringing a couple of bottles of his elderflower wine for the adults and cordial for the youngsters. Georgia and May biked down to the shop to tell Kenny and his family the news, then he returned with them, saying he would accompany May to Spare Penny later, while it was still light.

'Makes a big difference, though, that double summer-time the government announced,' Jube observed. 'We've got a couple of them land-girls on the farm now – you might be asked to take one of 'em to lodge, Phoebe, I suppose.'

'Not for a while,' she said firmly. 'I meant it when I said Georgia can come back, if need be. What about you, you've got a spare room, eh?

'You really mean that? A man on his own? Any girl would decline!'

'I'll try and get back to see you for your birthday in May,' Georgia told her friend. 'We'll *all* be eleven, then, eh?'

'I'll look after her,' Kenny promised solemnly.

Then all of a sudden, Eva burst into tears and Nell put her arms around her and said, 'There, there, dearie, it'll all come out in the wash . . .'

So there they were, Nell and Georgia in the train next morning and all the new friends – only they seemed like old friends now – waving goodbye as they steamed away. It was back to London and sandbags and air-raid shelters; to school in the mornings and more stringent rationing, for meat had been added to the list. But there was a grand reunion to come, with Dad, if not the boys, and Dusty the dog.

NINE

London didn't seem the same to Georgia. Her school remained closed, the playground deserted. Some of her former classmates, who'd returned earlier, had been re-evacuated much further away to the West Country. Children from several local schools were now grouped together in a church hall, but understandably tended to form little cliques. The teachers included one brought back from retirement. There was no mention of sitting scholarships and, in Georgia's view, too much copy work, spelling tests and endless arithmetic. However, there was a big map which unrolled down the blackboard, and each morning, the world at war was pinpointed by gnarled old Mr Jones, a veteran of Mons, who with his Welsh eloquence, held the attention of thirty children.

'It's geography *and* history, too,' Georgia told her mother enthusiastically. 'Mr Jones tells the background to what's happening *now*. Like Phoebe about Norway.'

Nell had a busy new job: she helped to sort, clean and distribute clothing donated for refugees. 'See, Georgia, no experience in life is wasted: all them years running the stall down the market means *I'm* in charge of all the girls!'

Georgia's father was busy towing barges from the warehouses, and he reported much activity on the splendid modern fireboat on the Thames. *'They'll* be ready, if, Heaven forbid, old London goes up in flames,' Georgia overheard him tell her mum.

At first, Georgia was at a loose end in the afternoons. Dusty dodged out when he saw her reach for his lead, being a street-rake, an independent dog.

'Can't dig for victory here,' Georgia sighed. 'There's hardly a book I haven't read in the library. Nothing going on like there used to be.'

'What about collecting waste paper?' Albie asked, rustling the depleted *Daily Mirror*, one evening after supper. 'I could look out that old haversack of mine from my boy scout days, unless your mother sold it when I wasn't looking?'

'Who'd buy *that*?' Nell retorted. She immediately urged caution. 'You mustn't go too far; stand on the doorstep unless you know who lives there; take Dusty if he's willing, *he* wouldn't let anything happen to you, but haul him well away from the pig-swill buckets; and mind you sling your gasmask on the other shoulder!' She paused, then, 'Leave a note to say where you're going, the key on a string through the letterbox, and mind you're back here before tea.'

'Rules and regulations, might as well be in the army with the boys.'

'Get the girl a whistle, Nell,' Albie said. 'Dusty's slunk off at the very idea.'

Georgia was now an official salvage collector: not 'any old iron' of course, because that needed to be carted away, but paper of all sorts and, occasionally, rags because these too could be recycled in the pulping factories. When she had sorted and tidied her spoils into neat packages, which occupied her most evenings, her father delivered them to the local salvage centre.

She even made a few friends on her regular route, while heeding her mum's warning. One day she was given a pile of pre-war girls' magazines, kept carefully and as-new, which she asked if she might read before she passed them on. 'You can keep them if you like,' the middle-aged housewife said.

'Thank you, but that wouldn't be right!' She was fascinated by the exploits of Mavis and Co. roaring around on powerful motor bikes pursued by wild men with spears, in the days when the Empire was there to be explored, or hurtling down the Cresta Run on a bobsleigh. Shades of Kenny and his sledge!

Perhaps the most unusual waste paper had intriguing pinhole patterns. 'Rolls for a pianola,' said the elderly foreign man with rheumy eyes, inviting Georgia inside for 'one last performance, yes?' Mentally crossing her fingers for ignoring her mother's strictures, Georgia sat down in what had once been quite a grand room, and listened enthralled to Brahms' 'Cradle Song', played by an invisible pianist, in sparkling form despite the patina of dust on the instrument.

'Are you sure you want me to take all this?' she asked, awed.

'The pianola was my late wife's. We found refuge here after the first war. We worked hard at our business; I bought this for her when we were past being poor. I have not played it in years. I am leaving London, going to my daughter's: I rocked her cradle to that music, but she says she hasn't room for it.' The old man rubbed his red-rimmed eyes. 'It has had its day, like *me*, young lady.'

I wish I'd practised more on the piano when I had the chance, she thought, wondering if Kenny and May made the keys fly up and down now. When she played her mouth-organ, Dad was grumpy because, as Mum said, he worked too hard, smoked a lot, got wheezy. He groaned, 'D'you *have* to, Georgia?' No playing his accordion either. Sometimes she wished she was back at Phoebe's . . .

She wiped away a stray tear with her finger, then licked it.

'Always made my wife cry, that tune,' her new friend said.

Norway, which hadn't been involved in war for well over a hundred years, and at that time had a pacifist labour government, was finally forced to make tentative, uneasy moves towards mobilisation. Although there were coastal defences, they were not manned at full strength. The Norwegian Navy patrolled still-neutral waters, and consisted mainly of seasoned vessels, unadapted for modern warfare. These had the backing of a few seaplanes. There were scarcely more fighter planes to combat any strike from the air. Norway firmly believed that the British Navy would come to the rescue in the event of aggression. Yet there was a traitor in their midst, and his name would become symbolic of his kind: Quisling.

One day, Churchill gravely announced that the navy was laying mines around the coast of Norway. Early the following morning, on Tuesday 9th April, the Norwegians awoke to the ear-splitting drone of wave after wave of German bombers en route to Oslo. There was no retaliatory anti-aircraft fire from the ground; this show of German force appeared to be totally unexpected. Rumours ran wild; some even thought that the planes were actually bound for England, for the long-awaited invasion there.

Jube called on Phoebe late that evening. 'I know you must be worried about your relatives there,' he said simply.

'There are a couple of elderly aunts and an uncle on a remote farm. At least they won't be affected by the bombing.'

She bit her lip. 'But, my cousin Nils works in Oslo, I've been thinking about him all day . . . He's probably been called up, he was in the Reserves.' She fiddled with the cord on her warm dressing-gown. She'd had a bath earlier, but she was decently clad, she thought. Anyway, Jube wouldn't get ideas. That was frustrating in a way, she realised with a start.

'You haven't heard from him for some time?'

'No . . . To be honest, he was rather keen on me when we were younger. I was fond of him, too, but not in the same way. My – long-time companion was jealous, he didn't encourage any familiarity. Eventually I felt trapped, I couldn't stand the constant suspicion. Now you know why I left him. Ran away home.'

'You're missing Georgia,' he said. 'She'd help to take your mind off things.'

'She certainly made me smile most of the time.'

'In a way she helped to put things right between you and me, Phoebe.'

'Was I as awkward as all that?' she asked wryly.

They sat at the table, sipping hot tea, looking across at each other.

'You'd been hurt. It takes time to heal,' he said, 'even though you had good friends willing to help.'

'Thanks to Georgia I found that out.'

'You're settled here now?'

'Seems so. But I can't say for sure . . . Why didn't *you* marry, Jube?'

'I suppose you want me to say because I never found a girl to live up to you! I did a bit of earnest courting, you know, years ago. She was the bonniest girl around, but I took too long about it and she married her childhood sweetheart.'

'Who was she?' she asked curiously.

'You know her now as Mona Button. She and Bob are a devoted couple' – he hesitated – 'though they went through a sticky patch early on. Still, he don't appear to have strayed since.'

'Bob Button – I find that hard to believe! He's a good husband and father.'

'So he is. Let's leave it at that. I shouldn't repeat idle gossip.'

'Anyone after Mona, for you, Jube?'

'I may look like one, but I'm no hermit,' he said. He put out a hand, gently tugged her damp hair, braided for the night. 'Like me to stay for a bit? Talk all you want, then you needn't *think* too much . . .'

She sighed. 'You know me so well.' Then she added, very quietly, 'I didn't mean to hurt you, all those years ago, it's just that –'

'You were too young, and I was too clumsy,' he said ruefully.

She awoke suddenly, just before dawn. Late last night they had both fallen asleep by the fire. She vaguely remembered stumbling up to bed sometime after midnight, leaving Jube where he was.

The door opened, diffusing light from the candle on the shelf outside, and Jube appeared with two cups of tea. 'Thought you could do with this, before I milk the cow, and then go to work,' he said diffidently. 'You can lie in a bit longer. I let the dog out, and made up the fire.'

'Thanks, Jube.' She sat up, accepted her cup gratefully. 'Sit down on the bed while you drink yours.' She sensed his embarrassment, knew that she must put him at his ease. When she'd broken down in tears during what had become a confessional, he had held her close, eventually stopping the talking when he kissed her.

'I don't presume anything, you know, after last night,' he blurted out.

'You don't have to make excuses, Jube, it's nice to be looked after.'

'You ought to see your brother, find out if he has heard anything.'

'I might. Coming to supper, Jube?'

He smiled. 'Yes. Glad to. You've buttoned your top all wrong,' he added.

'Oh!' Phoebe blushed now as she pulled the sheet up under her chin. What happened a few hours ago seemed so natural, she thought, and the memory of that awkward young man and her rejection of him years ago, was finally banished.

Beryl put down the telephone with a clatter. She was shaking with anger. 'If I'm not allowed to call on your superior in my own house, he can jolly well come round to see me! I wish to make a serious complaint,' she'd shouted.

'I wish you hadn't done that,' Lawrence remarked mildly, pouring coffee. He didn't expect to be offered breakfast.

'Why do you never back me up?' she demanded.

He sighed. 'You'd better get dressed Beryl, in case the top brass rushes round here to smooth things over.'

'Will you be in the room when he does?'

'I'm sorry, no. What can I say? I wasn't here, after all.'

'No, you were supposedly visiting your sister.'

'What d'you mean by that? I assure you I did spend the evening with Phoebe –' And Jube, he thought. That was unexpected.

As if she read his mind, she flared, 'Who else was there? Your not-so-prim little schoolteacher? People must be talking about you two, adding things up.'

'Don't be malicious, Beryl. You're wrong.' He rose from the table. 'Didn't you hear the knock on the door? You will have to conduct the interview in your housecoat. I'll let them in, that's all.'

The colonel was not in uniform; indeed he wore greasy overalls. 'I won't sit down, thank you. A complaint, you said?'

Beryl recognised him, despite his attire. He was very tall, good-looking, with a military moustache. 'Yes, indeed. Late last night there was a commotion in the lane, between here and Red House. Two men, obviously fighting, disgusting language, and a woman screaming.'

'Your husband didn't investigate?'

'My husband was out. I was on my own. *Terrified*,' she asserted.

'You assumed that the men were from the barracks?'

'*Barracks*? Is that what you call my house?' She was outraged.

He ignored that. 'It is highly unlikely that these were soldiers, madam. Fraternisation is not encouraged –'

'You make that clear, with all that wretched barbed wire! Do you intend to investigate, or not?'

'We have more important matters to concern us right now. However, if you can tell me the approximate duration of the altercation, and if you believe it led to something more serious –'

'It lasted perhaps half an hour. From some time after eleven o'clock. What I found disturbing, Colonel, was the sudden silence after the scream. For all I know, someone could have been *murdered*.' There were scarlet patches of agitation on her pale cheeks. She stood up, the kimono parting to give a glimpse of a revealing nightgown clinging to long bare legs, skimming mule slippers.

'Have you informed the police?' he asked abruptly, averting his gaze.

'Not yet.'

'Well, don't. Leave this with me, but rest assured, I saw no signs of any recent disturbance when I came along the lane. Drunks, I imagine, fighting over a female for her favours. Probably sleeping it off this morning. Goodbye, Mrs Bliss.'

'You will return to me, regarding this?'

'In due course.' He held out his hand. 'Forgive me, but what is an attractive woman like you doing in a backwater like this?'

For once, Beryl was speechless.

Early the following day, most of the troops left their quarters. There were no screams, only the continuous rumble of heavy vehicles going past the gatehouse and turning into the main road. Jube was forced to dismount and push his bicycle into the hedge as the lorries roared past him when he was on his way to the farm.

A skeleton staff remained in Red House, including the colonel, as Beryl learned when he telephoned her after lunch. She did not enlighten her husband immediately, but went off to get changed for going out.

'I've been summoned to see the colonel,' she then told Lawrence, with some satisfaction. 'You see, *he* evidently believed me.'

'See if you can find out what's going on now,' he suggested diffidently. She had certainly put on the warpaint, silk stockings, high heels, the lot. 'How long will you be? Remember I am teaching this afternoon.'

'That's your concern. What I do is my own affair. Is that clear?'

'Very clear,' he said.

'We should never have married, but you're not much of a man, are you? Despite Eva, and the whispers of you fathering a child before we met –'

'How dare you! Who told you that?'

'Your own mother. She suspected that you seduced a local girl, although you denied it. Hard to believe,' she taunted. 'But I couldn't let you – touch *me*.'

'You've got a wicked tongue. I never forced myself on you; isn't that enough? I knew you didn't love me, but I respected your wishes, then.'

'You don't need to pretend anymore. Can I be sure *you* weren't involved in that row last night? I shall leave you, oh, I haven't decided when, but there'll be no divorce. I've earned the right to my share of all your property.'

Then she walked out, leaving him a state of shock.

TEN

'*Heia Norge!*' was the defiant whisper, as the people of Oslo began their mass exodus. Yet there was little panicking on the day following the bombing and the arrival of a token occupation force, which had immediately taken over the city police headquarters, the radio station, the telegraph offices and the town hall.

The last train had steamed away earlier; the station was deserted. All kinds of vehicles were filled to overflowing, travelling at a snail's pace. Mobilisation was apparently rescinded: the despicable Quisling, long in league with the Nazis, claimed in a radio broadcast to have formed a government. Police patrolled the streets.

Enemy warships were already in the harbour. Nils Norland, wearing mountain boots, but with his army uniform concealed in his rucksack, was among a silent gathering there. Then warning sirens blared; there were rumours of British bombers on their way. That was great news, but now came the shout to '*Run for your lives!*'

It was a sunny spring day, but Nils was jolted in the back of a swerving lorry towards the designated military base, on roads which were still treacherous with ice. They passed many men along the route, marching resolutely, most in civilian dress.

On arrival, he discovered that the unit had received instructions to move on. Recruits were trusted to take uniforms and arms from the depot. Later, in pitch dark, they loaded supplies on lorries. Instructed to regroup in the morning, the men dispersed in a vain search for food, finally settling down for the bitterly cold night, in a cluster of isolated barns, in inadequate sleeping bags on straw-strewn dirt floors.

A rude awakening at dawn, to the realisation that the now deserted base was under attack. Men emerged from the barns, weaving instinctively over open fields to the woods, to staccato bursts from machine-guns as the planes swooped low. A pall of dense black smoke with a red core almost obscured their view of the pale Nordic sky.

A young recruit voiced his shock, his anger: 'Where is the RAF? Why are we told we will march back victoriously into Oslo by Independence Day?'

May 17th, Nils thought, not much more than a month away. Most of these volunteers had not handled a rifle before, feeding them was already a problem and they were ill-prepared for the conflict ahead. Then he saw all around him heads spontaneously bowed in silent prayer, and followed suit. The majority had left loved ones and young children behind them; Nils, in his early thirties, was unmarried, without close family. *At that moment he thought of Phoebe, back in England.*

There were soon pockets of resistance all over Norway, though the enemy was advancing. Norwegian Ski Troops played a vital part in reconnaissance. There were ambushes, several enemy detachments were destroyed, roads and bridges were blown up. But there was a desperate shortage of officers. The most experienced soldiers were those who had fought in the recent Finnish-Russian war.

The main route of escape from Oslo, for those trying to link up with the Norwegian resistance, was the Nordmarka, the great winter sports area, despite the presence of Nazi ski patrols. On arrival at Nils' latest camp, concealed in a snowy mountain valley, the first group of skiers to outwit these patrols were counselled, armed and instructed to return immediately to mount a rearguard attack.

Nils was one of those advising the raw recruits. There were no real guidelines. He did not voice the thought: We are being driven back. We will fight to the end, but that could be within weeks, not months. Where are the British?

It was official: Allied forces had landed on the coast of Norway. There was euphoria, soon dispersed when the enemy intensified its efforts and the number of casualties rose alarmingly. German planes released propaganda leaflets telling the Norwegian forces to give up. They were assured that if they surrendered without further resistance they would be allowed to return to their homes. But after a few days of this, bombs were raining down, thick and fast, on the besieged garrisons.

The nightmare retreat north began in earnest after three weeks of fighting.

There was definite talk of an amnesty, the surrender of arms, but there were those, including Nils, who were determined to carry on, to join their allies.

There were high banks of snow on either side of the road taken by Nils and two companions, who had requisitioned an armoured vehicle. It was a tortuous journey, with numerous stops and starts; laying planks of wood ahead when the wheels churned the slush. Through the mountain pass, then, in growing darkness and chill winds, they drove down a deserted valley road cautiously, towards a settlement where they hoped to find somewhere to stay until daylight.

Nils, who was driving, suddenly became aware of several men running towards them. Norwegians! In the familiar green, with peaked caps. He braked with difficulty as they heard not so distant machine-gun fire and explosions. 'We destroyed the bridge, but those bloody Huns swooped silently down the mountain on skis!'

'Are you sure they are enemy troops?' Nils asked.

'How can one be sure of anything, now? Turn back: we shall soon be surrounded.'

They marched resolutely over the mountains. When their transport ran out of petrol, they were forced to abandon it, together with the heavy artillery. Each man had a revolver and his rucksack. 'We must travel by night and hole up during the day,' Nils decided, as leader, despite the doubts of his companions who thought they should keep going. 'There is a hut I know of, over the next ridge. We will take it in turns to be on watch. Now we should share our rations.'

They approached the hut cautiously, pistols cocked. The door was unlocked, and there were signs of recent occupation. The dying embers of the fire were soon coaxed into flames. There were no skis hanging on the walls as they had hoped, but at least there was flattened straw to bed down on and tea was brewed, once they had melted snow. They dipped their hunks of bread in the remaining hot water and ate the cheese, rind and all, too weary to care that it was hard and stale.

The torch shining on his face was blinding for a few moments. Nils struggled to sit up, but was roughly pushed back on the straw. Then he realised his friends had gone.

'Hello, Nils,' his captor said softly in accented Norwegian, 'don't you know me?'

'Karl?' he asked uncertainly. The face was familiar despite the German uniform.

'Yes. I am as shocked as you are that we should meet like this. Don't be alarmed, I am not going to kill you, unless you prove troublesome. But I shall take your gun, because I am not foolish enough to think that you would not think it your duty to shoot *me*.' He removed the Colt from Nils' pocket. 'There, now you may get up and we will talk, while we decide what comes next, eh?'

'I am your prisoner,' Nils stated bluntly. 'Where are the men who were with me?'

'I spotted two fellows some distance from here. I had become . . . disengaged from my unit. I decided to return to this hut and stay put until morning. Would you like a nip of brandy to warm you up?' He held out a flask in one gloved hand. 'Look, I appreciate that we are not exactly friends, particularly not in present circumstances. I spare your life, Nils, because you are Phoebe's cousin and, in return, you shall give me news of her.'

'I don't believe she would want that.' Nils ignored the proffered drink.

'Look, don't be obstinate. I know she is back in England. I wrote to her old address, but my letters were returned. If it had not been for this war, I would have sought her out, in time.'

'That was the last thing she wanted!'

'And the last thing you want, is to be a prisoner of war
. . . I was considering letting you go. So, you would rather
I finish you off, after all?' He was actually smiling.

'I don't think you lost your way at all! You were always
a bully, I know how it was with Phoebe, remember. A man
who beats a woman is a coward. I suspect that you are a
deserter!' Nils shouted.

The flask struck him just above his right ear. Blood,
mingling with brandy, ran down his face, seeped under his
collar. Then they were struggling, each intent on overpowering the other.

The man on the bicycle was observed, but disregarded
by those on the look-out for strangers in the vicinity.
He was fair-haired, like so many in these parts, with
shirtsleeves rolled to the elbows as it was a fine day, and
wearing baggy khaki shorts. There was a green kitbag
fastened to his bicycle carrier. This was grubby and
water stained; again not unusual here where fishing was
a way of life.

He went into the village shop to ask for cigarettes, and
politely asked the helpful Mrs Button if she could kindly
direct him to the home of Miss Phoebe Bliss. His English
was perfect, but she would tell her husband later that, 'He
seemed a bit foreign like – reminded me of those Polish
chaps who were here a while back . . .'.

'Norwegian, I reckon,' he said. 'Refugee, probably. They say there's quite a few of 'em arrived in Scotland recently. Miss Bliss and her brother got connections in Norway, eh? Hope you did the right thing, sending him up there. Still, old Jube'll be around, won't he?'

'He had piercing eyes,' Mona told Bob. 'Dark blue. When he looked at me, even though he was smiling, I got a funny feeling . . .'

Phoebe and Jube were talking outside her back door.

'Heard from Georgia that both her brothers got back from Dunkirk, thank goodness, though the younger one was injured and is in hospital. Nell's visited him.'

'Who's this?' he cut in sharply, as he became aware that they were being observed over the gate.

'Hello Phoebe,' the stranger said, wheeling his bicycle through. 'I apologise for surprising you, but I know you will be pleased to see your cousin Nils again.'

Jube looked enquiringly at Phoebe. Her face was white as chalk.

'It's all right, Jube. Yes, this is certainly unexpected, but this is my cousin from Norway, the one I told you about, who taught me to ski – remember?'

'Aren't you going to invite me in?' he asked. 'Or, forgive me, do you wish to talk more to your friend?'

Do you want me to stay? She interpreted Jube's con-cerned glance.

'This is Jube, Nils, my neighbour. I – had invited him to supper.'

'I understand. I am hungry; have you enough for three?'

'Yes, of course. Where . . . are you staying?'

'My dear Phoebe, I am, as you say, at your mercy! I left my billet in Scotland because I wished to see you before I was sent to fight once more. I borrowed the bicycle and have travelled here mostly by that means, once I had spent all my money on the trains. You will please allow me to rest here awhile?'

'I suppose . . . Come in, both of you. Look' – she had to think quickly – 'I'm afraid you can't stay here long; you see, I need the spare room for my evacuee – she –'

'Will be back any time now,' Jube finished for her.

'Your friend took his time, I thought he would never go,' he said, just before midnight.

Phoebe was busying herself with the late evening chores: anything to delay the confrontation. He had followed her into the scullery, stood behind her as she rinsed the dishes.

Now she turned abruptly, almost colliding with him. 'Why are you here? Why the charade? Does Nils know?'

'My dear Phoebe, I can hardly announce that I am Karl Schmidt, lately a soldier in the German Army.'

'A deserter?' she queried sharply.

'He said that, your cousin Nils.'

'You were fighting in Norway?'

'He was fighting, I was, how shall I put it, "on the run". We met briefly, spoke of you, for your sake he let me go, gave me a comrade's uniform. Eventually, I joined a group of Norwegians planning to escape to Britain. Despite my story, which was good, I think that those who questioned me on arrival in Scotland were suspicious. In any case, I don't wish to be in combat again, especially on the other side.'

'You can't stay here!' She pushed past him, went into the living-room.

'You don't mean that.' His hands gripped her shoulders, turned her round. 'You may try to convince yourself that you despise me now, Phoebe, but I shall prove you wrong.'

'With force?' she flashed.

He smiled. 'I forgive you for that. We were together for a long time, neither of us can forget that. You need not worry tonight. Just show me to my bed. We will talk more tomorrow, yes?'

'I have to go to work.'

'Then I shall take the opportunity to sleep all day. And you will say nothing, nothing at all, to your friend Jube, your brother or to those who would take me away . . .'

ELEVEN

Phoebe decided to lock the back door, go out the front, pocket the key. The dog would have to be outside as she was unsure how he would react with a stranger on his own territory. Jube would be back to see to Sandy at midday, she thought.

Even as she removed the key from the lock, she sensed that Karl was standing there in the inner doorway. He wore yesterday's clothes, his hair was rumpled.

'Still creeping about?' she asked, angrily. She'd wondered how she would feel if she saw him again. Now she knew. The attraction was still strong, but the overwhelming realisation was that she would be forced to lie, to be devious. Where would *that* all end? She must endeavour to keep her distance, she thought.

'I had much practice, eh, when you came down early to the hotel kitchen and discovered me waiting there? You did not stay mad at me for long.'

'Not just one kitchen. I was inevitably forced to move on, remember, when it was discovered that I had a *man* staying in my quarters.'

He smiled. 'Here, it is a different story, I think. Then, despite your worry about your situation, you welcomed me, without questions, into your arms, your bed. Last night, you did not send me away, although you had your protector with you. You still have strong feelings for me, you can't deny it. Nor can I, my passion for you.'

'I *can't* go back to how it was – the undercover life you led . . . your . . . *moods*.'

'You say that now.' That dark gaze was disconcerting.

'I mean it! That's why I *had* to leave you. Don't try to force me, Karl.'

'I am at your mercy?' His tone was mocking, his proximity disturbing to her.

'Yes,' she said vehemently, '*yes*! I have to go now. You must be discreet, keep out of sight if anyone calls, though that's unlikely. We'll talk more tonight. Don't expect me until after six, because I promised to visit a friend after work who is expecting a baby shortly. From long experience, I know I have try to carry on as normal . . .

'Just remember that you can't stay here long – we actually have the military at the other end of the lane – but if you behave, I won't give you away.' She swallowed convulsively. 'I really must leave, or I'll be late.'

'Take care,' he said.

Did she imagine the hint of menace in his voice?

'Help yourself to food, but don't forget we're rationed; cigarettes, too.'

There were also unexpected visitors at Georgia's in London. Aubrey, her elder brother, who'd come through Dunkirk miraculously unscathed but now awaited the call back to battle, sprang a surprise on his family.

'Didn't even know you had a girlfriend!' Nell exclaimed, forthright as always, when he sheepishly introduced his new wife Eunice, on the front step, shaking confetti from her hat. 'Come in, so we can take a good look at you.'

'Then decide whether to keep me or not?' Eunice returned quick as a flash. She was a good-looking girl, bold-eyed, with short, newly-permed brown hair.

For a moment, Nell was taken aback, then she laughed and said to Aubrey, 'So you picked a saucebox, eh? Why the hurry? How long can you stay?'

Albie went upstairs, tipping Georgia the wink to follow. 'They'll say more to your mum, of course. Help me push the boys' beds together, Georgia, there's a good girl.'

'Oh good,' Georgia said. 'I thought, I bet they'll expect her to share my bed!'

'Ain't Mum had that little talk with you yet?' They yanked sheets over the flat, flock mattresses on the narrow iron-bedsteads. Boys didn't sleep on feather beds.

'About where babies come from? Yes, but they only got married this morning.'

'You'll learn,' Dad said enigmatically.

'Five days' leave, that's all,' Aubrey said, lounging back in his father's chair, the privilege of the returning hero. 'Then I hope you'll let Eunice stay on here with you, Mum. She'll look for a job, of course, but she'll have my allowance so she can pay her way.'

'What about your brother, where's *he* going to sleep? When he comes home it'll be for good. His war is over, thank God.'

'Mum, you know Martin'll be in hospital a while yet. By the time he's discharged, Eunice will've set us up with a couple of rooms of our own.'

'No particular reason for marrying quick, is there?' Nell asked, looking keenly at Eunice, who returned her stare. The girl was reed slim in her smart grey costume.

'No babies until after the war; I promised my mother,' Eunice said.

'Don't she still need you at home? You said your dad worked away.'

'There's six younger kids. I've had enough of their racket, and there's nowhere private there for newly-weds, Mrs Smith.'

Nell appreciated her honesty. 'Well, if we're going to live together, you'd best call me Nell. It'll take me a bit of time to realise there's two Mrs Smiths in this house – but only room for one in the kitchen, mind . . . What kind of work do you want?'

'In an office, if I can get it. I can touch-type and I'm quick with figures.'

'Your lucky day! The agency I work for is wanting someone in Records! That'll count as war work, too. I'll take you along with me tomorrow. All right, Aubrey?'

'Mum! Let's have our honeymoon first. Now, how about a nice cup of tea?'

She's older than him, at least twenty-five I reckon, Nell thought. He's all starry-eyed, can't believe his luck, but she's the one with the experience, I can tell . . .

Georgia pulled the covers over her head. The walls were thin; she was aware of sporadic giggling and the creaking of the improvised double-bed from the next room.

She thought: I'm not sure I like her. Dad obviously thinks she's pretty and she can hold her own with Mum. But it won't be just us any more, once Aubrey's gone . . . I'll write to May, tomorrow, and say I'm sorry I couldn't come to see her on her birthday, but Phoebe's invited me to stay for the summer holidays. Then, maybe when I get back here, Eunice will have found a flat.

An alarming thump from the next room, as if someone had fallen out of bed.

Georgia couldn't help herself. 'Want any help?' she called out.

'Your dear little sister, Aubrey' – sharp and clear – 'needs putting in her place!'

Much later, after Georgia finally dropped off to sleep, she was wakened by the sound of shouting. Then Nell was knocking on the newly-weds' door and anxiously calling, 'Are you all right?'

She heard the door open and Eunice's voice. 'He has nightmares, Nell, about Dunkirk, he ain't got over them terrors yet. You go back to bed. I can cope . . .'

'If you're sure,' Nell said. 'I could make a cup of tea?'

'No thanks. Goodnight.' The door closed smartly.

As Georgia thought, Mum'll be hurt, she became aware of muffled sobs and a hoarse whisper, 'Think about *this* instead . . .' Then, more intimate sounds.

She stuffed her fingers in her ears. *She* didn't want to think about it.

Phoebe was collecting her things from the Spare Penny kitchen, thankful that it was Friday and she had Saturday off, when May burst in, all out of breath.

'Phoebe! Eva wasn't in school today, and Miss Worley kept popping out to see how she was, then the nurse arrived when we were off to our music lesson, and –'

'Slow down!' Phoebe advised. 'Are you trying to tell me the baby's on its way?'

'Yes! Miss Worley said to tell you to come, as Eva's asking for you!'

'Helga, give the girl a glass of water! I was actually going to see her anyway.'

'Will you let us know what the baby is?' May asked.

'I'll tell Kenny to pass on any news when he makes his delivery, will that do?'

May nodded. 'Oh, and tell Eva good luck from me and Helga, won't you? Won't Georgia be disappointed to miss all the excitement!'

'She certainly will! Cheerio, then.'

'Oh, and Mr Bliss knows, 'cause he asked where Eva was,' May called after her.

Eva hauled on the plaited sheeting tied to the bed rail. Nurse Carroll had protected the mattress with layers of newspaper and pulled the nightdress unceremoniously above Eva's waist, but she was past caring what she was revealing. She just wanted the pain to go, the little being who was causing it to be pushed head-first into the world. She clung tight to Phoebe's hand, her nails digging into the other's palm. Her eyes were closed, sweat poured from her, and she was groaning in her agony.

Miss Worley left quietly, when Phoebe arrived, to see to her father. 'Call me, if you want me.' She looked in first on another visitor, waiting patiently in her sitting-room. Lawrence Bliss had called in to see how things were when he left the hut. 'I'm sorry,' she said, 'no news yet, I'm afraid.'

'How long has she been in labour?' he asked.

'More than twelve hours. Nurse is debating whether to call the doctor now.'

'Shall I do that?'

'Best not to interfere,' she told him in her dry way, but he sensed her concern. Then she added, 'I'm not sure you should be here at this time, you know. There could be speculation.'

'I don't care,' Lawrence said.

'Your wife –'

'Can speculate all she likes!'

'I should tell you, I know you are not the man responsible, but I also know that Eva values your friendship.'

'Thank you,' he said simply.

Sighing, Miss Worley left to reassure her father about all the hustle and bustle and to give him his tea.

Eva struggled as the rubber mask was held in place and she breathed in the stupefying fumes against her will. 'I don't want Phoebe to go,' she tried to tell the doctor who took her place. It was he who was administering the gas.

She was barely conscious when she was asked to 'give one last push', before forceps were threatened. The pain was all-consuming, but now she was strangely detached from it. The contraction propelled the baby into waiting hands, subsided briefly and then intensified to expel the placenta. It was all over. She turned her face to the damp pillows, began to weep weakly.

The baby was briefly examined, wrapped in a towel and placed across her flaccid stomach. Nurse Carroll gently moved her arms to hold the bundle. 'You have a little daughter, Mrs Stedman. Get to know her for a few minutes then, while I bath her, Doctor will do the necessary stitching for you. Your friends may pop in to congratulate you when I've tucked you both up . . . Have you a name for the baby?'

'Winifred,' she said. 'Win, after my mother.' This little soul must be determined to win through all future adversities, she thought, learn to be strong, like her late mother. '*Win*,' she repeated.

'She's – very nice,' Miss Worley observed, looking in the cradle. 'Smaller than I expected.' She didn't ask if she could hold the baby.

'Six pounds seven ounces,' Nurse Carroll smiled. 'Could I ask you to make tea in a while? Doctor couldn't stop, he had to go on to another maternity case, but he'll call in tomorrow morning, he said.'

'Thank you for coming, Phoebe.' Eva looked up at her, standing by the bed.

'I'm so glad everything went well in the end. Look, Eva, I have to go now, in case – Jube is worrying I've fallen off my bike, or something – but I'll see you both again soon! No tea for me, thank you.'

'You'll be her god-parents, you know, you and Miss Worley – that's if you agree.'

'You bet! Give Win a kiss from me.'

'I'm going to take two weeks off, with the head's permission.' Eva smiled at her other friend. 'Then the baby can come into class with me, be parked in a corner in her pram, until the holidays begin and we can make other arrangements . . .'

It was 7.30 when Phoebe left for home. What would Karl be thinking?

When Miss Worley went to tell Lawrence the news, she found that he had gone. Perhaps because of what she'd said. The poor man, she thought, with a sigh.

He arrived at the gatehouse just as Beryl came out of the door.

'Don't worry about being late,' she said sarcastically, 'I've been invited out for dinner. I just came home for a few things. I shall stay overnight.'

He didn't ask with whom, or where, as there was no need. Since she had been working as the colonel's private secretary at Red House, they had eaten few meals together. But this was the first time she had let him know that she would be away all night. It didn't mean, he imagined, that this was the first time she and her employer had slept together. In a way, it was a relief that she had a lover: for the moment, anyway, she appeared to have lost interest in his affairs.

Jube was keeping Karl company in the kitchen. Karl had obviously made friends with the dog, who was lying at the foot of her grandfather's shabby old chair, which he had brought in from the living-room.

'Making yourself at home, I see,' she told him. Jube looked at her in surprise.

'You locked the back door, not thinking,' he said. 'But I used my key and Nils was able to spend the afternoon in the garden. Sandy was no trouble, as you can see.' Sandy's ears pricked up and he wagged his tail.

'We shared a rug, sunbathed together under the tree. As you thought, no one came to disturb us. It was most pleasant.'

'I made supper,' Jube continued. 'Yours is keeping warm on the stove. Young Kenny called with your order, I put it all away for you.'

'Oh.' She'd forgotten that, and what about her promise to May? 'Did you –?'

'Pay him? No, he said it'd do when you were next in the shop. He'd spotted the doctor leaving the schoolhouse, and asked if the baby had come. He also heard that you were there. Good news, eh? All well?'

'Yes. Are you off now, Jube?'

He didn't take offence. 'I'll leave you to catch up on all the family news. Nils has been a mine of information about Norway!'

'I have made another good friend, I think,' Karl said smoothly. 'See you tomorrow, Jube. Don't forget the wine you promised for me to sample! Now,' he said to Phoebe, 'we will settle down and talk, while you eat, as Jube suggested . . .'

He came to her room that night as she had known he would. The talking earlier had ended in an argument. 'Don't you think you have caused me enough grief?' she cried, then stormed off upstairs and closed her door firmly. No lock, she regretted.

'Phoebe, are you awake?'

'Go away,' she muttered.

'My bed is hard; my legs too long.'

'It's a child's bed. It was mine, when I was young. It's Georgia's now, I told you. That's why you can't stay indefinitely. She'll be back here soon.'

In the dark, she was aware that he was moving closer. Then she felt his fingers caressing her face. 'Your cheek is wet. Why are you crying, Phoebe?'

'You really want to know?' She thrust his hand away, sat up. 'I am crying for my friend, who looked so happy with her new baby. I am crying because all too soon she will remember that the baby has no father, that she will have to bring her up by herself. I am crying because it reminded me that I will probably never have a baby of my own. How can I feel jealous when she's gone through so much, and now her life will be even more difficult?'

She did not demur when he slipped into bed beside her, and put his arm around her slumped figure. 'I didn't know you wanted a baby.'

'I thought I was pregnant once, when we were first together. The sickness I suffered was due to shellfish, eaten on a hot day. The doctor told me that I was unlikely to conceive, or would need an operation to correct what he termed "an irregularity" first. As I was unmarried, he intimated that this condition had its benefits: I could enjoy unbridled love-making.'

His lips were warm on her bare neck. 'And so we did. I would never have been the perfect husband or father, eh? As for the perfect lover, you are the judge of that.'

She felt her resolve melting away. 'Karl –' She didn't struggle as he drew her to him, what was the point? She wanted this as much as he did. Tomorrow was another day.

TWELVE

Georgia's hand went up. Mr Jones did not sigh his disapproval, as other teachers did, that she was always first to ask a question or to give a smart answer.

'Yes, Georgia?' His finger still lingered at a point on the globe.

'Please, sir, d'you reckon Hitler'll invade us soon?'

'It's almost two months since Dunkirk, Georgia. Much going on in the home front since then, eh? Munition factories working all-out; the production of many more aeroplanes; there's the new Local Defence lot; and our navy is ever-vigilant.'

'Yes, but my dad says they might decide to attack from the air,' Georgia declared.

'We have to be prepared for all *eventualities*,' Mr Jones said. His pronunciation of the last word was fascinating. Welsh, she appreciated, was a musical language.

'But you should all go now and enjoy your summer holidays. I don't believe invasion is imminent. See you all in September. Class dismiss!' Mr Jones suppressed a yawn. He was returning to the Valleys for the summer.

'What are you doing home already?' Eunice asked sharply, when she came in.

'I could ask you the same thing. Where's Mum?'

'Don't be cheeky. I had a headache. Nell said to go. Where's the aspirin?'

Georgia reached down the old Oxo tin from the high shelf in the kitchen. 'You were late home last night,' she ventured, as Mum was not around to reprove her. She'd heard Eunice stumbling around in the bedroom in the early hours, and Dad's voice: '*Put that light out!*' as he arrived back from his patrol. Then Mum saying, shocked, 'She's had one too many!'

'Not down the Albert, she ain't,' Dad had replied.

Eunice swallowed four tablets with water. She did indeed look pale round the gills, accentuated by the letterbox-red lipstick.

'*Snoop*, you are, Georgia. Dunno why Aubrey thinks so much of you. Well, get the tea made and bring me one, I'm going to have a lie-down. I'm likely to be busy tonight on other essential war work. The kind that gives me a bit of cash of my own; I'm sick and tired of being poor, and living here. And don't think about telling tales to Aubrey when you next write, will you?'

Georgia thought, I'm glad I'm going to Suffolk this weekend; trusted to travel on my own and all, though they'll see me onto the train, before Mum and Dad go off to see our Martin in hospital. They're afraid of upsetting Eunice, with Aubrey out in the Middle East in the burning-hot desert. I ain't making *her* no tea, no fear!

Albie was right. Hitler was about to attack from the skies, preparing the way for invasion by sea. The bombardment began on the 12th August, 1940. Over two months what came to be known as the Battle of Britain was fiercely fought in the heat of summer, in the cloudless skies over the south-east. Despite being grossly outnumbered, the courage and skill of the young British pilots eventually won through. Radar, giving advance warning of an attack, proved its worth, over and over again.

As Nils had witnessed in Norway when the army depot was bombed, dense columns of smoke billowed above blazing buildings and stricken planes on targeted airfields, but still the pilots 'scrambled' and the Spitfires and Hurricanes engaged the enemy in aerial combat, which was thrilling to witness from the ground.

All this seemed remote and unreal to Georgia, reunited with Phoebe and May at the end of her journey. To her delight, she learned that May would be keeping her company at Phoebe's. She'd written to Georgia about the Norwegian, now occupying Jube's spare room. However, before Georgia could meet him, Jube rushed over the next morning to tell Phoebe, 'Nils has gone! Taken all his stuff and his bike. We had callers last night, the colonel from Red House, and another chap, a civilian, who made notes. The colonel was very polite, but he asked lots of questions. He said he'd like to talk to you, as well, but wouldn't trouble you then as it was very late.' He wouldn't say in front of the girls that his wage packet, tucked behind the clock on the mantelpiece, had vanished with her cousin in the early hours, along with some food.

'It's fortunate I'm on leave. I'd rather talk to him here, than at Spare Penny,' Phoebe said evenly.

Georgia and May, finishing breakfast, were obviously intrigued.

There was another unexpected early-visitor: Phoebe's brother Lawrence. He appeared agitated and asked to speak to his sister privately.

'I was just going,' Jube said tactfully, departing. 'See you later, Phoebe.'

'Perhaps you could wash-up girls?' Phoebe suggested. 'Then go out to play.'

Plenty of whispering went on over the dishwashing. Then they went into the field with Sandy and tirelessly threw the india-rubber ball Georgia had brought from home.

'Haven't seen you for ages,' Phoebe began, opening the curtains in the living-room.

'You didn't choose to inform me that our cousin Nils was here with you,' he said, somewhat stiffly. 'I heard on the grapevine, of course, drew conclusions –'

'Lawrence, I'm sorry.'

'So am I. I imagined we had, well, agreed to forget the past.'

'It seems to catch up with you, inevitably,' she said almost inaudibly. 'Look.' She cleared her throat. 'I've got to tell someone, and you're family, after all. Sit down, Lawrence, because you will no doubt be as shocked as I was . . .'

Later, she buried her face in her hands, trying hard not to cry.

'It's even worse than I thought,' he said, and she felt a comforting grip on her shaking shoulders. 'I imagine if he were Nils, he would have been severely reprimanded for disappearing like that, but eventually returned to his compatriots. They didn't take him into custody immediately, after all. This – man – could be shot as a spy. And you, accused of harbouring the enemy! What happened to the real Nils?'

'I-I don't like to think about that.'

'Why did you allow him to stay here? Didn't Jube suspect anything?'

'Karl can be violent, Lawrence, I was afraid.'

'Has he *touched* you?' he asked urgently.

'Not, not like *that* ... I didn't put up any barriers, I *couldn't*,' she admitted. 'Jube and he actually got on well together; he didn't suspect anything. I always feel safer with Jube around. Lawrence, what should I say to the colonel?'

'Be careful, or you'll be in grave trouble, Phoebe. I'll support you, whatever you decide, but my instinctive feeling is that you should stick to the story that he is our cousin Nils, from Norway. Jube will have confirmed this, in his innocence.'

'Promise you'll keep this from Beryl.'

'I promise, but I have to say she's very much in the colonel's confidence,' he said drily. 'I expect you'd heard that – and more?'

She nodded. 'Forgive me, doesn't that leave the way open for you and Eva?'

'*More* complications? What a pair we are!'

'She's disappointed you haven't been to see the baby yet.'

'Best wait until all this is behind us,' he said.

'I'm glad he's gone anyway: it would have been awkward with the girls around.'

'I wonder where he is right now? A long way from here, I hope. I must go. I don't want to be here when the colonel comes.'

'*You* were in trouble once, weren't you?' she said impulsively, as he moved away. 'I wasn't here, so I don't know the ins-and-outs.'

'And you don't want to know them now. What hurt most was Mother's attitude. Grandpa was too old to talk to by then. If I learned anything from that experience it's that telling the truth doesn't mean you'll be believed, Phoebe.'

'I understand,' she said. 'But I always thought you were Mother's favourite. She couldn't relate to me like Grandpa did – and Grandma, of course, adored you because you inherited her musical talent.'

'Mother said I was a coward. Beryl agrees. I'm not stubborn like you.'

'You're unworldly that's all, Lawrence. Eva likes you for that, I know.'

'We seem to have reached an understanding, in adversity,' he said, unexpectedly kissing her goodbye. 'I'm not jealous of you anymore.'

'I imagined it was the other way round.' She essayed a tremulous smile. 'We're family, in the real sense, now.'

Kenny joined the girls, having heard their voices from the garden. '*You*'ve shot up, Georgia; you're as tall as me, now!' He sounded a bit put out at the thought.

'Girls mature quicker than boys,' she returned. 'In brain power, too!' She hoped he wouldn't notice that she'd developed the slightest hint of a bosom during the four months she'd been back home. Mum had embarrassed her by whispering, while they waited for the train, 'Tell Phoebe if anything, *you know*, happens: you're growing up faster than I thought you would.'

May was still as skinny as ever; Georgia had turned her back on her when she undressed last night. Another thing, why did she feel not quite at ease in Kenny's company, she wondered? Almost as if she were shy, which was daft.

'Hear the lodger's gone. Know anything about that? Mum saw him the day he arrived; she thought he looked suspicious,' Kenny asked them.

'No,' May said. 'I never met him.'

'Nor did I,' Georgia added, regretfully.

'Oh well – plenty of other interesting things going on. Did you know that there's more soldiers at Red House? Dad says they're not like the regular army. More like a secret force. They train here, then just disappear.'

'I do know that Jube's joined the Local Defence Volunteers,' May put in.

'Well, he's well qualified, isn't he? Knows the countryside like the back of his hand, and he's a crack shot. Any Nazi parachuting down near him – and *bang*! He won't get far! Fancy going for a bike ride?'

'If Phoebe says we can.'

'Oh, she will – when I saw her just now, she said she'd be busy today and why didn't we go for a picnic lunch.'

'Sounds like a good idea,' Georgia thought.

'Don't go too far,' Phoebe counselled them, as Kenny put the provisions and the old rug, which smelt of dog, into the delivery basket on his bike. 'And don't forget your gas masks! Be back in good time for tea, eh?'

'I won't be able to stay for that.' Kenny assumed he was invited. 'Dad said five o'clock was the limit.'

They cycled along Middle Moor in a leisurely fashion, three abreast, so they could chat, until they reached Spare Penny.

'I know Helga'd like to see Georgia – can we stop off for ten minutes?' May asked.

Not only did Helga hug Georgia, she gave a quick look round, then presented them with a bag of still-warm jam tarts, carefully placing sticky sides together.

'Getting on all right with the cooking on your own?' May asked.

Matron came in, beaming, just at that moment and answered for her. 'She certainly is. Numbers are going down, of course, and we won't be taking in any more long-term residents. Reckon they'll close Spare Penny after the war . . . Don't worry, Helga my dear, I believe there's a job coming up shortly that might suit you. Do you good to get back into the outside world again, I think, meeting folk your own age.'

'But what about Phoebe?' Georgia mused, as they resumed their ride.

'Reckon old Jube might have the answer there,' Kenny grinned.

'They'll get married, you mean?'

'Who knows?'

'Where are we going?' May asked.

'Isn't it obvious?' Kenny teased.

'To the cove? You're not allowed there without permission.'

'Jube still fishes from there, and others do, too.'

'Yes, I know, but the coastguard will be looking out.'

'He'll turn a blind eye. He's my dad's mate, and we're not taking a boat out.'

'Could the Germans land there?' Georgia asked.

'Hardly think so,' Kenny replied. 'That small jetty and miles of open heath before you get to the lane; they'd be spotted immediately and repelled. Now, the south coast, they say, is all barbed-wire.'

The winding lane was hardly wide enough for a small car to pass along, let alone a tank, Georgia realised with relief. On either side there were prickly gorse bushes and, beyond, great swathes of bracken. 'Got to watch out for adders, there,' Kenny warned them.

Then before them was the beautiful purple heather, sea birds wheeling and calling stridently overhead and beyond that, as they dismounted and pushed their bikes along a narrow track, the sparkling sea, glimpsed through the crumbling gap in the sandstone rocks. Further to the left was a marshy area and high above this, a row of tiny cottages, with windows watching the sea. COASTGUARD pronounced a sign, pointing in that direction.

They left their bikes in a dip – Kenny padlocking his and removing the things from the basket – then they descended the treacherous steps and almost tumbled onto the soft sand below. There were a couple of beached boats, tarry patches to watch out for, but the jetty was deserted, like the cove. A path meandered off to the right and in the distance was a black shack, where Kenny said the fishermen kept their tackle.

They settled down on the spread rug and ate their sandwiches and plum jam tarts. The thermos tea had that rather funny taste, due to the added milk, but it all went down well. There were a few flies to bat at, which tended to alight on bare limbs, irritating them, so they took off their shoes and dug their toes into the damp sand beneath the powdery, warm topping.

The heat of the sun became more intense after midday. 'Let's have a dip, cool off,' Kenny suggested. The tide was right, just on the turn.

'We haven't got a towel,' Georgia said quickly, 'and don't say we can use the rug, Kenny: Sandy has rolled on it once too often.'

'We'll swim in our undies – we'd soon dry off after-wards. No one'd know.'

May looked at Georgia. 'I ha'n't got a bathing costume, anyway.'

'Can you swim?' Georgia asked.

' 'Course I can. This is where we and all the other kids learned, eh, Kenny?'

'Safe as houses,' he assured Georgia. He peeled off shirt and trousers, stood there, knobbly-kneed in vest and baggy pants, then he waded in the water.

May followed suit, in skimpy vest and voluminous navy bloomers.

'Come on!' they called to Georgia, stirring up the water around them.

'I'd rather go for a stroll,' she said airily. Besides, she thought, I left my vest off this morning, as I was too hot, and I can't get my dress wet.

'Don't go out of sight, then,' Kenny cautioned her. He ducked underwater, came up to splash May, but she returned the compliment.

The sound of their laughter followed Georgia as she scrambled along the path: she'd make for the shack she decided, then turn back.

The shed was long and low, smelled rankly of fish and oil. The door was locked, but she peered into the interior through a crack in the side-boarding. She made out a dinghy, covered over; a stack of old cans, nets, fishing gear. There was a sudden flapping sound, and she looked up to see a white gull land on the ridge of the roof. Then she lowered her gaze to the gap and became aware that someone was staring back at her. She gave a strangled shriek.

'Stop that!' a man's voice said.

'Who – are you?'

'None of your business. Why are you spying on me?'

'I'm – not . . .'

'You won't tell *anyone* you saw me here,' he stated. 'Or' – his face receded, was replaced by the muzzle of a gun – 'I won't hesitate to use this.'

Georgia dodged aside. 'I'm going, I won't say anything – honest! I promise!'

'Good, because I know who you are and where you live.'

'How?' Her mouth was dry with fear.

'Because Phoebe told me about you. Red hair, she said. Georgia, isn't it? If you care for her, remember, tell no one, no one at all.'

Then she was running and May saw her coming and rushed up to her. 'You look like you've seen a ghost!' she said.

THIRTEEN

The colonel and his assistant were just leaving when Georgia and May arrived back at the cottage, having parted company with Kenny by the gatehouse. 'I understand you've been out and about today,' he observed. 'Not wise to venture too far in these troubled times, eh? I'm sure you are aware of the restricted areas. Well, enjoy the good weather!'

When the men were out of sight, the girls took off their canvas shoes and shook the sand out into the garden border. 'I'm sure he guessed where we'd been, May,' Georgia said. 'Better go and see Phoebe's all right after her interrogation,' she added dramatically. 'At least she's not been arrested!'

The door opened and Phoebe stood there, smiling. 'Not quite that, Georgia. 'They were actually very pleasant; just asked to see any photographs I had of Nils. Not that my snaps were of much use. Taken by me, when I was around your age, mainly spectacular views of Norway and tiny figures you need a magnifying glass to identify. Just a couple of Nils and me taken by Grandpa, which were clearer, but none of him over fifteen years old. Well, come in, and tidy up before tea.'

She sounds cheerful and relieved, Georgia thought. 'You're not in any trouble then?' she asked.

'Not at the moment, anyway,' Phoebe said.

'Perhaps your cousin'll give himself up,' May suggested.

'Perhaps. *He's* not in too much trouble either, I think. But you can't go wandering about in wartime Britain without the proper authority, you see. Don't go writing to your mum and worrying her about it, will you? Now, I bet you're hungry, so let me dish up the shepherd's pie then you can tell me all about your day.'

Georgia gave May a warning nudge.

'We went to see Helga,' May began, 'then we had our picnic.'

'On the moor?'

'Mmm. We picked you a bunch of heather, but left it in Kenny's basket.'

'Never mind. It'll bring me luck, I'm sure.'

Georgia thought fervently, I hope it brings *me* luck too, then that scary man'll leave his hiding place and go far away . . . or *maybe*, I *did* see a ghost?

The summer days passed with intermittent bursts of energy, when the children climbed trees and dangled dangerously from bending branches; picked early plums in Jube's garden; stretched out in the sun and dozed like puppies; braved the gnats and fished in the field pond; helped Jube with the milking, one morning.

One afternoon, the girls and Phoebe went visiting, 'all starched up', as Georgia put it, in clean cotton frocks. Miss Worley and Eva had invited them for afternoon tea.

They were not the only guests, for others had arrived half an hour earlier. Helga was standing irresolutely on the step, clutching a letter in her hand, when she was joined by Mona Button who'd watched out for her from the shop window.

'It's good to see you again, Helga,' she said warmly, jerking the bell-pull. 'Miss Worley thought you might be glad of a little moral support.'

The glum sitting-room was transformed. Miss Worley had been busy in the school holidays, brushing the walls with cream distemper, while Eva had washed the net curtains shades lighter and opened windows to air the room. 'You can't sit in your bedroom all day,' Miss Worley said, 'and Win won't disturb Father down here.'

Little Win was in her pram, just waking from her afternoon nap, wearing a cambric nightgown with minuscule lace-edging. Eva lifted her up and proudly showed her off. 'Like to hold her, Helga?'

Helga cradled her carefully in her arms, her freshly washed hair, trimmed by Matron, dipping round her face and hiding her expression as she watched over the baby. Mona, beside her on the sofa, exclaimed, 'I'd forgotten how tiny new babies are!' Her cheeks were pink as she added impulsively, 'Oh, I must tell you! Soon the whole village will know, of course. I'm expecting a baby myself next Christmas – after all these years! Bob doesn't appear too put out, nor Kenny, which is a relief!' It wasn't such a surprise, for her expanding waistline had already caused speculation locally. Then, seeing the sheepish smiles, she said, 'You guessed, I can tell!'

Helga murmured something, and Mona patted her arm, encouragingly.

Miss Worley's expression warned them not to comment. 'Let's get down to business,' she said briskly. 'Eva, over to you.'

'Well, I can see that you and Win look comfortable together, Helga, and we – because after all, this *is* Miss Worley's home – hope you will agree to come in on a daily basis when the new term begins, as Win's nanny. The job involves bathing and changing her; making up bottles and so on; doing her washing; but we don't expect you to cope with the housework as well. Hours from eight thirty to four, to fit in with school, Monday to Friday. Thirty-five shillings a week, midday meal provided; is that all right?' She sounded anxious.

Miss Worley looked at Helga, just as if she were still at school. 'Well?' she asked, obviously expecting an answer.

'All right,' Helga said, clearly this time, and her sweet smile illuminated her face.

'It won't be too long before we can wheel the babies out together,' Mona beamed. Then she saw Eva's lips tremble: *she* was the one who would miss out.

Miss Worley cleared her throat. 'If you would be kind enough to look in occasionally on my father, and alert me if necessary, I would be grateful Helga. I could give you an extra five shillings –'

'No! Thirty-five shillings is enough. It's what I'm used to,' she said simply.

'It just came back to me,' Georgia whispered to May, 'when Miss Worley asked me my name and said, "*I'll remember that*"...'

'She didn't say, "I don't care for you, Georgia Smith!" did she? She soon got to like you, I can tell.'

'Good! She ain't a bad old stick.'

'What are you two conspiring about?' Phoebe asked, as they approached the schoolhouse.

'Not much. Just wondering what there'll be on the table for tea,' Georgia said.

'That's Helga's bike. Wonder what *she's* doing here?' May asked.

They were soon enlightened. However, Helga didn't say another word for the rest of the afternoon. Maybe it was enough for that day.

The two girls took their turn holding the baby. 'I suppose you're looking forward to becoming an aunty.' May sounded wistful: no chance of that for her.

Everyone looked at Georgia in surprise when she said explosively, 'If you mean my sister-in-law Eunice, well, I'm *not!*'

'Obviously no love lost there,' Miss Worley said. 'Now, hand Win back to her mother, she's puckering her face to cry, and it's time to pass the sandwiches, I think.'

Georgia wrote:

Dear Mum and Dad,

Having a lovely holiday. My turn for the camp-bed tonight. I am writing by torchlight because May is already snoring. (She does too.) This afternoon us and Phoebe went to tea at Miss Worley's. She actually said it was nice to see me again! And was I going to stay on because of all the bombing and that in the south, but I told her, not in London so far and you need me at home, well, I hope you do? Anyway, Phoebe (see, I can spell it now) has got a PROBLEM, only I'm not supposed to say, and worry you. Eva's baby is sweet, but she gets all het up when it cries, which it does if you speak too loud. Guess what? (Well you won't!) Kenny's mum is PREGNANT! (She says, expecting.) I would have thought she was too old, like you, Mum.

When we got home, Jube was upset because he was going fishing and found his boat had been pinched from the beach. But he hasn't got much time for that now, as he has joined the LDV (they call it the home guard.) Being a bit of a poacher helps, Kenny says.

With love to you both, but not to you-know-who, and Martin when you see him, Night night,

Georgia xx

PS Watch out SHE don't kick poor old Dusty.

PPS Helga is going to be Win's nanny. And she (Helga not Win) actually spoke today! May told me, SHE knew she could if she wanted to.

Jube was sitting in the kitchen with Phoebe. 'I can't help thinking,' he said tentatively.

'I know, you can't help thinking that Nils might have taken your boat.'

'It must have been him. Someone had broken into the tackle shed, too. Phoebe – isn't there something you should have told me?'

She sighed. 'You've guessed, haven't you?'

'Not exactly. But there was a sort of suspicion lingering in my mind, I must say.'

'You liked him, didn't you?'

'I made sure we got on all right together, for your sake. I could keep an eye on him in that way. I wasn't sure he was really your cousin Nils. Those people who spoke to us, they're pretty high-up, aren't they? If he was Nils, wouldn't it have been the local bobby making enquiries?'

'I wanted to tell you, but I – couldn't, Jube. I had to confess to Lawrence the other day; it's very awkward, you see, with Beryl working for the colonel.'

'Surely you can tell *me* now?'

'He wasn't my cousin Nils – you really would have liked *him*, you know, he's such a good person. The man who was here, Jube, was Karl Schmidt, my . . .' She faltered.

'Your former lover? The one who hurt you so much?'

'Yes. He threatened me, but I was concerned for you; it wasn't fair to let you become involved.'

'How could you think that? You know my feelings for you, surely?'

'I'm sorry . . .'

'Look, I need to know, even if you don't think I have any right to: did he take advantage of you?'

'Oh, Jube, does it really matter now? Can't we just be thankful he's gone?'

'It's not the end of the story, Phoebe,' he said heavily, sadly.

'I realise that. Please forgive me, Jube.'

'You know the answer to that . . . But, I thought, that night before he came, that I was getting somewhere with you at last. I could have been the one to have taken advantage of you then. I don't think you would have said no. It was the closest we'd ever been, wasn't it? But I respected you too much for that.'

'Don't be bitter, Jube. I can't bear it.'

'I won't desert you, but I'm not sure how long it will take me, us, to get over it.'

'I can do with a hug right now,' she said in a small voice, as he rose to go.

For a moment he stood irresolute, then, '*You* come to *me*, Phoebe.'

'I *am* very fond of you,' she insisted, pressed against his chest.

Some time later, he released her gently. 'Now, I believe you . . . Just recalled another thing I should've told you.'

'What's that?'

'The coastguard told me he'd spotted three children playing on the beach the day after – your cousin ran off. He recognised Kenny, so decided just to keep an eye on them. He said that Kenny and one of the girls had a dip in the sea; the bigger girl went off on her own, towards the hut. She came running back, then they all packed up quickly, collected their bikes and went home.'

'Georgia! It must have been. She didn't say anything to me. I assumed they were on the moor. D'you think she saw something, *someone*?'

'You'll have to ask her, but gently does it, Phoebe, you know.'

'Don't you think I've learned that from you?' she said quietly.

As she climbed the stairs, Phoebe saw the flickering light under the door in Georgia's room. She entered cautiously, candlestick in hand.

'It's all right,' Georgia said. 'I'm still awake. I heard Jube go. I know it's late, but I can't get off to sleep – May went off straightaway tonight.'

'Is something worrying you?' Phoebe whispered. 'Why don't you come in my room for a chat, then we won't disturb May.'

She lifted a pile of laundry from the bentwood rocking chair. 'There, sit down.' She perched on the end of her bed. 'Is it all this business about my cousin disappearing and me being questioned about it?'

'Sort of.' Georgia leaned back in the chair, so that her face was in the shadow. 'We went somewhere we shouldn't have, I'm sorry, I should have told you.'

'To the beach? The day of the picnic?'

'Yes. Oh, you guessed!' She sounded relieved.

'Sort of,' she echoed wryly. 'Is that all? Nothing happened, did it?'

'I didn't want to go swimming like the others; anyway, I didn't want to admit I can't, swim that is, so I – went for a walk along the cliff track, to the hut.'

'And,' Phoebe prompted.

'I looked in through a split in the boards to see what was inside. It was all dark and gloomy and I thought I saw a face, eyes staring back at me.'

'You imagined it, you mean?'

'No! I mustn't tell you!' Georgia was panicking now. 'He said so! He knew who I was, that I was staying with you! I thought he'd come and get us!'

Phoebe was kneeling beside her now, holding her hand firmly. 'He's gone, Georgia. Where, I don't know, or care. He stole Jube's boat; got away. He – he wasn't the person I believed I knew ... I'm so sorry he frightened you, but you see, you had to confide in me in the end, didn't you? He won't come near here again, because he knows the authorities are looking for him and, anyway, we have Jube next door, eh? Feel better now? Then back to your bed, and have a good night!'

Georgia's mum, reading between the lines in her letter, but none the wiser, thought it was maybe time to fetch their daughter home. 'Sounds as if Phoebe's got something to sort out, doesn't it?' she said to Albie. 'Georgia's been away a couple of weeks, and yes, I do miss her.'

'So do I,' he agreed. 'But we did promise her she could stay all of August in Suffolk. How about one more week? Specially with these air battles going on, a bit too near home, like?'

'Our pilots are more than a match for the Luftwaffe, everyone knows that.'

FOURTEEN

Late on Saturday afternoon in Silvertown, the dockland area's street-market was still bustling, despite the previous night's raid, when the sirens sounded again. It was 7th September, 1940. Georgia's mum was helping out on a friend's fruit and veg stall, on the promise of a few leftovers at the end of the day. The *ack ack* began as a massive formation of enemy bombers roared overhead. Sticks of bombs rained down.

There was an overpowering smell of burnt caramel and boiling oil as the sugar factory and fat refinery ignited. Clouds of flour mingled with smoke from the mills.

'Take your pick!' Nell's friend yelled above the din, 'then get going!'

Nell ran for home, spilling carrots and potatoes, not stopping to retrieve them, shouting unnecessarily, '*The Thames is on fire!*' to folk staring mesmerised from doorways.

The Smith family home, originally three flats, was in a shabby Victorian terrace some way from the docks. Nell had begun married life in the basement, now unoccupied due to rising damp. They'd moved to the ground floor after they had the boys. Later, when Georgia started school and their sons were in work, they took on the whole house. The landlord turned a deaf ear to pleas to convert a box room into a proper bathroom, but Nell had made a real home for them here.

A cobbled yard, with a back-gate opening into an alley to facilitate deliveries to the coal shed, meant no space for an Anderson shelter. The dank basement was designated a refuge for the family and their neighbours, but rarely used until now.

'Georgia!' Nell yelled, as she fumbled for her front door key. She turned at the rapping on the basement window.

'Down here, Mum! *Hurry!*' Then a shutter blacked out the window.

The former kitchen reeked of bleach, which Nell had applied to the fungus on the walls. There were two benches, with folded rugs to sit on; assorted chairs; an old table laden with necessities; pails of water; and a covered bucket in a corner for emergencies. There was a single, low-watt light bulb and a battery-radio crackled. Mr P had dragged his precious motor bike down there and Georgia had staggered after him with Dad's accordion in a blanket, her harmonica stuffed in her pocket.

Mrs P from next door was keeping Georgia company; the husbands, who'd been up all Friday night, were back on duty again, armed with stirrup-pumps.

'Mum!' Georgia cried. 'Dusty rushed out when Mrs P came and she wouldn't let me chase after him!' An ominous *crump!* not far away, made her clutch her mother's arm.

'I should think not,' Mum scolded her. 'Got the primus lit? I need a cup of tea.'

'Only condensed milk,' her neighbour jabbed the tin with the opener.

'Don't care, my throat feels full of dust. Where's Eunice?' Aubrey's wife had still been lying in bed when Nell left for the market. Eunice had stayed in the West End overnight after hearing the East End had been hit; arrived home with the milkman, who told them of dockside houses destroyed, casualties, families made homeless taken to the crypt of a local church. It was shocking, but life had to go on: hence the market that day.

'She went out; we couldn't stop her, either. Said she wasn't sitting down here with that stink, but going back up west. Reckoned it was safer.'

'That darned nightclub I reckon,' Nell sighed.

'You're only young once,' Mrs P said, passing her a mug of tea. 'Sounds as if she had a tough life before she married your boy.'

'Would you and I have behaved like that, with our husbands away at war, Phyl?'

Mrs P shook her turbaned head. She kept her curlers in all day on Saturdays, until it was time for a good comb-out before her weekly visit with Reg to the pub.

'Well, then . . . Now, what've we got for high tea – bombs or no bleedin' bombs?'

Georgia was relieved Eunice wasn't there. She'd peeked in her room after she'd gone. She wouldn't tell Mum she'd spotted Eunice's wedding ring glinting on the chest of drawers. She tried not to think of poor old Dusty scared out of his wits and cowering somewhere. At times, despite the thick walls, the furore outside was deafening. And Dad, she remembered belatedly, guiltily, where was he? A tin hat wasn't much protection against chunks of falling masonry; a stirrup pump and bucket of water to extinguish fires was, well, a drop in the ocean.

The jangle of fire engines racing past down the road. Mum stopped slicing cheese and observed, 'The fireboat's come into its own, too, they say . . .'

'Plenty of water in the old Thames,' Georgia quoted Dad. We're shut off from it all, she thought, but if the house is hit, will anyone think to look for us down here?

The raid was over. They trooped up the uncarpeted stairs. 'Stay with us, Phyl, till Albie and Reg get back,' Nell said.

There'd been no time to blackout the living-room. Georgia looked out. The houses opposite were there. 'It's still light,' she observed, in amazement.

'We need some more comforts down the basement,' Nell said. 'I wish we had a spare double mattress.'

'Got one next door,' Phyl said. 'Let's trundle it round while we got a chance.'

'Glad I put the sacks on the floor. Georgia, while we do that, boil lots of water, Dad'll need a good wash when he gets in. What about an eiderdown, Phyl?'

'Mm. And a cushion or two: them hard benches'll give us all, 'scuse me, piles.'

Georgia lit the gas under two big pans. 'I'll see to the windows,' she offered. The women expecting her to do her bit, treating her like an adult, made her glow.

Her father suddenly appearing in the doorway, made her shriek. He was almost unrecognisable, for he was smothered in black dust from head to foot. He slumped down on the nearest chair, without a word.

'Your hands, Dad!' Georgia cried. 'They're *bleeding*!' She snatched a clean tea-towel and wrapped it round them. She gently removed his tin hat. His balding head was slippery with sweat. Then a whining at the door made her whirl round.

'The dog,' Dad said faintly. 'Met up with him ... Tried to get him to go home, but he was scrabbling and digging – we didn't know, but *he* did, there was someone trapped in all that rubble . . .'

Dusty's paws were red and raw, too. He limped over to his water bowl and began to lap thirstily. He was all of a shake, Georgia saw.

'Good idea,' Dad said. 'Dying for a drink, gal.'

Then Mum was back and clucking in concern when she saw him. 'He don't mean *tea*, Georgia, get the whisky from the top cupboard!'

While Mum helped him out of his clothes, Georgia fetched a blanket to cover him, averting her eyes as she handed it to Mum. She'd never seen either of them unclothed, she thought. She busied herself with pouring cold water into the enamel bowl on the table, then carefully added boiling water, before she tested it gingerly.

'There's a new flannel in the dresser drawer,' Mum directed Georgia, 'and a bar of Lux. I'll see to his hands first. Oh, and that tin of Vaseline – thanks! Then tear some long strips from that old sheet I keep by me.'

Her father was shaking now, like the dog, his teeth chattering in his head. Nell knelt by his feet, stretching up to rinse and wring out the flannel in the water. To Georgia, sitting opposite, determinedly ripping the white cotton into pieces, it was a scene which would be imprinted on her memory for ever. Mum bathing Dad's hands, as gently as if he was a baby, with a soft cloth and perfumed toilet soap, instead of the carbolic Dad usually scrubbed himself with. Then she anointed and padded his sore palms before attending to the rest of him.

'Let's get you in your night things,' Mum decided, when the last bowl of filthy water had been tipped down the sink.

'No! Might be needed again tonight. You mustn't argue about it, Nell.'

'You ain't putting that lot back on again. Fetch his work things, Georgia, and they'll have to do. We'll rinse the tin hat under the tap.'

When Dad was eating the cheese sandwiches they'd saved for him, Georgia tended to the dog. Dusty was already licking his paws, but she followed Mum's example with washing and applying Vaseline.

'It won't hurt him if he licks that off, it ain't poisonous,' Mum reassured her.

'Dusty's a hero,' Georgia said huskily. 'Like Dad.'

'Meant to tell you, Georgia' – Albie's voice was hoarse, too – 'the accordion's for you, if anything happens to me.'

'Dad, *no!*'

'He always wanted to go there, you know, to America,' Mum added. 'It wasn't just because of the song we named you that.'

'It was when we saw your flaming hair; the soil's red in Georgia, they say.' He wasn't trembling any more, the spirit had done the trick.

There were rival sunsets that evening. The glorious tints of the sky in the west, which promised a fine day on the morrow, and the ominous glow from the still-raging fires in the dockyard.

Eunice failed to show up on Sunday. They had to believe that 'no news is good news', when they learned of the mayhem all around them. No lessons now for Georgia: the church hall that had been her classroom was obliterated one night, when it was crowded with those earlier made homeless. Old Mr Jones, the Welsh teacher, there to help as always, was among the missing.

The days went past, with still no sign of Aubrey's wife, but eventually a letter. *You can tell him I'm not coming back . . .*

'How can I do that?' Nell asked Albie, who had no answer, just shook his head.

When Georgia and her mother went into the basement that evening – their new routine, siren or no siren – Nell, who'd looked distracted all day, suddenly told her, 'We should've left you with Phoebe; you shouldn't have to go through all this.'

'I'm not leaving you and Dad now, Mum!'

'I must say you're a comfort to me, dearie, when Dad's out at nights.'

'There you are then.'

'Poor Martin, stuck in hospital, though he's fairly safe there. He must wonder why we haven't been to see him lately. He can't come home, even if they say he can.'

'I wish we could shelter down in the Tube,' Georgia said. 'They get entertainment there, eh? All the best acts from the Empire theatre, they say, when they're forced off-stage.'

'Well, Mrs P and me have got *you*, gal, buzzing away on your mouth organ!'

The bombs were hitting much nearer to home. Shouts and pounding on the door alerted them that the coal shed had been torched by an incendiary. The hoses were playing on that and on the back of the house. At first they imagined it to be torrential rain. Advice was: 'Stay where you are!' There was no sleep that night. Georgia tried bravely to drown out the threatening discordant sounds with her harmonica while accompanying some wavering singing, like 'Rock of Ages', from her companions. Perhaps the words 'cleft for me' were rather unfortunate, but hymns were easier than prayers, it seemed, for the words were written for them.

In the morning, when the bombers had gone, Georgia looked out over the road, as usual. It always reassured her to see the solid houses opposite still untouched.

'Mum, come and see!' she cried out, in shock.

There was a gaping hole near the end of the terrace. The last house was detached from the rest, windows blown out, tiles off the roof. Rubble was strewn all over the road. Picking their way home across this scene of devastation were two figures, Albie and Mr P. Then behind them emerged another familiar sight, the postman, with letters in his hand, gazing up helplessly as if expecting the missing house to materialise.

'Bring the poor chap in for a cup of tea!' Nell bellowed through the window.

There were two letters from Aubrey, both addressed to Eunice. Georgia saw the tears welling in her mother's eyes and knew she was tempted to open them, but she turned away to the stove and fried up their week's ration of bacon for the exhausted men. Their neighbours had as good as moved in with them now: it made sense for the two women to have mutual support. 'Surprised the gas ain't cut off,' Mum said, prodding at the fatty slices because the only lard she had was that clinging to the wrapper.

'Could be, later.' Dad was taking first turn to wash at the sink. Georgia hadn't washed yet, or cleaned her teeth, but Mum didn't reprove her. There were more important things to see to, right now.

'Any coal left, Albie?' Mum asked. The two men would have to share an egg – and she couldn't be sure that was fresh until she cracked it.

'Sorry, Nell. Can't even use the shed wood, that went up in smoke, too.'

'Laid the table, Georgia? Sit down and read your letter from May, then.'

Dear Georgia,

The news about the London bombing has alarmed us. I hope you are all right? I wish you were back here, so does Kenny. He is a bit fed up with all the baby talk, he says. Miss Worley is going to put us in for the grammar school exam next spring. She says it is not too late. Just in case, she has got your name on the list, as well. Anyway, I expect you would like to hear all that has happened since you went home?

Helga loves looking after Eva's baby. Win is very good, but she does not sleep much. Still, that means that Helga has to talk to her so we are all pleased about that. I am so glad Helga got the job, because Matron is ill, and they are moving the residents to the cottage hospital, and Spare Penny is being taken over by the army, like Red House. Don't worry about me and Helga not having anywhere to stay, as it's not happened yet. The council have promised us a house, as Helga has a job in the village.

Now you will say, what about Phoebe? She is going to help out with the cooking at the hospital. I know she writes to you, but I don't suppose she tells you that she misses you a lot. And did you hear about Jube's boat? It was found, all smashed up, further up the coast. They think that cousin of Phoebe's must have been drowned. Jube is upset about the boat, as it was his dad's.

Mr Bliss has given up the music lessons and Kenny says he has become a hermit. He has given up shaving anyway, and he and Eva don't seem to be meeting up any more. Maybe his wife has put her foot down! (Though there is a lot of gossip about *her*.)

To finish, guess what? I am Head Girl! So watch out, if you do come back!

All the stuff above is really just to cheer you up. I miss you!

Lots of love from May.

PS Remember me to your family and Dusty. Sandy is well.

'That kept you quiet a long time,' Mum said, passing Georgia a bacon sandwich.

Then came the knock on the door, and they all stopped eating and wondered who it might be.

'Mrs Nell Smith?' the stranger asked. 'Mother-in-law of Eunice Smith?'

FIFTEEN

'I'd rather not say what I have to, on the doorstep,' the unfamiliar police officer stated.

Even as Nell hesitated, because of the crowded kitchen, her husband, still in his shirt and braces, joined them. 'It's all right, Nell.' he said. 'The neighbours are off. They'll take Georgia. We couldn't help hearing what this gentleman asked you.'

There was the sound of the back door closing. 'Please come in,' Nell told the caller. She was wearing her pinafore, which normally she would remove hastily before opening the door, but it didn't matter, because it was obvious something serious had happened. She still had Aubrey's letters in her pocket.

Georgia and Mrs P had hastily cleared the table of crocks and crumbs. The smell of the frying bacon lingered. The teapot wore its cosy. 'Cup of tea?' she asked.

'No, thank you.' The policeman sat down, indicating they should do the same. 'I'm afraid I have some bad news. As you are aware the bombing has become more widespread; London is not the only target –'

'But Eunice *is* in London,' Albie interrupted. 'She went up west the night after it started, didn't she, Nell?'

'We got a letter a week later, saying she wasn't coming back,' Nell added.

The policeman waited patiently, aware that they also wished to delay the moment of truth. Then he took a notebook from his breast pocket and read aloud:

'The Cockatoo Night Club received a direct hit three nights ago. Mrs Eunice Smith, a hostess at the club, was among the casualties . . .'

'We read about that in the paper, said it was packed with servicemen.'

'That is so, Mrs Smith. Regrettably, there was much loss of life.'

'Why weren't we informed at the time?' Nell demanded.

'I regret – identification proved difficult. Eventually, her escort, who was taken to hospital, recalled the clothes your daughter-in-law was wearing that evening.'

'You said *casualties* – d'you mean, she's *dead*?'

The police officer sighed. 'Again, I regret – yes. It would have been instantaneous. There is no need for you to, ah, visit the mortuary, indeed, it is best that you do not. I do need your permission to make arrangements, and an address for your son, so that he can be officially notified.'

Nell brought the letters from her pocket, placed them on the table. 'These came this morning . . .' Her voice trailed off.

The policeman glanced at them. 'I'm so sorry,' he said sincerely.

Georgia's dad had at last gone off to work: not to the familiar routine he'd followed since he was a lad, but directed wherever help was most urgently needed in the area.

When Georgia returned, her mother could see by her look of apprehension that she'd guessed about Eunice. 'Oh, *Mum!*' She flung her arms round her.

Mum repeated the brief, shocking story, leaving out the bit about Eunice being a hostess at the club. She didn't want to conjecture what that really meant. She added, 'You don't want to be around, Georgia, when we have the funeral. This has made us realise that we really should send you back to Suffolk.'

'I can't leave you now, Mum, you do need me, don't you?'

'Of course we do, but we need even more to know you're safe, dearie. Besides, what about your schooling? It could be some time before you can pick that up again here. You were doing so well at the village school, weren't you?'

'May said, in her letter, that Miss Worley has put me down for the scholarship next spring,' Georgia conceded.

'There you are then. Not much chance of that locally, eh?'

'No. I can't help thinking about Mr Jones, he was everyone's favourite teacher, even though he was so old . . . Can't *you* come with me to Phoebe's, Mum?'

'Now you know I can't. What about Dad? And visiting Martin? I've got Mrs P for company when the men have to go out at nights, I won't be on my own.'

'Dusty will look after you, too!'

'I know I shouldn't say this, but I won't have to worry about Eunice now, poor girl. I can't imagine how our Aubrey will take the news . . . I'll have to get in touch with her parents, too – what a shock for them. There's something else I must brace myself to do, sorting out her things in her room.'

Suddenly Georgia was sobbing her heart out, against Mum's comfortable shoulder. The wedding ring Eunice abandoned, she thought, Mum'll find *that*. Mum never takes hers off; well, she couldn't now, she says, it's stuck fast.

'Oh, Georgia, I never thought you were really fond of her!'

'I wasn't!' Georgia wailed. 'She was always nasty to me when you weren't around. I never liked her, right from the beginning. But now I feel guilty because I didn't *try* to become her friend. I couldn't understand why she went out enjoying herself when Aubrey was fighting in the desert and in mortal danger! I thought she couldn't love him.'

'We don't know that, dearie. It was, well, just the way she was . . .'

'Well, all I know is, *I* won't ever be like that!'

'We mustn't judge her now. We can only do our best with whatever life chucks at us, dearie. You never know.'

After what came to be known as Battle of Britain Day, 15th September, 1940 – when the full force of the Luftwaffe targeted London and were taken on by the greatly depeleted RAF, who, miraculously it seemed, saved the day – the daylight bombardment dwindled. The imminent invasion of Great Britain was called off by Adolph Hitler.

Now, the arrival of the bombers synchronised with nightfall, establishing a pattern. Sleep deprivation meant pale faces, dark-circled eyes as folk carried on as best they could. All around was devastation, many lives were lost, yet morale remained high.

Georgia was still in London at the start of November. After much agonizing, her parents decided that they couldn't bear to part with her just yet. Her twelfth birthday came and went, a subdued affair this year.

She overheard her father saying to Nell, after a particularly bad raid, 'Well, at least if we go, we'll go together, Nell.' Then he picked up his accordion for the first time in ages and played the rousing 'Keep the home fires burning!' The fires were burning in other British cities, now; and in Berlin, too.

Albie wasn't feeling too good. 'Stay put,' Mr P advised. 'A night off won't hurt you, and it looks as if old Hitler agrees. They're late tonight, eh?'

When he protested, Nell wouldn't stand for any argument either.

'Well, I ain't lying down on that mattress, hemmed in by you gals,' he asserted. 'I'll sit in the old easy-chair, if you give me a cushion to put over the springs.'

Mum sighed. 'Go on, then.' Adding sharply, 'Why're you clutching your chest?'

'Bloomin' indigestion! Got a peppermint, Nell?' His face had a grey look.

'You had the last one earlier. Have a little nip of whisky, eh? And Georgia, get a nap in while you can.'

Georgia had become so accustomed to the nightly concerto that she was barely aware of the rise and fall warning notes of the siren later on, followed by the All Clear shortly afterwards. 'False Alarm,' she heard Nell mutter sleepily.

She must have drifted off again, until she was disturbed by the sound of stertorous, rattling snoring and alarmed voices. Neither her mum nor Mrs P were lying beside her on the mattress. She sat bolt upright, calling out, 'What is it?'

A torch momentarily flickered in her direction. 'Go back to sleep,' Nell said.

The harsh noises abruptly ceased.

'Is Dad all right?' Georgia asked urgently.

There was no reply. The two women closed ranks around the chair. After what seemed an eternity, Georgia heard desperate sobbing.

'Mum!' she pleaded. 'Please . . .'

Nell didn't answer. She was on her knees by the chair, her arms round her husband.

Mrs P came over and looked down at Georgia. 'Be brave, dearie. Your dad's had a heart attack, I reckon – he's . . . *gone*. Nothing we can do, until morning. You must be strong for your poor mum.'

There was a long drawn-out howl from a corner of the dark room. *Dusty knew.*

Georgia didn't cry until after it was all over. She hadn't been expected to go to Eunice's funeral, but had made tea and sandwiches when her parents brought her family back afterwards. They'd sat, shocked but stoical, saying little, and later took Eunice's possessions away in a single, small case. None of them could bring themselves to say they would keep in touch.

No one asked if she wanted to attend this time, despite her youth. She sat silently beside her mother during the brief service, holding tight to her arm, while Nell wept softly. Just one hymn, 'The Lord Is My Shepherd', sung unaccompanied, for Georgia's teacher, the late Mr Jones, had been the organist in this little church. Some of Dad's workmates and pals from the Albert sat at the back, paying their respects.

The boys should have been here, Georgia thought. How was Aubrey coping, after yet another awful shock? This had set her younger brother back in his recovery; Mum said she must go to him as soon as she could.

'You'll come back to the house?' Nell asked Albie's friends.

'Got to get back to work,' one of them said. 'But thank you, Mrs Smith.' He cleared his throat. 'We had a collection for you.' He passed over a brown envelope.

'Thank you,' she said simply, accepting it. She shook hands with each in turn.

The tears came at last when she and Georgia were on their own. Nell held her tight and rocked her in her arms as if she was a baby again.

'Let it out, Georgia, it helps . . .'

'It's not fair, Mum!'

'No, it isn't. Not at forty-three years old. But at least he went with us there. That's a comfort, ain't it? There's something I got to tell you, Georgia, that's hard for me to say . . . We can't afford to stay on here without your dad's wages coming in. The landlord has agreed to re-let the place furnished –'

'With our furniture you mean?' Georgia interrupted.

'Yes. He's offered me ten pounds for the lot. We'd take all the personal stuff, of course. It will mean us being parted again for a while: you'll go back to Phoebe and school, and I'll visit you as often as I can.'

'But where will *you* go, Mum?' she asked anxiously. 'And what about Dusty?' Those living in heavily bombed areas were advised to have their pets put to sleep. Just then, she felt the dog's cold nose touch her hand, as if he needed reassurance.

'Phoebe has suggested he stays with Jube, that way you'll get to see him whenever you want. As for me, I'll rent a little flat near the hospital, so Martin has somewhere to come, away from the bombing, when they discharge him. I'll have to find a job, of course, but I've got enough to get by on, for now. There's your father's insurance, not much, but . . .'

Then they were both sobbing their hearts out. Finally, Nell took off the unfamiliar black hat and Georgia noticed for the first time that there were streaks of grey in her auburn hair. She eased her feet out of her best shoes, the brown ones Mrs P had blacked over for her. 'This won't do, eh? Don't forget he left you his precious accordion, Georgia – you should learn to play that, as soon as you can.'

'Oh, Mum! I-I put my arms through the straps and it was too *heavy* for me.'

'Like our hearts right now, dearie. You'll grow into it, you really will.'

They struggled with the accordion onto the train. Georgia carried the same case she had before – was it really only sixteen month ago? So much had happened since then. The train was packed with servicemen and women in uniform, and they had to stand in the corridor most of the way.

She and Mum didn't talk much. They stared out of the grimy window as the scenery flashed by. The trees were leafless once more, the skies leaden. The countryside looked barren, not lush and beautiful as it had when Georgia travelled back to London last summer. Had they left their London home for ever, she wondered? Family life would never be the same without Dad, and now she was, however you looked at it, losing Mum, too. She thought of her mother tenderly washing her husband that day, and how it was obvious then how much they loved each other.

The feather in Mum's hat tickled her face as she bent to whisper in Georgia's ear. 'Just think how lucky we were to have him as long as we did, dearie.'

Then the soldier on her other side tapped her shoulder and asked, 'Would you and your mum like a bar of chocolate? I got plenty.'

Eating milk chocolate was a comfort, even though it made them thirsty.

There was quite a reception awaiting them on the platform when the train stopped: Phoebe, hugging them both; Jube with his bike; and Kenny with the shop handcart, waiting to stow their luggage and wheel it home. Georgia retrieved Dusty from the guard's van and May patted him, asking if she could hold his lead. They had to steer him away quickly from the tempting flowerpots to a patch of grass beyond.

Everyone was very tactful and only said it was so nice to see them again. Then they began the long walk home.

SIXTEEN

The old routine was slowly being re-established. Georgia kept her chin resolutely high after her mother left to join Martin.

The two dogs eyed each other warily through spyholes in the dividing hedge, when they were out in their respective gardens, but Jube soon decided to take Dusty with him to work. 'Plenty of space there for him to run around, but nowhere to go, eh?' This meant Jube's chickens could scratch around undisturbed all day, too.

He tied Dusty to the post outside the gatehouse one evening. He waited for a good five minutes before his rap on the door was acknowledged.

'Yes?' Lawrence asked. He had lost weight: his clothes hung loosely; his face was haggard. Jube would tell Phoebe later on, 'He's not looking after himself.'

'Can I come in a minute?'

'What about the dog?'

'He won't mind. He's used to being tethered now and again, for his own good.'

'I'll come straight to the point,' Jube stated, when they stood in the hall. 'The Home Guard needs you. You can shoot, can't you? I recall you going out as a lad with your grandfather.'

'It wasn't something I liked doing.'

'Maybe not, but it's a skill you don't forget. You'd be helping your country.'

'Invasion seems more remote as time goes on.'

'Bloke in charge – Bob Button – says we mustn't become complacent. And there's the *hidden enemy* – we can't trust folk like we did.' He decided to be frank. 'You'd have to pull yourself together, Mr Bliss, smarten up. You can't let *her* win.'

'My wife, you mean? You've got a cheek, you know.'

'I got through to you, didn't I? I'll call for you at seven, take you to the meeting.'

'What does my sister say about this?'

'She doesn't know I'm here. But I know she's been worrying about you since your wife moved back next door . . . So has the young teacher,' he added slyly.

'Ah, Eva. Nothing can come of *that*, I'm afraid.'

'At least you can prove to them you're a real man, eh?'

'That's enough, thank you.' Lawrence opened the door. 'You'd better go.'

'You'll come?' Jube said, as he untied the dog.

'All right!' Lawrence almost shouted, shutting the door.

Georgia and May were hanging about outside the school-house, waiting for Helga to join them after she finished work. They'd observed Eva hurrying home to her baby, so it shouldn't be a long wait. Miss Worley knew they were there too, but she wouldn't ask them in, despite the cold wind whipping round their ears on a typical December afternoon. As Georgia said, 'She's had enough of us lot, I reckon, after a day of it.'

It was Friday. She was disappointed that the music lessons in the hut had been discontinued in her absence. She had something important to ask Mr Bliss. That was another thing: he didn't come round to Phoebe's any more. It was a shame, she thought, just when they seemed to be reconciled at last.

The door opened and Eva beckoned to them. 'Don't stand out there in the cold, girls. Helga wants to finish off some ironing. I told her not to bother, but she insisted. Come and have a quick cup of tea – I'm dying for one, myself.' She smiled as they hesitated. 'Miss Worley spends some time with her father directly she gets in.'

They hadn't been in the kitchen there before; it was cosier than the sitting-room. There was a pull-down airer above the stove, where the flat-irons were heated in turn, full of small garments and nappies. Helga was pressing and folding more of these on the table, protected by an old blanket. The baby was propped up in her high chair.

While the children talked to Win, and obligingly picked up the rattle and toys she threw overboard continually, Eva poured the tea, adding sugar to the girls' cups. 'Excuse me, while I take the tray upstairs for the others,' she said.

There were three items left in the ironing pile. 'I'll do those,' May offered.

Helga still didn't talk much as a rule, but she looked at Georgia as they sat side by side at a corner of the table, and asked softly, 'How are you? And your mother?'

'It helps, being here,' Georgia replied. 'Mum was right about that. My brother's being discharged from hospital tomorrow, but he won't have to go far. Mum's got a cleaning job there, and a little flat. A bed and a put-u-up she says. It'll do for now.' She didn't like to think of her mother scrubbing and polishing floors, on her knees, silently pushing along clanking buckets of dirty water. She deserved better. She'd really enjoyed her sales pitch at the market; it suited her lively, sunny personality.

Then she added, she didn't know why, 'I've got my dad's piano accordion, did May tell you? I hoped Mr Bliss would teach me how to play it, but he's given up the music lessons . . .' Tears welled in her eyes, and she rubbed them away fiercely.

Eva came back just then and looked at her with concern. 'Don't worry, Georgia, we understand . . . Finish your tea and get off home, all of you. It'll soon be dark.'

The three of them cycled along, expecting to meet up with Phoebe on her way back from Spare Penny. When they came to the gatehouse, Helga waved them to a stop. They left their bikes by the gate and she went ahead of them to the front door. They glimpsed a shadowy figure in the sitting-room window, then Lawrence greeted them.

'Visitors two days running!' he said warily. 'Come in, then I can turn on the light.' There was an exclamation of surprise. '*Helga*?' he queried.

'We can't stop long, as Phoebe will wonder where we are,' May told him.

'Georgia, I heard you were back. I'm –'

'I know, you're sorry, everyone is.' She had her feelings under control now.

He turned to Helga. 'I haven't seen *you* for years,' he said simply.

She finally found her voice. 'Not since I used to come here – to play the piano.'

'It wasn't your fault,' he said, almost inaudibly.

'I didn't tell *them*. The girls miss their music. Georgia wants to learn the accordion. Please –'

He nodded slowly. 'Not back at the hut. I'm not – ready for that.'

'Come to Phoebe's,' Georgia suggested impulsively. 'Tomorrow afternoon.'

'You've persuaded me.' He made an effort, smiled. 'I'll see you then.'

Phoebe came upon them at the gate as they disentangled their bikes. Helga and May went off up Middle Moor, and Phoebe and Georgia wheeled their bikes along in the gloom, for the ruts were difficult to discern after dusk.

Georgia related what had happened, and then a thought struck her. 'Phoebe, shall we ask Eva and Win round? Make it a surprise, or Lawrence won't come!'

'Oh, I *am* glad you're here!' Phoebe exclaimed, but didn't enlarge on that.

'We ought to have asked Kenny,' Georgia remembered belatedly, when May arrived.

'I popped in the shop for some chewing nuts and he was behind the counter – his dad was with his mum, waiting for the nurse – the baby's coming!' May said, excited.

Georgia helped herself from the proffered poke bag. 'Mum says these'll ruin your teeth, but thanks!' A couple of ounces of the little bullets of toffee, coated in something that looked like chocolate but wasn't, outlasted most sweets. Her teeth already glued with caramel, she mumbled, 'Was Kenny excited?'

'Not exactly. 'Specially as his mum says his dad always wanted a girl, and she's sure that's what it is!'

'Rather tactless, eh?' Phoebe lifted the lid of the piano. 'There, have a practise, before Lawrence puts in an appearance. I thought Helga would be with you?'

'She's not saying much today, just shook her head when I asked,' May said.

'Maybe it unsettled her,' Phoebe began. Then, 'Got your music book? Good.'

Lawrence was walking slowly along the lane when he became aware of a trundling noise behind him. He turned to see the raised hood of an old-fashioned black pram, and beyond that the person pushing it – Eva. He stopped in his tracks, waiting for her to come alongside.

'Need any help?' was all he could think of saying.

The cold air had put colour into her cheeks. She'd turned up the fur collar on her tweed coat which, despite the severe style, failed to disguise her more womanly figure. She was no longer, as Georgia's dad had remarked, in need of a 'spot of mum's steak and kidney.' Strands of hair escaping her woollen cap softened the prim look of a year or so ago. Then she yelled at him, 'I thought you were my friend, I believed you even wanted more than that, you – you – cut me out of your life, after the baby was born, you didn't come to see me.'

He caught at her hand as she made to push past him. 'Eva – *I was there*, waiting for hours, in the schoolhouse, the day you were in labour –'

'Miss Worley didn't say!'

'I don't wish to criticise her, because she has obviously been so good to you, helped you in ways that would not have been possible for me, but, she made it clear that she thought I would only make things more difficult for you if I persisted.'

'She was probably right,' Eva said. She tugged her hand free. 'I was going to Phoebe's, but it's obvious that you are headed in that direction, so –'

'Don't go,' he pleaded. 'I think about you all the time. I do care for you, Eva. But there seems no hope of marrying you eventually, because Beryl has refused to divorce me. It wouldn't be right for me to ask you to move in with me.'

'You could take the initiative, you certainly have grounds for divorce!'

'You don't know how devious Beryl is. She would destroy both our reputations.'

There was a wail from the pram. Eva lifted the baby, adjusted the pillow. 'There, look at Win, Lawrence. Are you brave enough to take us both on? She needs a father, and I – I'm asking for commitment. *He* wouldn't give me that, but then, he didn't love me. Let's get on now, eh? But don't take too long to decide.'

Lawrence had adjusted the straps so that Georgia could handle the accordion more comfortably. He showed her some simple fingering, then left her to explore its possibilities while he instructed May at the piano.

Eva, the baby and Phoebe were in the kitchen. His sister was making sandwiches and baking rock-cakes for tea. They'd closed the door so he couldn't hear what they were saying, but Lawrence guessed Eva would confide in Phoebe.

'You've remembered quite a lot,' he told May.

'Helga made me practise now and then. Was *she* very good?'

'Very good, I wish she hadn't given it up. And I believe you will be, too.'

Then Kenny came bursting into the room. 'Mum's had the baby, it's a *girl*! We're calling her Dinah! Dad's shut the shop early and sent me out of the way for a bit!'

It turned out to be a celebratory tea in more ways than one.

The slightest noise had the night patrol of the Home Guard on full alert: the whip-crack of a fallen branch underfoot; a rustling in the grass; a strangled cry from some small creature seized by a predator. The moonlight, glimpsed through the trees, silvering the patches of frost, made them more uneasy.

Lawrence had taken the message on the transmitter: *Lone German plane, jettisoned load in sea, brought down by us. Two crew killed. Another baled out, believed in your area . . .'*

They hunted in pairs, spreading out to the perimeters of the wood. Jube and Lawrence crept along stealthily, the novice shadowing the poacher, taking his cue from him. Yet they almost passed the great tree where the mushrooming canopy, with a suspended figure jerking futilely, was snared. Then Lawrence spotted it.

'*Jube*,' he shouted, before he could stop himself, 'there he is!'

The parachutist's response was quicker. He had a revolver clutched in his hand. The first bullet dented Lawrence's tin hat; the second hit Jube's raised right arm as he responded with his rifle. The figure spun round, then hung limply.

Jube's involuntary exclamation of disbelief as he recognised the man, startled Lawrence into action, to shout, '*Here!*' They were surrounded by the rest of the platoon. Jube waved away immediate first aid. 'It can wait. Get him down.'

It was a situation none of the Home Guard had dealt with before. They gathered round the dead man. He was in civilian clothes. This did not concern them at the time. The important factor was that the enemy had fired first; the return fire had been in self-defence.

'I shall have to report back to HQ,' Bob Button said at last. He put a reassuring hand on Jube's shoulder. 'You must get that arm seen to.'

Both Jube and Lawrence were in shock. They would keep the knowledge of who had injured Jube to themselves, for Phoebe's sake.

'I thought you were happy here,' Miss Worley said help-lessly, as Eva collected her possessions together.

'I was – oh, I can't thank you enough for all you've done for Win and me. But we did disturb your peaceful exist-ence here, it was quite an upheaval, I know –'

'My dear, it did me good!'

'I can still carry on at the school as usual?' Eva asked, suddenly anxious. 'Helga can look after Win as before, but in her own home now. I'm going to leave her there now, while I find my way round the gatehouse.'

'Of course you can continue teaching here. I intend to make sure you are in line to take over from me when I am finally able to retire.' Miss Worley was holding Win in her arms. This was unusual, but the pram was full of her para-phernalia. She suddenly bent her head, kissed the baby's cheek. 'I shall miss you, both of you. I hope you're doing the right thing, Eva.'

'I hope so, too.' Eva had to be honest. 'He's a good, gentle man.'

'You'll need to be strong, for both of you.'

'We love each other.'

'Then, I suppose that's all that really matters. Come on,' Miss Worley added briskly. 'Let me give you a hand, or you'll never get going today.'

'I thought you could have my room, it's bigger for you and the baby,' Lawrence said diffidently. 'I'll move a single bed into my study next door.' He left unsaid, but she guessed, that they would keep the door closed on Beryl's room.

You need to be strong for both of you, Miss Worley's words echoed in her head.

'You and I will share this room, as it's got the double bed,' she said firmly. 'The small room will be fine for Win, as it's close by. Don't move the bed yet, she's still in her cot, remember.'

'I-I didn't want to presume,' he said softly, moving closer, as she sat on the bed to test the springiness of the mattress.

'That's why I said it! I know how you feel, what your needs are, Lawrence. We both deserve that happiness, I think. This is the time to take a chance.'

'Then I *will*, darling Eva,' he said, as his arms went round her firmly.

After a quiet Christmas, when Jube, recuperating but still with his arm in a sling, joined them, Georgia wrote to her mother:

I still miss you a lot! But now I have to work hard and catch up at school with the exam coming up. It's good you and Martin are together, and in a safe place away from the bombs, same as here. Spare Penny has closed, and Phoebe likes cooking at the hospital. May and Helga love their new house. They wanted to be by themselves, Christmas Day. It's nice to have them nearby. Dusty is being good, and I think Jube still has HOPES as you say, regarding Phoebe. She has looked after him since his MYS-TERIOUS accident. (Kenny thinks he was shot by a German spy!) Red House is empty again since that horrible Beryl went with the soldiers!! Hurrah! I hope it is all right to pass on that Mr Bliss and Eva and the baby are all living together now in the gate-house. I wonder what Miss W thinks about that!! But I mustn't gossip, must I? Looking forward to seeing you soon, and playing for you on the accor-dion, I know Dad would be pleased I can.

Your ever loving (only) daughter, Georgia. xxx

PS Helga looks after two babies now, when Kenny's mum has to serve in the shop!
PPS HAPPY *PEACEFUL* NEW YEAR, 1941!

PART TWO

SEVENTEEN

Georgia could not have envisaged that the war would drag on for another four and a half years and that by VE Day, 1945, she would still be living with Phoebe in Suffolk. She and May were at the grammar school and their education was almost complete.

Word went round: *Victory Party Saturday, 12th May, in the hut!* Georgia and May were among the eager volunteers decorating that squat, plain building, with bunting on the outside and well-worn decorations within. There were clusters of rather limp balloons; twisted, faded crepe paper; and a giant poster painted by the school children on VE Day itself: DANCE AND BE HAPPY! embellished by their footprints.

The workers were entertained during the afternoon by Lawrence, with a medley of wartime tunes. 'When the lights go up again, all over the world,' the girls sang and, 'We'll meet again,' in a fair imitation of the Forces' Sweetheart, Vera Lynn.

Some wouldn't meet again, Georgia thought, like Aubrey, whose war was not over yet, not until Japan was defeated, and Eunice. Others, like Martin, suffered from recurrent bouts of depression. He still needed his mother to be with him. Georgia accepted that without resentment. She hoped they'd be together as a family again, one day, but it was a disturbing thought that there was no place to call home.

From ten to sixteen years old, apart from the tragic events in London during the Blitz, her life was here. She'd changed so much during that time; in appearance that is, for she'd retained her impulsive, outspoken, cheerful nature. The skinny youngster with flaming, frizzy hair was now an attractive young woman with definite, delicious curves and hair that had darkened at adolescence to a deep chestnut, as Mum predicted it would. The frizz remained, of course, but as May pointed out ruefully, with her own fine, straight hair in mind, 'You don't have to curl yours every night, and go to bed looking like a porcupine.'

May was shorter than Georgia, still slightly built; not well-developed like her friend. 'With your name,' Georgia had remarked tactlessly recently, '*you* should have the Mae West shape, not me – but I guess I take after my mum, more and more.'

May flashed back, 'I'd rather be brainy, know I *could* go to college, though I've decided not to; Miss W says *you* haven't lived up to your promise lately.'

'I want to get a job, help Mum out,' Georgia said, but the truth hurt.

They soon made up, because their friendship meant a lot to them both.

She was wavering about on the top of the hut's rickety stepladder when Kenny exclaimed, 'Watch out!' and obligingly held it steady. She jabbed the last, bent drawing-pin into a streamer on a beam and descended smartly. Kenny might be a mate but she was wearing a short skirt and he was grinning, she thought.

'What're you doing here? What about the shop?' she asked, because his mother was busy in the hut kitchen, helping Helga, Phoebe and Eva wash all the crockery. His young sisters, for Mona had produced Annette a year after Dinah, were jigging to the music along with their friend Win, watched over by May. They had unwittingly decided Kenny's future. At fourteen he'd left school to work full-time in the shop.

'Dad said, "get along and enjoy yourself", no customers anyway,' he replied. 'He thinks there's a box of Christmas lights under the stage somewhere. You can crawl in the cavern with me, and hold the torch.'

It was dark and dusty under the floorboards, and there were boxes everywhere. They inched their way to the far side and a trap door, which connected with the tiny room backstage where the meters were on the wall and broken chairs were stacked. There had been no concerts in the hut for the duration, as folk called it.

'Lights!' Georgia told Kenny, shining the beam on a long box. 'We could have got at 'em from the other side. We wouldn't have ended up nearly as grubby.'

Then they heard voices. 'Shush!' Kenny warned her. They hadn't sought permission to be where they were. He switched off the torch.

A male voice, hoarsely whispering. 'You'll have to tell her some time.'

'*They* said: best to leave it as it is.'

'*Helga*?' Georgia mouthed at Kenny, but of course he couldn't see her lips.

'Don't you understand? I *want* to acknowledge her,' the man said.

Another voice, louder. 'Found the tools, Helga?' Mona asked. 'Can't get that top cupboard open. Oh, good, *you're* here, too – we can do with some more help.'

They waited in the dark. Georgia suppressed a sneeze. She was about to say, 'Can't we get out of here?' when Kenny's arm squeezed her round her waist. 'You don't need to help me, Kenny, I can manage, thank you,' she hissed indignantly.

'Oh, do shut up for once,' he said, before he kissed her, experimentally.

To her mortification, she didn't struggle much; there wasn't room.

'There, you enjoyed that, didn't you?' he challenged her.

'I've got cramp in my legs,' and I'm trembling, she realised, surprised.

'Let me rub them for you.'

'Certainly not! Open that bloomin' door, Kenneth Button, or I'll scream!'

'Admit it first, you actually liked being kissed, Georgia Smith!'

'You need a bit more practice,' she retorted. 'And what about May?'

'What about her?'

'She's your girlfriend; everyone thinks –'

'May wouldn't let me kiss her as you did,' he teased. 'And folk can say what they like, *you're* the girl for me . . .'

The door opened, and they blinked in the light. 'Stuck in here?' Lawrence asked. 'May was worrying where you'd got to, but when your dad arrived, he guessed!'

They clambered out, dusted themselves down sheepishly. Bob Button came along, took the box of lights from his son. 'You'll need a bath before the shindig,' he said, looking at him keenly. 'I suggest you make it a cold one!'

Someone said it was a pity the Yanks weren't still around: they'd taken over Red House in 1942, but left before D-Day, a year ago. The Americans had been generous with sharing their rations with the villagers, particularly on special occasions. Still, Bob and Mona Button had delved deep under the counter, come up with some rationed goodies and whispered, 'Blow the points!'

When the tables were laid, and everything ready, Georgia and May went back with Helga to her house in the small, council development off the main street, to change into their party clothes. Georgia was staying the night there for the first time.

The house was more modern than the cottage; it even had a small bathroom, with a high-sided tub on four splayed feet and, Helga's pride and joy, a noisy gas water heater, which ignited with a frightening *bang!* but provided lovely hot water. Georgia had been well primed by Phoebe: 'That costs a lot to run, remember.' So she said politely that the handbasin would be fine for her needs.

'How on earth did you get so dirty?' May exclaimed, sitting on the cork-topped stool, awaiting her turn. 'Mind you clean the basin after you.'

'Kenny and I were searching for something in the glory-hole under the stage,' Georgia said casually, reaching for the towel to dab her flushed face.

'You look so pretty,' May said approvingly, later, of her multi-coloured rayon dress with the sweetheart neckline, gathered skirt and short sleeves.

'Pity about all the freckles on my arms,' Georgia sighed. She looked in the long mirror brought from Spare Penny. All bounce, she told herself: hair bouncing on my shoulders, bouncing bosoms, and feet already tapping to the music in her head.

'Aren't you girls ready yet?' Helga called up the stairs.

It was an emotional evening: much embracing, kissing in corners. The girls danced together for the boys gathered at a table to watch, scoffing the remaining sandwiches and slyly sharing a bottle or two of Jube's homemade wine. The younger children were determined to stay to the end, but one by one dropped in action and were lifted onto parents' laps. Mona played the piano now, while Lawrence sat with Eva.

He stroked Win's dark hair off her damp forehead. 'Wide to the world,' he said.

There was no one close by. Eva looked at him. 'Let's go home,' she said softly.

'You think we should? This could go on for an hour or two yet.'

'Lawrence, we can't go on, as we are –'

'Why not? I'm happier than I've ever been in my life. You and Win –'

'I want us to be married. I want another baby, *your* baby, I want –'

'I *know* what you want. So do I. Yes, let's slip away while we can,' he said.

He carried Win tenderly, her head against his shoulder. Eva walked close beside. She thought, we're a family anyway; we've been through so much together.

There was a light on in the front room of the gatehouse. No blackout tonight. But, 'I'm sure I didn't leave that on,' Lawrence said, puzzled. Before he could insert the key in the door, it opened. '*Beryl!*' he said, in disbelief.

'You must have known I'd be back one of these days. The colonel is with the occupying forces. I can't join him yet, so I decided to sort things out here. You've got away with it for long enough. I suggest you put that child to bed and then we'll talk . . .'

'You keep out of this, Eva,' Lawrence said. 'Go to bed yourself.'

'Yes, you go, Eva. But, I promise you, he won't be joining you there for some time,' Beryl said, and the malice was unmistakable.

The hut doors were open to cool the overheated atmosphere. A long line of giggling dancers swayed out into the garden to the beat of the Conga. Georgia was on the end of the snake, and she let go of the person in front to walk round the side and look up at the stars. What a magical evening! One she would never forget. She leaned against the wall, took a deep breath. The heady smell of roses! Bushes planted to commemorate those lost in the Great War. Then she sensed that she was not alone. This time she didn't resist as Kenny drew her close. She was vibrantly aware that his heart was beating as fast as her own as he kissed her parted lips.

They sprang apart as they heard Phoebe call out: 'Georgia, are you out here? May's been looking for you. They're going home now, and so are we, Jube and me. The poor old dogs will be wondering where on earth we are.'

'Just as well,' Kenny whispered. 'Powerful stuff, Jube's wine . . .' He snatched another brief kiss.

'I must go,' she managed. 'You stay here, or they might think.'

'I get you,' he said.

As she went back into the hut, May said reproachfully, 'There you are!'

Here I am, Georgia thought; I mustn't let it happen again, for her sake. She recalled those whispers, overheard. May might be about to be hurt in other ways . . .

'Well, goodnight. It's been a great day,' Jube observed, at Phoebe's gate.

'Aren't you coming in for a nightcap?'

'Haven't we had enough of those?' he smiled, but followed her in anyway.

He sat down in Grandfather's chair and stretched out his legs. 'Getting ancient – I'll be stiff tomorrow from all that dancing, I reckon. Did you say tea? Yes please.'

She stifled a yawn. 'I can't really be bothered to make it, Jube, sorry.'

'You'd best get off to bed, then. See you tomorrow?'

'You don't have to go – not if you don't want to,' she said, tentatively.

'Well, I *was* thinking of asking you, after such a good day, will you marry me?'

'Oh, Jube, you poor chap: I've kept you hanging on another seven years and –'

'You still haven't made your mind up,' he sighed.

'I'm sorry. I suppose I should have said, because I don't have any proof that Karl was drowned, I-I've been afraid he might come back eventually, when the war is over, which it is, now, of course, or almost, and –'

'You still love him?'

'*No!* Don't you understand, Jube? I thought we might take the chance, with Georgia away – I really want you to stay here tonight.'

'You're so beautiful in that red dress,' he said, gazing at her. 'Like a girl.'

'Oh, you've seen it before, it's pre-war! And *you've* looked younger, ever since you joined the Home Guard: short back and sides and clean-shaven! Jube?'

'I'm not sure this is the right moment, even though we both wish it was.'

'I'm getting on for forty, you're more than that; we're wasting time,' she said.

'I shouldn't say this,' he began, then stopped abruptly. He'd been sworn to secrecy about the events of the night he was shot.

'Then don't,' she told him, unaware of what he had been about to divulge.

'Go and let Dusty out, and I'll see to Sandy, then . . . Just tonight, as I said: I wouldn't like to upset Georgia at such an impressionable age . . .'

Georgia was restless in her narrow, hard bed, alongside May's. The spartan furniture in Helga's house had been given to her when Spare Penny closed.

'Are you awake, May?' she murmured.

'It's long past midnight, Georgia! What d'you want?'

'Don't you ever wonder, you know, about who your parents are?'

'I know who my mother is,' May said, in a matter-of-fact way.

'You never said. I thought we told each other everything!' She felt a pang of guilt. She couldn't confide in May about what happened with Kenny tonight.

'I only found out recently. I had to take my birth certificate to school, when the head wanted me to apply for that college course – actually, I never told you that, either; they turned me down, because of it.'

'Why? I don't understand.'

'I did, because I opened the envelope after Helga gave it to me and read the form. I suppose I wasn't that surprised, because we've always been so close. My real name is May Hazlitt. I expect Matron invented "Moon".'

'You mean, *Helga's* your mother?'

'Yes. I imagine Matron wanted my birth kept secret, because of the man involved – it just said "Father unknown", well, that didn't shock me because I guessed I was born out of wedlock. Some people take against you because of it, of course.'

'That's not fair! Weren't you upset that Helga didn't tell you?'

'No, I realise that's why she hardly spoke at all, at one time, you see.' May leaned out of bed towards Georgia, said in her ear, 'I haven't spoken to her about it yet. I'm waiting for the right time. *You* won't tell anyone, will you, not even Phoebe?'

'I promise.'

'I'll tell you something else, then. I believe my father is *Mr Bliss*! Remember that evening when Helga asked him to teach us music again, and some other things they said to each other, which we couldn't make head nor tail of?'

'Well, if you're right, he let Helga down badly; I hope he won't do that to Eva!'

Georgia lay awake for some time after May went to sleep. May's so good at accepting what happened in the past, she thought. How could that college turn her down because her mother wasn't married to her father? How can *she* be blamed for that? I'm so fortunate to have had two wonderful parents, even though I lost Dad when I was only twelve years old. Phoebe's like a second mother to me, too.

EIGHTEEN

Phoebe lay contentedly in the circle of Jube's strong arms; awake, but not wanting to break the spell. A breeze billowed the curtains inwards from the open windows. She wondered what the time was. Her face was pressed against Jube's broad, bare chest, rising and falling in the gentle rhythm of sleep.

Downstairs, Sandy gave a sudden, plaintive bark. Jube's eyes flickered open. His lips brushed her hair. 'Have we overslept?' he asked, as if he didn't really care.

'Probably. Does it matter? It's Sunday.'

'I'll be late with the milking . . .'

'Don't leave me yet,' she said softly. 'Are you happy about last night?'

'What do you think?' His hands caressed her shoulders.

'I think I should consider your proposal very seriously . . .'

Later, after pulling on his shirt, while she brushed and braided her hair at the washstand mirror, he couldn't resist coming up behind her, sliding his arms round her seated figure, hugging her tight. 'You know what came into my head last night?' he asked, his voice muffled as he lifted the heavy plait to kiss the nape of her neck.

'I can guess, Jube,' she replied demurely.

'No, I don't think you can. I suddenly thought, I'd love to have a son before I get too old to teach him all the things a boy should know, like my dad did for me.'

She swivelled round. 'Would it matter to you if we didn't have children?'

'Let me make an honest woman of you first, eh? A family will follow!'

She kissed him fiercely, before he could see the sudden tears in her eyes.

After a mainly sleepless night, aware that Lawrence had not come to bed at all, Eva rose at her usual time before Win began calling out. She dressed in her room as she didn't want to meet up with Beryl while still in her nightgown.

The bathroom was empty, she discovered with relief. She'd tiptoed past the sitting-room, where the door was firmly closed. No voices. Was that ominous, she wondered? 'Let's get you bathed first,' she told Win, locking the door.

When Win was dried, dressed and playing with the damp rubber toys, Eva washed herself. Her reflection in the glass over the basin was wan.

The handle on the door turned. She stared at it, too nervous to speak.

'Eva?' Lawrence asked urgently.

She flew to the door, opened it. 'Lawrence! I was so worried about you!'

He clasped her convulsively. 'It's all right. She's gone.'

'Gone where? When?' she demanded.

'To Red House, five minutes ago. She wants to see what state it's in, before –'

'Before what? Don't tell me she intends to move in, spy on us,' she gabbled.

'Look, we can't talk in this cramped space. Let's have breakfast. Hungry, Win?'

Eva was suddenly furious. '*Breakfast!* I couldn't eat a thing!'

'Perhaps not, but Win can't go without. Be sensible.' They went into the kitchen.

'What I want to know is, did you know she was coming?'

'Calm down! Of course I didn't. It's Beryl's way, she likes to spring nasty surprises. Here, give Win her cereal, while I boil the kettle. Then I'll tell you all.'

Eva reluctantly ate the toast and honey he offered. '*Now*,' she insisted.

'The colonel's divorce is through. He waited until his children were old enough. If he wants to marry Beryl after five years together – *he* must be a match for her!'

'So, she wasn't tearing you to pieces last night? I imagined –'

'Well, don't. She did indeed come out with a few home truths and made me fully aware what an inadequate person I am. She brought Phoebe into it, said we'd both made a mess of our lives due to our upbringing: no father figure, dominating grandparents and a mother who resented us, tied to a house she hated.'

'What comes next, Lawrence?' She felt impatient with him now.

'I can have my freedom, but at a price. She says she'll cite you. Oh Eva!'

'I don't care! Let her do it! Changing my name by deed poll was a wise move.'

'What about your career? You can't keep *that* quiet.'

'We won't contest it. It'll all blow over. We'll get married; you can adopt Win.'

'She made certain stipulations. We sell Red House, auction the valuables, as she calls them, and we divide the proceeds between us.'

'That doesn't sound too bad. We'll still have the gate-house, I presume?'

'I didn't say "divide equally". Beryl demands a settlement of seventy-five per cent. Yes, we'll have this place, it's not worth much, but we'll lose the rest. The only good thing is, she's not asking for maintenance. The colonel, she says, can provide *all* the things I couldn't. I can guess what . . . ' Suddenly he was weeping, his head in his hands.

'Daddy!' Win cried, alarmed.

For a moment Eva sat there, undecided; then she shifted beside him, put her arms around him. 'You provide for *my* needs very well, darling. Don't we have an inspiring love life? Money, Red House, who cares? Home is *here*, with you two.'

'Why don't you go and talk to Helga now?' Georgia urged May. Helga had gone downstairs a little earlier, to start cooking breakfast. 'I'll keep out of the way – I'll have a bath, eh? Helga said I could, last night.'

'Let me light the geyser then, I've got the hang of it.'

When she knew Georgia was safely wallowing, May went to find Helga. She was basting stale bread in the bacon fat. The eggs were cooked, ready to slide on top.

'Shall I make the tea yet?' May asked casually.

'Leave it a bit, I gather Georgia's having her bath.' Helga carefully lowered the gas, then turned her flushed face to look at May. 'Everything all right?'

'Sit down a minute, Helga. I want to tell you something.'

May hadn't really noticed it before, but now she saw how similar they were in looks. The same dark-blonde, fly-away hair, high cheekbones and wary, blue eyes.

'I know you're my mum,' she stated.

'You – you looked at your birth certificate?'

'Yes. Don't be upset, because I wasn't. I couldn't ask for a better mother.'

'I wanted to tell you, years ago.'

'It doesn't matter now. Though I can't call you anything but Helga. You didn't give me away, you cared for me yourself, that means a lot. If you want to tell me about it, that's all right; if you don't, that's all right, too. I can guess who my father is – was. But he doesn't come into all this. Let's leave it at that. You weren't much older than I am now, when it happened. He's the one who should have known better.'

Cheerful whistling along the landing: Georgia letting them know that she was out of the bath, about to get dressed and would be down shortly.

'I bet she didn't wash the bath round,' May sighed. 'I'll make the tea now, shall I, and you'd better see if the fried bread has burned.' She added, 'Thank you, Helga.'

'What for?' Helga was wiping her face on her turned-up apron.

'Being with me,' May said simply.

School was out for the summer and the girls would not return there in September. They deserved a holiday, Georgia's mother, Phoebe and Helga told them. They were hopeful of good results in the Oxford School Certificate and job-seeking could wait. Anyway, the war with Japan hadn't ended yet, and business prospects were still uncertain.

'You're lucky,' Kenny said mournfully. 'I'm stuck behind the counter, or pouring paraffin into cans; there's still rationing, but Dinah and Annette raid the sweet jars and I get a thick ear from Dad. When I go out on my bike, it's only on deliveries . . .'

'Got any pipe-cleaners?' May asked.

'Blimey, you taken up smoking – what does Helga say about that?'

'Nothing, 'cause I haven't! I want to try curling my hair with 'em.'

'Seen smoke-rings coming out of *your* ears lately,' Georgia grinned. She knew he was looking surreptitiously at her long, bare, tanned legs. She was wearing shorts and a sun top today, which left nothing to the imagination. She'd learned to accept admiring glances now, since Nell had reassured her, '*Big is beautiful*', on her last visit.

'Roll-yer-owns: all I can afford if I'm to treat you girls to the pictures one evening.'

The next day, Tuesday 6th August, the first atomic bomb devastated Japan. It was followed by a second bomb three days later. On 14th August, Japan surrendered.

Mum's letter to Georgia did not mention the A bomb; she had surprising, happy news.

Dear Georgia,

You will find this hard to believe! There is a lovely young nurse we have known since Martin was first in hospital. She lost her husband in 1942. I guessed M was sweet on her, but he didn't have HOPES (as you and I say). Well, they got together at last at the Hospital VE party, and they aren't wasting any time. They are getting married at the end of August! She is just the girl for him and, as he is so much better now, I'm sure he can get a job and help support a wife – and who better than a nurse to support him on his not so good days? Her name is Elizabeth, but she is known as Lizzie. I am going to ask them if they would like to take over this flat. If they do, it will mean you and me will be able to be together again. Where would you like to live? Come up with some ideas! It won't be a big wedding, but it will be in the hospital chapel, and Lizzie would like you and May to be her bridesmaids. (Just wear your best frocks.) I am enclosing a note for Phoebe, to invite her too, so she can bring you by train. I will pay your fares, and arrange bed and breakfast nearby for two (you can stay with me, of course). Will be writing again soon with final details.

Fondest love from Mum xxx

PS Let's hope Aubrey will be as lucky, when he comes home, to meet the right girl second time around.

Georgia spent her days with May now that Phoebe worked at the cottage hospital. She did a few chores for Phoebe, after she left first thing, like taking Sandy for his walk, making the beds and washing up; then she went down the lane, calling via Button's store for the shopping.

Kenny, in his clean white apron, wrapped bread, checked the coupons in their ration books, weighed sugar and biscuits, packed her basket on the counter. She couldn't keep it to herself, although she'd intended to tell May first.

'Had some exciting news today!'

'Good. You've got a job?'

'Not yet! My brother's getting married, and May and me are going to be bridesmaids, only she doesn't know yet, and Phoebe – she doesn't know either – is going to escort us to Hertfordshire for the wedding. Then Martin and his new wife, she's a nurse, which Mum is glad about, Martin being not so well at times still, are going to take over Mum's flat and then *we'll* find somewhere to live together!'

'You're not going to move away from here, I hope?' he asked sharply.

'Why, wouldn't you like that?' she teased.

'You know I wouldn't!'

'You can make do with *one* girlfriend, can't you?'

Before he could respond, his mother came through into the shop from the back and asked, 'What's that about girlfriends? Not yet, I hope. We don't want him mooning about the shop. Georgia dear, can you take the little girls with you down to Helga's please? Thank goodness in September it'll be one less pickle to cope with. As Dinah's starting school, I did wonder, as Win will be going to, if Helga might be willing to come back to work in the shop. We could both keep an eye on Nettie then, and I might catch up on the housework at last. We'll need two behind the counter when all the menfolk come back from the war, eh?'

'I'll drop a few hints for you. Are the children ready?'

'*No!*' Helga said immediately, when Georgia told her of Mona's hopes. 'There'll be other little ones for me to look after; I've already been asked. I prefer working at home here.' But she was pleased to hear about the wedding, and encouraged May, who expressed some doubts about her new role. 'What can I wear?'

'Phoebe'll come up with something for you both, she always does.'

Phoebe was pleased, too, because a great idea had struck her. She decided she mustn't say anything to Georgia, raising her hopes, until she'd spoken to Jube and written back to Nell with her acceptance.

She had her chance when Kenny called round unexpectedly that evening, and he and Georgia took the dogs out for a run.

Phoebe and Jube hadn't actually been on their own since the VE party, three months ago, now. There was a great deal of pent-up feeling released as they embraced, knowing there was no one to see. She gave him a little push. 'I'm not sure we should get carried away like this . . .'

'You haven't changed your mind?' he asked anxiously.

'No, and you've been very patient! Jube, it looks as if Nell and Georgia will be reunited very soon; read this letter and find out why. *We* can get married too, as soon as possible, after things are settled.' She waited until he'd perused the note.

'Which side will we live? Yours or mine?' He had a broad grin on his face.

'We'll toss for it! Oh, Jube, don't you see, we could offer the vacant cottage to Nell – she may not like the idea, of course, maybe she wants to go back to London, but Georgia is so settled here, and that would mean we wouldn't lose her altogether.'

'Stop talking, come here,' he said. 'Let me show you how happy I am . . .'

'You won't go back to London, promise me,' Kenny insisted. They were stretched out on the meadow grass, watching the two old dogs ambling about rather than running after interesting scents.

'Well, I've got so used to living in the country I'm not sure I want to be crowded in by city buses and busy roads, and blocks of new flats the new Labour Government say they are going to build to replace what they call slums . . . I hope we won't have to move far away from here but, remember, Mum and I will both be looking for jobs.'

He flicked an ant off her arm. 'Make sure you do something more exciting in your working life than I am . . . I didn't want to leave school so early, but I had no choice. At least you'll have a certificate to show you passed your exams.'

'I hope you get another chance later on, Kenny,' Georgia said.

'That would be good. Georgia –'

'Mmm?'

'Can I kiss you? I don't suppose I'll get another opportunity.'

She leaned towards him, smiling. 'Go on then! But be quick about it. I want to go home and write a letter back to Mum!'

NINETEEN

Lizzie, the bride, wore what she termed 'the communal outfit': a good quality, if rather heavy, costume in heather tweed, donated by a senior nurse before the war.

'It'll never wear out,' she told them all, ruefully, 'but, as it's the second time, I didn't want to wear the wedding gown which goes the rounds.'

'Hope you won't get too hot,' Nell worried, for they were sweltering, crowded in the bedroom in the flat. She applied face powder liberally to the bride's shiny nose.

'*We're* all right,' Georgia said cheerfully, as she and May dodged about trying to get a glimpse of their splendour in the wardrobe mirror. Phoebe had ingeniously unpicked the full skirt of a once-worn ball dress – kept in tissue paper since she was seventeen – to fashion two pretty, if skimpy, dresses in pale-blue taffeta.

'Keep still,' Nell reproved them, pinning a single white carnation to each bodice. 'Now, sit on the bed and don't move again until I say! Well, Phoebe, let's leave 'em to it, shall we? I'll check if Martin's finished in the bathroom and hasn't cut himself shaving. Only half an hour to go!'

They delayed calling the bridegroom for five minutes, because Phoebe wanted to tell Nell her own good news. 'Jube and I are getting married next month, Nell.'

'That's *just* what I hoped to hear! You've decided you love the bloke after all?'

'I'm very fond of him, Nell; I really regret sparring with him in the old days, before Georgia came and told me firmly how nice he was.'

'I'll be taking Georgia off your hands soon. It'll be just you two then, eh?'

'Look, I won't be upset, well, if I'm honest I *will* be, if you say no to this suggestion, but we wondered if you might like to take over the spare cottage? Probably mine, because Jube has worked so hard on the garden, his side.'

'You can breathe again, dearie, because I always make my mind up fast. It's a lovely idea! Mentioned it to Georgia yet?'

'No. I didn't think I should, until I had spoken to you.'

'I missed out you know, on all these important years, my daughter growing up, but it couldn't be helped. Still, it was a comfort to me that she had you to get her through all that, and I do thank you for it, Phoebe. We'll work it all out, eh, after we've waved the happy pair off on their honeymoon! Now, where's that boy?'

The little chapel was crowded with nurses, all in uniform. Lizzie was obviously a popular member of staff. Dressed in that stuffy outfit, with her everyday, black stockings and sensible shoes, she dabbed at her damp forehead continually. But when she turned to look at Martin, also uncomfortable in his best suit on a warm day, her face was radiant. It was obviously a love-match.

Georgia was suddenly reminded of Eunice and Aubrey. Now she was older she could think of her first sister-in-law in a more charitable way: marrying Aubrey to escape from the demands of her family, maybe, but making him happy for the short while they were together.

The modest wedding breakfast was served in the hospital canteen: Spam sandwiches, sausage rolls and a Victoria sponge without icing but plenty of decoration. Phoebe provided two bottles of Jube's elderberry for the toast: 'To the bride and groom!' Nell beamed and glasses chinked. The chairs and tables were pushed back against the wall and there was much laughter and impromptu dancing to a gramophone, even though men were still thin on the ground. May danced with the hospital's elderly consultant, who turned out to be a bit of a twinkle-toes, Georgia mirthfully observed, as she winked at her over her mum's shoulder. Lizzie, discarding her jacket, drifted by dreamily with Martin, only startled by applause when they kissed.

After the couple's departure, they returned to Nell's for a cup of tea before Phoebe and May went to their bed and breakfast next door. Now the girls learned the exciting news about another wedding, and the proposed move for Nell and Georgia.

Georgia was so thrilled she gave a twirl, clapping her hands above her head because space was restricted. 'Yippee!'

'Not too much of that!' Phoebe laughed. 'You'll be wearing that dress again soon, I hope, and you, too, May, of course, only *you* don't need to be warned that too much exuberance could result in great splits under the arms!'

Phoebe visited the gatehouse shortly after they arrived back, to ask Lawrence if he would give her away. When he hesitated, Eva gave him a nudge. 'Of course, he'll be delighted! You'll have to ask Mona Button to play the organ in church, though.'

'It won't be a big wedding, no white dress, a minimum of fuss,' Phoebe said. 'Just two attendants, Georgia and May – and we'd like Win to be a flower girl.'

'When is this happening?' Lawrence asked abruptly. 'Jube's said nothing to me.'

Phoebe was surprised. 'You mean, you expected him to ask your permission?'

'Yes. Tell him to come and see me this evening. You still haven't said when.'

'Four weeks from this Saturday. September's a nice month for a wedding. You might show a little more enthusiasm, Lawrence.' Phoebe sounded hurt.

'I'm sorry. A lot on my mind. I was going to tell you when it was all settled, but I think you should know now. I – we had an unexpected visitor after the VE party: *Beryl*. You don't need to hear what was said, most of it unpleasant as you might suppose. Our divorce is going through; Beryl made some unreasonable demands, threats, you could say, but our solicitor has dealt with those firmly. Red House is in the process of being sold; I will receive half of the proceeds.'

'So you and Eva will be able to marry, too. I'm so happy for you both!'

'You make me feel guilty for my ungraciousness earlier.'

'It doesn't matter.'

'Yes it does. I've talked it over with Eva, and we agree that you were not adequately provided for when Grandfather died. I intend to give you a three thousand pound settlement. I don't imagine you will waste it as once would have been likely . . .'

'That part of my life is well and truly over, Lawrence. Thank you!'

'Jube is a good sort. Our grandparents were snobs – oh, don't deny it – it was that class thing, with their generation – but I believe they would have approved.'

When Jube arrived, Eva tactfully whisked Win off to bed, despite her protests that it was too early. Lawrence and Jube went into the sitting-room to talk.

'Drink, Jube?'

He shook his head. 'Rather not. Let's get on with it, Mr Bliss.'

'I think you should call me Lawrence, as we are to be brothers-in-law.'

'You mean you don't object to me marrying Phoebe?'

'Of course not. She's well past the age of needing my permission.'

'That's a big relief! We didn't mean to offend you.'

'You didn't. The – *other one* – was a scoundrel. You're a decent fellow.' He paused, thinking maybe that sounded patronising. 'And you asked her to marry you, before you heard about the money; that's good.'

'What money?'

'Oh, she hasn't told you yet? Perhaps she thought you'd call it off!'

'No fear of that, after it took her so long to say yes.'

'Good. I just want to be sure, Jube, that the *secret* we share will remain unrevealed. We had to swear that at the time, remember?'

'I do remember. It still troubles me though; I was the one who fired the shot.'

'You were exonerated from any blame, remember that, too.' Lawrence rose, held out his hand. 'I wish you both every happiness, Jube.'

September was a very busy month, culminating in the wedding. Nell joined Phoebe and Georgia, and a gap was made in the dividing hedge because of all the toing and froing. The old dogs, rather bewildered, wandered from one cottage garden to the other, and eventually ended up sharing a basket in Jube's kitchen, where they observed all movements, curled round each other, head on paws. Furniture was shifted, with some Red House additions; curtains and coverings were cleaned.

Phoebe gave notice at her job, while Nell went to work at Button's store on a temporary basis. Kenny was released from behind the counter, and his father, in a reckless moment, bought a motorbike and sidecar; not for outings, as Mona hoped, but for more speedy deliveries to a wider area. Kenny learned to ride it in a very short space of time, before Bob could change his mind. It would be useful for courting, too.

Jube's unexpected wedding present from Phoebe was the field he leased, the chance to be his own boss, with a proper smallholding and the promise of a partnership in a different sense, with his new wife.

'You deserve it,' she said. 'It's our investment for the future.'

As for Georgia and May, they received a summons from Miss Worley. 'Time you two girls were employed. After Miss Gathercole died last spring, her cousin decided she needed help in the post office. She would like to interview you, May, for the job. I know it is not the exciting career you envisaged, or what you merit after all your hard work at school, but it would be a start.'

'Why did she choose *me*?' May dared to ask.

'Because you are mature and bright, she said. Eva – er, Mrs Bliss, put in a good word for you, too. Now, Georgia, when I was in Goodbody's Bank a few days ago, the chief clerk mentioned that they were looking for a suitable candidate for the junior position. One lady works there at present; she was taken on during the war, when the younger men were called up. Until that time the bank was an all-male preserve.'

'It sounds very stuffy,' Georgia said frankly. 'I don't expect they'll think I'm suitable at all.'

'You'll have to convince them of that.' Miss Worley was actually smiling at the thought. 'These prejudices must be swept away. Women's wages are less than men's, are you aware of that? It is difficult for them to rise to the top in any profession, including mine. Men with inferior qualifications are preferred.'

It was a challenge. 'When do I start?' Georgia asked.

'Oh, you have to undergo a medical first, and a lengthy interview.'

'I'll get through, I'll show 'em!' Georgia declared.

'And I'll prepare you both, as much as I can,' Miss Worley told them, satisfied.

The medical over, with Georgia pronounced healthy in all respects (which Nell said she could have told the doctor anyway and saved her daughter embarrassment), Georgia was summoned to see the manager at Goodbody's Bank in Woodberry, the bustling market-town. The building was a gloomy Victorian one, looming over the market-square, with granite steps up to a massive double door. JEREMIAH GOODBODY'S BANK, the highly polished brass plate proclaimed: FOUNDED 1854.

Nell, who had accompanied Georgia, was asked to wait in the banking hall. The magazines on the small table beside her chair were mostly pre-war vintage and very dull. 'Couldn't even chew my nails,' she would say later, 'with those grim faces gazing at me from behind the counter.'

The chief clerk, a remote relative of old Jeremiah, ushered Georgia into the manager's sanctum. Georgia didn't know it then, of course, but she would not see the manager, Mr Puddefoot, again for many months, though she would often hear his sonorous voice, which made the bank employees quake, with the exception of the supercilious chief clerk.

'Ah, Miss Smith, please be seated,' Mr Puddefoot intoned, in a room hazy with cigar smoke, without looking up from a letter he was tapping with a bony finger. Finally, he cleared his throat making Georgia jump, for she was studying the dark oil painting of the bank's founder, hanging on the wall behind him. 'Ah, Miss Smith,' he said again. 'Your references are excellent. However, I note that you merely achieved a pass in maths in your school certificate and, as you are no doubt aware, this is a manual branch and accurate, painstaking bookkeeping is essential.'

Primed by Miss Worley, Georgia reassured him, 'I enjoy mental arithmetic.'

'Diligence is the quality we require in this junior position; enjoyment can be equated with frivolity, which is frowned upon. Banking is a very serious business, and I am still not convinced that women are suited to the profession. I am offering you this position, Miss Smith, on the understanding that you will keep your, ah, feminine side firmly in check. Your first month will be spent at the City Banking School to learn the history of banking and how to tackle long columns of figures. Your train fares will be refunded.' He rose. 'My chief clerk will go over the details of your contract with you.'

'Not finished yet,' Georgia mouthed at her mother, after emerging from the manager's room. 'Got to sign on!' She inclined her head slightly at the tall, black-clad figure of the remote relative, waiting for her to accompany him to the offices beyond, where clerks perched on high stools behind lofty desks, poring over hefty ledgers. Miss Wood, her immediate superior, was the only one to look up and smile.

The duties required of the junior were mundane indeed, ranging from: keeping stock of the post book, with the terrifying responsibility of balancing this to within a half-penny; collecting envelopes on a daily basis, bearing in mind the continuing serious paper shortage, to glue on economy labels for re-use; addressing all outgoing post; to answering the telephone, a daunting task as she was not familiar with its use. Consequently, she often failed to take down the correct name of the customer calling because it was hard to balance the heavy receiver and manipulate her pencil. Once a week, Georgia had to clean the inkwells, replenish them with ink and renew the pink paper on the much-used blotters. But, as Monica Wood whispered in her ear on her first morning, 'Your most important job is to make the tea!' For all this, including the extra hours when the bank door was locked on a Saturday afternoon until all the books balanced, Georgia received £3. 12s. 6d. a week, paid monthly, which was considered an excellent salary for an almost-seventeen year old.

There were few light-hearted moments but, while two of the three male clerks considered themselves vastly superior to the lowly junior, the youngest – newly demobbed from the RAF – was kind to Georgia. He was in his late twenties, lived in digs locally and was supplied with a substantial packed lunch by his motherly landlady. He passed on little treats to Georgia and Monica, when Georgia delivered him his cup of tea, like hard-boiled eggs and wedges of cake. His name was Malcolm, and the girls called him Mal. The other clerks were Mr Thomas and Mr Ledward.

One afternoon, as she was about to finish work and looking forward to meeting Kenny at the Regal, a regular weekly treat, the chief clerk requested that she dash to the post office before it closed, for stamps. 'There are some late letters for you to address and post, when you get back, Miss Smith.'

She ran all the way to the post office; ran back to the bank. Mal let her in. The rest of the staff had gone home. 'Thought you might need some help, Georgia,' he said, noting her tear-stained face, but not commenting on it. She was upset because by now Kenny would have been waiting half an hour for her to join him.

They sat side by side on the stools, and he copied out the addresses in his neat handwriting while Georgia folded the letters, stuffed them inside the envelopes and stuck on the stamps. 'Thanks, Mal!' she said gratefully.

'Care to come with me to the British Restaurant?' he asked. 'A nice sticky bun, a decent cup of coffee; that's what we both need.'

'Oh, Mal, I'm sorry, I'm meeting someone, that's why I was upset.'

'A young man?' he asked.

'Yes.' She suddenly realised that he was looking at her intently. He really likes me, she thought. Of course, he's much older than me, but he's very good-looking and he's a really nice chap, too. 'It's only Kenny,' she told him, feeling disloyal. 'He's not my boyfriend, though I know he'd like to be, but we're the same age and I've known him for ever. Anyway, my best friend is keen on him.'

'Are you trying to tell me you'd like to come out with me another time?'

'I-I suppose so!'

'Let's make a date, then. And you can let down your lovely hair, and wear something other than that black skirt and white blouse, eh?'

Whatever will Mum say? But he's not as old as all that, she thought, as she hurried to the Regal. Faithful Kenny was still there, and relieved to see her. All through the picture she kept thinking of a sandy-haired young man, who must have looked very dashing in his pilot's uniform. Imagine flying in a plane: sitting on the back of a motor bike, roaring home, was not the same thing at all

TWENTY

Nell popped next door to see if Jube needed any help, or moral support. Phoebe had arranged to leave for her wedding from the gatehouse, after her friends reminded her that she could hardly cycle to the church in her wedding finery. Kenny had the same thought for Georgia, arriving on his motor bike, minus the sidecar, just after breakfast to take her to Helga's, so that she, May and little Win could get ready together. That left Eva free to take care of the bride. Nell wouldn't say, but she felt a little left out.

Jube was endeavouring to knot his tie neatly, when Nell opened the back door with a familiarity she'd quickly adopted. They got on well; he reminded her of her dear Albie in that he was down to earth. He'll calm Phoebe down, she thought with a smile. You have to accept that the Blisses are upper crust types and *they* always get het up!

'All right, boy?' she joked, the usual greeting in these parts. 'Here, let me tie that for you! You've made a mess of it.'

'Don't usually wear one, feel as if I'm choking myself,' he groaned.

'Got to look nice for your bride.' She felt him shift slightly, as she attended to her task with her ample bosom pressed against his starched white shirt. 'Oops, sorry!' she said. 'Didn't mean to crush you!' She looked up with a comical expression, feeling unusually flustered when she saw him grinning at her.

'I never noticed before: can see where Georgia gets her hair – and her spirit!'

'Go on with you! *I'm* old and grey!' she retorted. 'There, you'll do!'

'Don't say that, about being old. I reckon we're around the same age, and I'm getting married for the first time today!'

'You've got a lot of catchin' up to do. My eldest is twenty-five. You'll have to get a move on.'

'I know that. Phoebe intends to work alongside me, but I hope she'll soon have, er, family things to attend to. We'll need a proper bathroom with that in mind.'

'Good luck!' Nell said. She couldn't help herself; she gave him a quick hug and a smacker on the lips, which he warmly returned. Phoebe's been a wonderful second mother to Georgia, she thought, but she was ten years old when Phoebe took her on. She couldn't somehow picture Phoebe with a *baby* . . . 'Now, I'll go and put on my hat, then I'll fix your buttonhole and we'll walk down to the church together, where I guess Bob Button will be waiting as your best man and looking at his watch, eh?'

The church bells were ringing as Lawrence and Phoebe emerged from the gatehouse, where the wedding car was waiting. Eva had joined the bridesmaids and Helga a while back. Five minutes to go, Phoebe thought, leaning on her brother's arm.

'Who asked for the bells? I really didn't want any fuss. And the car, Lawrence.'

'Shut up, Sis,' he said, as he had in the old days. 'Relax and enjoy it all!'

There was a crowd outside the church, a shout of: 'Here comes the bride!'

'Whatever are all these people doing here?' she whispered.

'Come to pay their respects to the old squire's granddaughter, I suppose!'

Then they were crunching up the gravel drive, the doors swung open and they stepped into the cool interior of the church, fragrant with flowers. The organ music swelled; she looked down the aisle at the two men standing there, and then Georgia passed her bouquet while May held firmly onto the flower-girl's small hand.

The pews were packed, but there was the reassurance of familiar faces. Helga, with the little Button girls; Kenny, eyeing the bridesmaids; Miss Worley, sitting with the now frail matron from Spare Penny; Eva with Nell, in the front row; and just a glimpse of Mona's swaying back, seated at the organ.

Then she was standing next to Jube, who towered over the rest of them, and he squeezed her hand and smiled happily. She was glad that her friends had persuaded her to accept some of their precious clothing coupons, that the outfit she wore was old stock and thus better quality than the utility clothes now in the shops. She'd had second thoughts when she showed the linen two-piece to Nell, when she brought it home.

'Green – I've just realised: isn't that supposed to be unlucky for a wedding?'

'Don't be daft,' Nell said firmly. 'It's just your colour, and fits you perfect.'

She didn't wear a hat on her glossy black hair, but a wreath of green leaves entwined with yellow mimosa from the conservatory at Red House, which she intended to press and keep as a memento of her old home.

The minister taking the service was the same one who had baptised her as a baby, and confirmed her at thirteen. She hadn't been to the church much since then, only at Easter and Christmas, but she and Jube had attended together to hear their banns called. She mustn't recall the past today; she was marrying a good man – one who maybe couldn't understand her complex character, but who was prepared to accept her for what she was.

'Therefore if any man can show just cause, why they may not lawfully be joined together, let him now speak, or else hereafter for ever hold his peace.' Why did these solemn words always cause those present at a wedding to hold their breath for a few seconds in an awesome silence? At that moment, although neither would ever speak of it, both Phoebe and Jube thought of Karl.

The priest continued, 'I require and charge you both, as ye will answer at the dreadful day of judgement, when the secrets of all hearts shall be disclosed . . .' They could not know that these particular words struck home to others present, too.

The marriage vows were exchanged, the ring slid smoothly onto Phoebe's finger and suddenly she was radiantly happy. '*I love you*,' she murmured for the first time, as she and Jube kissed.

She'd asked Georgia to choose her favourite hymn, and they all rose and sang together, 'All Things Bright and Beautiful'. *The rich man in his castle, / the poor man at his gate, / God made them, high or lowly, / and ordered their estate.* Those differences in class, of birth, meant nothing now, Phoebe thought. The war had blown those distinctions, restrictions away, and thank God for it.

Out in the sunlit churchyard, blinking; confetti blowing in what was undoubtedly an early autumn breeze; then a procession to the hut where the Buttons had taken care of the refreshments, as their wedding gift.

Phoebe took it all in, bemused, with Jube's arm firmly round her waist. She caught snatches of conversation: Kenny boldly asking Georgia and May if he could kiss the brides-maids; Eva looking at Lawrence, and the question, 'Will it be us next?'; Nell calling the girls to watch out for the young 'uns, dancing behind the curtains on the stage; Mona urging everyone to queue up, take a plate and as much food as they could cram on it. Then, as Jube led her towards the top table where they would be served as the privilege of the bride and groom, she saw Bob catch at Helga's arm and overheard him plead, 'Why will you never speak to *me*?'

There was dancing at this wedding, too, as there had been at the last one. Jube wasn't one for dancing, but he encouraged Phoebe to take the floor with partners young and old. Lawrence and Mona took it in turn to play the piano, and those who didn't dance, sang. It was late even-ing, and dark outside, when the party finished.

'Got to go and feed the dogs,' Jube said innocently, elicit-ing much laughter.

'Can I stay the night with May, oh please, Mum?' Georgia pleaded.

'You realise I'll be a gooseberry, walking home with the happy couple?' Nell joked. 'Oh, go on then! Bring Helga and May back for Sunday dinner with us, eh? I don't want to eat on my own.'

'Been a long day,' Jube said reflectively. They'd called good-night to Nell and locked up, after the dogs had been in the garden. Then they went straight upstairs.

'It'll take me time to get used to being this side,' Phoebe said. 'But at least I've got my own bed.' She took off her jacket and skirt, hung them up.

'Our bed, I hope.' He sounded quite shy. That bit about secrets, he thought, during the service. Would she have married me, if she'd known about me and Karl?

'We must get a generator,' she said, 'modernise this place, and next door. But now, I'm glad it's candlelight, it's much more romantic. Hurry up Jube, let's get into bed. I'm worn out, and I can see you are, too.'

'Not too tired, I hope,' he dared to say. He nipped the candle out. It was easier to ask her the next question in the dark. 'Phoebe, there's no need is there, for us, you know, to be *careful*? What I said, about us not wasting any more time, trying for a family right away – is that all right?'

He felt the warmth of her body, as she moved closer. As Lawrence said to her earlier, she repeated fondly, 'Shut up, Jube! *You're* the one wasting time, now!' It was not the moment to divulge secrets, to disappoint and hurt him.

Nell surprised herself, crying into her pillow that night. She'd hardly spent a night on her own since she married, she thought. She wondered if this was the first time those two next door had come together. If it was, she hoped all would be well. She couldn't help recalling that odd feeling when Jube had returned her kiss earlier. Don't tell me, she said to herself sternly, you're a bit sweet on the bloke!

There'll never be anyone like Albie. I always vowed he'd be the first and the last man in my life. Too late now, anyway, Jube's married the one he's waited for all these years. Get a grip on yourself, Nell Smith. You've got Georgia to yourself at last, even though she's becoming a woman so fast; there'll surely be wedding bells ringing for her soon.

'Oh do go to sleep, Win.' Eva was tired. It had been a long day. She wanted nothing more than to climb into her own bed and to cuddle up to Lawrence. He'd been rather withdrawn lately, and she suspected this had a lot to do with the statement Beryl's solicitors had sent to his. They wouldn't dispute it, they just wanted to get the divorce over and done with.

At last the little girl closed her eyes. Eva gently removed the remains of the posy she still clutched in one hand. Then she tiptoed next door.

'You awake, Lawrence?' No answer. She wrapped her arms around him anyway. He turned, and his passionate response surprised, thrilled her.

'I'm so lucky to have you, Eva – I'm sorry you've had to endure all this mess.'

'Shush. We love each other, that's all that matters.'

May sat up in bed. 'Can you hear anything, Georgia?' But Georgia was out for the count. May pushed back the bed-clothes, crept out of the room. There it was again, muffled sobbing coming from Helga's room. She opened the door cautiously. 'Helga, whatever's wrong?' She sat on the edge of the bed, felt for her hand, gripped it.

She sensed that Helga was shaking her head, couldn't tell her.

'I thought you were happy, like me, at Phoebe and Jube getting married at last.'

'I am,' Helga managed at last.

'Is it because you wanted to marry my – father – but couldn't?'

'I – *never* wanted that.'

'He's a rotter, whoever he is,' May said angrily, 'if he still makes you feel like that. I shan't ever get married. I couldn't leave you on your own.'

'You'll meet someone one day.'

'Well, I suppose I already have, but he's only got eyes for my best friend . . .'

TWENTY-ONE

There really wasn't much to smile about at Goodbody's Bank, but Georgia managed to relate incidents to Nell and May, not funny at the time, which made them laugh.

The chief clerk, always referred to as the remote relative, actually had a wife. 'She's dressed in black, too, and she's tall and thin like he is, and they live in the flat above the bank – he got that privilege, not the manager, because of the family connections. I've come to the conclusion that they look as if they are permanently in mourning, because of their hobby.'

'And what exactly is that?' Nell asked, intrigued.

'Well, quite regularly, he pokes his head round the office door and says, "We are going to a funeral." Walking behind him is his wife, carrying a sheaf of lilies – it makes you *shiver*! She doesn't acknowledge our existence; she has her nose in the air as if there's a nasty smell. Then they disappear for a couple of hours. It's really weird! I must admit I'd like to see him caught by the manager one day.'

'What, for *not* going where he says he is?'

'Well, I have to admit he probably is, what with the lilies and all, eh? No, I'm thinking of his *most* disgusting habit.'

Nell looked apprehensive. 'What's that?'

'He's always sticking one of those menthol inhalers up his nose and sniffing loudly, especially when he's going to make a telephone call. Sometimes he forgets he's left it dangling from his nostril, and he talks away, while we are expected to keep quiet, but are about to *explode*, as it waggles!'

'Ugh!' Nell exclaimed.

Georgia confided in May alone regarding another matter. 'If I tell Mum, she'll be down there to see the manager, and I'll get the sack.'

'You'd like that, wouldn't you?' May sounded wistful. Goodbody's sounded superior to the post office, where she was on her feet all day, date-stamp in hand.

'Well, no, I wouldn't. Mal makes up for a lot . . . Anyway, as I was saying, only the two cashiers have keys to the strongroom, so only they can open the security iron railings in an emergency. Sandwiched between that and the book room, where the handwritten ledgers are kept – they have to be brought out every morning, and taken back there each night – is the *communal* lavvy. The inside wall dividing it from the book room is made from thick, smoked glass: *bullet proof* Monica says, but this isn't the

Wild West, eh? You can just see shapes moving around on the other side and hear voices, so it's obvious they know we're in *there*. It's horribly off-putting, especially for us girls. No one's bothered to change things; it's just as it was when it was all men on the staff. But you have to laugh!'

'*I* couldn't,' May said earnestly.

Mal did indeed make up for a lot. Georgia didn't tell her mum about *him*, either. He was twelve years older than she was, he'd been to war – gone straight there from his public school in Somerset. Mal was in line for the under-cashier's job when he retired in a few years' time. Maybe he'd even be manager one day, but not in this rural bank; he had ambitions, hoped to progress to one of the big, city banks.

Monica, who'd been friendly to Georgia in the beginning, became off-hand with her. Georgia was mystified by the sudden coolness between them, until one afternoon she caught Monica's jealous glance when Mal bent over her desk and whispered, 'Care to accompany me to the town hall tomorrow evening? Local operatic society, Gilbert and Sullivan, *Mikado*, should be good. You play an instrument, I hear?'

'Yes,' she managed, wondering if a piano-accordion counted.

'Good. Starts at seven. Not worth you going home after work. Come and eat at my landlady's. You can get changed there. I'll escort you home, of course.'

'Mr Barton, a word, if you please.' The chief clerk's voice made them jump.

'Mal's in trouble, I reckon,' Monica said, 'and it's all your fault, Georgia.'

Regal night, Georgia suddenly remembered. She'd have to put Kenny off, and would Mum actually allow her to go out with Mal?

She didn't mean to lie; it was more a case of her mother assuming that Monica would be going with them to the concert.

'Nice of this Mr Barton to offer to see you home, but –'

'He's got a little car, Mum. I said about all the ruts up the lane, but he said his bone-shaker was up to it, if I was.'

'Couldn't you make a foursome, ask Kenny to join you?'

'I stopped off at the shop to let him know I can't go to the Regal tomorrow, and he was a bit huffy and said he'd ask May to go with him, instead.'

Nell looked at her daughter keenly. 'Didn't that rile you, Georgia?'

'Why should it? He was May's friend before he was mine.'

'Well, you can't blame dear May if she seizes the opportunity.'

'What d'you mean?' Georgia demanded.

'She thinks a lot of Kenny, but to him she's just a good, loyal pal. He hasn't eyes for anyone but you, and you –'

'I'm not ready to be serious with any boy yet! He shouldn't assume that we'll end up together. I can't see that happening, can you?'

'It's your life,' Nell said, dodging an answer. 'Now, what do you plan to wear?'

As Georgia and Mal came down the steps of the bank, she saw Kenny parking his motor bike in the square. It was a typical late afternoon in November, cold and damp, but fortunately not foggy. A few leaves from the solitary tree in the centre of the empty market-place were blown around their ankles.

Kenny glanced up as he helped May out from the side-car. Georgia thought, oh, he doesn't expect her to ride pillion, but I reckon he likes *me* to perch on the back, because I have to hold on tight round his waist!

'Hello, you two,' she called. Kenny gave a sketchy wave, before they went off.

'So that's your boyfriend, is it?' Mal sounded amused. 'He didn't look too pleased to see us.'

"That's Kenny, yes. And the girl with him is a *friend*, too,' she emphasised the word 'friend'. She couldn't help feeling disloyal. Why didn't she call her May?

'This way,' he said. 'It's not far. Take my arm. It's slippery underfoot.'

She was glad to have his support, because she wore court shoes given to her by Phoebe, who had smarter things than Mum, and she was not used to heels.

Mal's landlady was younger than Georgia expected, probably about Phoebe's age. Mal might have implied she was motherly, but voluptuous was more the word, in a low-necked dress stretched to the limits. The searching look she gave Georgia was unsettling. However, she seemed pleasant enough. 'Let me take your coat, dear. I should say I do not permit visitors to the paying-guests' rooms. After supper, you may get changed in my room, off the hall, here.'

Rissoles, cabbage and potatoes, with a tasty thick gravy: the food here was good. The gooseberries in the tart were sharp, but the crust was fine and flaky.

'Coffee?' Mrs Grant offered. There were six of them at the table, for there were three other, silent, male lodgers. 'Camp, I'm afraid, Georgia, but real cream. Lionel here kindly brings me a jar now and again, because he says I'm so good to him. He works in the dairy.' Lionel looked down at his plate, embarrassed.

Later, she escorted Georgia to her bedroom. 'A word of advice, dear; how old are you, by the way?'

'Seventeen,' Georgia said. Well, she would be that in a week's time. She stood there, bag in hand, for she didn't want to take off her top clothes in front of Mrs Grant.

'Don't mind me, dear,' Mrs Grant said, amused, reading her thoughts.

Georgia had no alternative. She whipped off her office clothes. Her hair shone, sparked with electricity as her head emerged from the neck of Phoebe's best cream, silk blouse. Mum had given her locks the hot almond-oil treatment to quell the frizz, before the henna shampoo.

'Don't you use a spot of Mum, dear?' Mrs Grant reproved her. 'You don't want to rot that pretty garment under the arms. Here, take your arms out of the sleeves, then you can apply under cover, as it were.' She handed her the deodorant. 'Got a lipstick in your bag – oh good. Hope it goes with your hair, dear. Now, what was I going to say? Oh yes, you should bear in mind that Malcolm is *experienced*.'

'At what?' Georgia asked bluntly. That was Nell coming out in her.

'Matters of the heart, dear. *Flirting*. Why, he's even made advances to me.'

'I don't believe that.' Georgia knew exactly what Mrs Grant was up to, now.

The smile vanished from the landlady's face. 'Don't let him take liberties!'

'I'm sure he won't, and even if he did, my mum told me what to do.'

'No need for vulgarity. You'd better go. But don't forget what I said.'

As they went out of the front door, Mrs Grant called after Mal, 'I'll be waiting up for you as usual.'

'Aren't you enjoying yourself?' Mal asked in the interval, as they drank their tea, the only refreshment provided.

'Oh, Mal, of course I am. A real orchestra, those dazzling costumes and the lovely backdrops, and the *singing*! They sound professional.'

'A couple of the older members of the cast once were. It's the first concert the society have put on since 1939. More women members than men. I'd join, but my voice is not good enough. I meant, you've been very quiet ever since we left my digs.'

'Have I? I was just absorbing the atmosphere, as I said.'

'I wondered if you were intimidated by the fact that the chief clerk and his wife are in the front row, but I don't think they've spotted us.'

'Stop worrying Mal, I'm having a lovely time.'

'Good,' he said. 'Because I'd like to take you out again . . .'

They had to walk back to Mrs Grant's house to collect the Morris Eight, parked in the drive. There was still a light in the front room, and Georgia hoped Mal wouldn't suggest going in there again. There was no need. Her carrier bag was in the car.

'Better get straight off,' Mal said, to her relief. 'If you're to be home by eleven.'

It was dark up the lane: the lights were out in the gate-house, and Red House was still not occupied by the new owners. It was a bumpy ride and Mal drove cautiously. Finally, they saw the upstairs windows illuminated in both cottages, no black-out nowadays, and a light left on downstairs their side, as Nell had promised.

Mal turned the car just before they reached the cottages. 'There, facing the right way! Well, Georgia I've appreciated your company very much tonight.'

She guessed what was coming. 'Are you?' she asked ingenuously.

'Am I what?' He pulled her to him, undid the top buttons on her coat.

'Experienced? Mrs Grant said ...' His arms encircled her, under the coat.

'Never mind what *she* said,' he murmured. 'It's only natural I want to kiss you.'

It was the most natural thing in the world. His hands on her back, but not straying; the firm pressure of his mouth on hers; the whispering when they came up for air at last. 'I wouldn't take advantage of you, Georgia, I promise.'

'I must go,' she said. 'Mum must know we're here.'

He deftly fastened her coat. 'Let me take you to your door.'

'No,' she said. She wanted to compose herself before she saw her mother.

'See you tomorrow.' He wound up the car window. Drove off.

Nell was in the kitchen, making cocoa. 'Had a good time?' she asked, deliberately casual. 'I put a hot-water bottle in your bed.'

'Thanks, Mum. Oh, I *did*! I'll tell you all about the concert at breakfast.' She didn't need the hot-water bottle, she thought happily, she was all aglow, surely Mum could see that!

May invited Kenny in for a few minutes; Helga had gone to bed, but she wouldn't mind, she thought. She put the kettle on. 'Good picture, wasn't it?' she asked.

She had her back to Kenny. He turned her round, took the spent match from her hand. 'Yes it was. Look, May, I'm sorry –'

'You don't want to go out with me any more? Honestly, Kenny I don't mind.'

'Of course you do! So do I. It wasn't nice of me to let you down.'

'What d'you mean?'

'I mean, me being all for Georgia, practically ignoring you these days. I've been a silly fool, wasting my time. I'd forgotten how well you and I get on. May, d'you want to come out with me again? How about the Regal next week?'

'Won't Georgia expect –'

'She'll be glad to have an excuse, I reckon, to go out with *him*, all dressed up. Why can't *you* have some nice clothes? I know the answer to that, you give Helga all your wages.' He suddenly hugged her to him. 'There's nothing of you, May! You need me to take care of you, like you do Helga. We can help one another to achieve what we really want to in life. I've got national service to do next year, after that, I want to go back to full-time education. You deserve that, too. I know you wanted to teach.' He parted her fringe, looked searchingly into her eyes.

She faltered, 'I'd . . . like that, Kenny. I really would.' It was the promise of a new relationship, their first real kiss, uncertain at first, then with a definite frisson of excitement. She tried not to think of the real reason he'd turned to her: she'd noted his hurt expression earlier, when he saw Georgia on the arm of that smart chap in the grey suit and trilby hat.

Did Helga suspect what was happening now? Would she fret about it?

'Would you like a party this year?' Nell asked, as Georgia's birthday approached.

'Mum, would you mind? Mal would like to take me to a dinner-dance on the Saturday, but we could have a special birthday tea on the Sunday.'

'Will you invite him to that? I'd like to meet him.'

'I'm not sure I'm ready for that, yet. Oh Mum, that sounds mean!'

'Dearie, I know you better than anyone. Better than this Mal does! I don't want you to get hurt, go too far, too soon,' she paused.

'Mum, haven't you drummed all that into me? Mal's just a good friend. He respects me, honest.'

'Well, always remember you can talk to me, about anything, any time.'

'I will,' Georgia assured her mother.

'Oh, I've got some good news: Aubrey's coming home on leave shortly. He won't be demobbed just yet, but at least he'll be in this country. He's going to see Martin and Lizzie first.'

'I thought you were going to say that they're having a baby.'

'Not as far as I know. I do hope Aubrey will meet some nice girl and that he'll be lucky the second time around, don't you?'

'Would you ever get married again, Mum?'

'Right now, I think "no", but then, things change unexpectedly; look at us settling here – if you'd asked me before the war, I'd have said I could never live in the country. Too quiet, not enough going on. But there's a lot bubbling 'neath the surface, folks with secrets, just like in London, ain't there?'

'You can't be lonely, you've got me!'

'You'll be spreading your wings any moment now, dearie. I accept that.'

'Enjoyed yourself last night?' Monica asked Georgia on Saturday morning.

Georgia yawned. 'Well, I'm glad we're only working a half-day. Yes, I did.'

'He took me to a dance before you came here. I wore a long dress. I met his landlady.'

'So did I.'

'She tried to warn me off.'

'Me, too.'

Monica leaned over the desk. 'She was right. I expect you found that out, too.'

'I don't know what you mean!'

'Oh, yes, you do. He tried to take liberties.'

'Well, he didn't with me, I assure you. Now, if you don't mind, Monica, I've got the post to sort.'

Monica had the last word. 'Don't you wonder why he stays in that boarding-house? He could afford a flat.'

Georgia refused to answer. But it made her think.

'Had a busy morning at the post office?' Helga asked May.

'Mmm. Why do people always rush in five minutes before we close?' She didn't wait for an answer. 'I'll get you some more coal in, shall I? It's much colder today.'

'May, just a minute ... Was that Kenny I heard you talking to, last night?'

'Who else would it be? He's the only boy I know.'

'I thought he was walking-out with Georgia ...'

'That sounds so old-fashioned! You know we've always been good pals. He's more like a brother to me –'

'Can't – can't you leave it like that?'

'I imagine we will. We've both got high ideas, I suppose you could say, and we'll encourage each other to achieve those. Don't worry, Helga. I said I won't ever leave you, and I won't.'

TWENTY-TWO

Phoebe and Jube were gathering dead wood in the plantation beyond the meadow. It was just on freezing, that day in December. Jube had allowed his beard to grow again, and they wore layers of clothes, with woolly hats and fingerless gloves.

She made to swing a full sack of wood over her shoulder. 'That's enough, eh?'

'Leave it for me, Phoebe. Don't want you putting your back out,' he said.

'I'm not *pregnant*, Jube, you'd be the first to know if I was. If it happens, well, it does, but it doesn't look likely. I'm thirty-eight; that's getting on, for a first baby. Oh, I suppose I might as well tell you – Eva confided in me, a few days ago – she's expecting a baby next summer. Of course, she's younger than me.'

'Does Lawrence know?' He fastened the sacks together with stout twine, slung that round his shoulders. Even loading, that was the trick.

'I'm not sure. If not, she'll have to tell him soon. He insisted they should wait until they were married; she thought he might be upset.'

'What's the matter with the fellow?' he demanded.

'He's got a lot on his mind, with the divorce and the new owners of Red House wanting to buy the gatehouse, too. They've made him an offer, which he's refused.'

'He, Eva and Win like it there, I suppose. It's home, like the cottage is for us.'

They trudged back. No dogs today, they were too comfortable by the stove.

'I'm going to get you a tractor in the spring,' she told him. 'And a van to take produce to market, or to deliver locally.'

'Bob Button won't like that! Anyway, you sure we can afford it?'

'I'm talking about second-hand vehicles, Jube. The horseless kind!'

'Another thing, I can't drive.'

'I can. I learned when I was overseas. I'll teach you. And before you say it again, even if I do fall for a baby, it won't stop me from getting behind the wheel.'

He put the sacks down. 'Come here. Did I tell you lately, I love you?'

'Actions speak louder than words,' she teased, but she held him tight.

'Fancy fish and chips tonight?' Phoebe asked Nell, when she returned from the shop.

'Do I! Can't face cooking; we've had a busy day. Things are picking up. Where's the nearest chip shop, though? I'm not capable of remounting my bike.'

'Jube's offered to go. "Tabby's a'fryin'", they say. Decided to go back in business, now the war's well and truly over. I can almost taste that crispy batter, those chips . . .'

They provided Jube with an oil-cloth bag and several sheets of newspaper. He cycled off down the lane, whistling, for he guessed he'd meet Georgia on the way.

'Where are you off to?' she asked, as they swerved round each other.

'Getting your supper, young lady; you and Nell're eating with us. It's a surprise!'

Tabby lived in the end one of the Brook cottages. A queue had already formed outside, the tail a good way up the street. Hands in pockets, feet stamping in boots, breath wreathing like smoke, torches flashing at each new arrival. 'Evening, Jube!'

An old chap paused by Jube, stuffing his newspaper bundle up his jersey. 'That warm my cockles, boy, do it be a long way home.'

'How're them hosses, Toby?' These were a pair of Suffolk Punches, beautiful horses whose days were numbered; modern farms wanted jobs done yesterday.

'Getting on, like me, boy ... You catch the fish for tonight, did you?'

'Never got another boat; I give up that lark, when I got wed.'

'Done well in that direction, boy, I hear – Miss Bliss, no less!'

So *that's* what they think about my good luck, Jube mused ruefully.

Tabby, in her seventies – so her mother, still spry, must be over ninety, Jube conjectured – was a stout, cheerful woman, scarlet-cheeked from bending over the sizzling great cauldron of chips, turning them in the bubbling, boiling beef-dripping, collected over the last months. Mrs Tabby, senior, chopped peeled potatoes with a will, lifting them from the bowl of cold, salted water, then swaddling the chips in a cloth to remove excess moisture. Their neighbour, called in to help, handled slippery fish on a slab of marble, filleted them swiftly, tossed the discarded bits to the waiting she-cats, heavy in kit, who crouched at their feet. Then Tabby dipped the fish in the bowl of thick batter, shook off the excess and fried them in a huge, cast-iron pan.

All this achieved in the cottage outhouse, with a stove fired by wood, water still pumped by the bucket, and no electricity. The flaring gas-lamps were a luxury to Tabby. The smell of the frying fish and chips brought folk hurrying from all over the village.

They ate their feast straight from the paper, sitting round the kitchen table. 'No knives and forks needed,' Nell declared, 'just rinse your own cup out, that's the ticket!'

Georgia sprinkled on more salt and vinegar and licked her fingers. 'I like the scrunchy bits as much as anything.' She took a long draught of her tea.

'Friday night used to be your evening out,' Jube observed slyly.

'Oh well, May and Kenny go to the pictures together now. I decided I'd rather be on good terms with the other girl at work, than fight over one of the men clerks!'

'He was too old for you,' Nell said, 'in my opinion.'

'Who asked for that, Mum? Anyway, I prefer fish and chips to romance!'

'You'll find the right one eventually.' Phoebe looked fondly at Jube.

'But don't take as long as she did over it, eh?' Jube advised.

'Oh, I *am* enjoying this, us like family all together! Just wish Dad was here.'

It gave Georgia an idea. After the paper was screwed up, fed to the fire, and the table wiped over, she fetched the accordion from next door and played it for them.

'Not bad,' Nell said huskily, 'not bad at all. Your dad would be proud of you . . .'

'Fish and chips?' Eva exclaimed. 'The very thought makes me feel sick!'

'It was only a suggestion. Tabby's frying tonight. You know, you've been off your food lately,' Lawrence said mildly. 'Maybe you ought to see the doctor.'

'Don't tell me what to do! Win, eat up that poached egg, then get ready for bed.'

'Can't cut the toast,' Win said mutinously. 'I want *chips*!'

'Do as I say!' Eva told her, then saw the tears in her daughter's eyes.

'Let me help you,' Lawrence said, flashing Eva a reproachful look. He cut the toast into little squares. 'Eat up, Win, there's a good girl. You can do your piano practice tomorrow morning.' He dried her face gently with his clean handkerchief.

He washed up while Eva saw to Win. No story tonight, he noticed. He made coffee, took it into the sitting-room. Eva had her head turned away from him.

'Now *you* are crying. Come on, tell me what's wrong.'

'I'm having a *baby*, Lawrence, and that's not in our schedule, is it?'

'Whatever are you talking about?' He set the tray on the table.

'We had it all planned: the decree nisi, me taking over next year as headmistress, we'd get quietly married, I'd really be Mrs Bliss. *Then*, we'd have a baby.'

'We'll manage somehow,' he said helplessly.

'Can't you say you're thrilled at the news?'

'Of course I am! I'm – just taking it all in, Eva. You must go ahead with your career, you've worked hard for that through adversity, and you deserve it. I could look after the baby myself.' He tried not to sound doubtful.

She was smiling now. 'I don't think it'll come to that, Lawrence!'

'Why not? I think of Win as my own daughter, don't I?'

'There's always dear Helga; she cared for Win so well. It was even better when she was able to look after her in her own home, especially when we moved in with you. *You* didn't have to deal with all those nappies!' she reminded him.

'I'll never be the perfect husband, or father,' he said ruefully.

She held out her arms. 'That's where you're wrong, darling, you *almost* are!'

'I just wish, you know, that Helga had the chance to fulfil her potential like you. She might have changed her whole life through her aptitude for music.'

Eva felt a moment's disquiet. 'She couldn't have wanted that enough.'

'I think she just accepted her lot, but retreated from life for a while.'

'Stop philosophising! Let's talk about *us*, Lawrence – *our* future. We can probably still get married before the baby comes. Win will be thrilled, I know.'

Phoebe stared incredulously at the letter, addressed to Miss P. Bliss at next door. The postman knew of the change, of course. She placed it unopened on the table. She'd wait for Jube to come in for his elevenses. She ought to be euphoric, for she had long feared the writer to be dead. Would there be news of the other one, inside?

'What's up?' Jube wrestled with his muddy boots on the door mat.

'It's that obvious, is it? A letter, Jube, from my cousin Nils in Norway.'

He sat down heavily at the table, lifted the steaming mug in both hands. 'Open it, read it then. He's alive, that's obvious, after all your worrying, Phoebe.'

'You want to hear it?' She began to open the envelope carefully.

'Only if you want me to. Read it to yourself, first.' He slurped his tea.

That set her teeth on edge. She wouldn't tell him, as she would have, once. After scrutinizing the two flimsy sheets of paper, she read aloud:

Dear Phoebe,
    It will be a shock to you, I think, to hear from me after so long. In 1940 I was with the Norwegian Army. We were in retreat, heading towards Narvik, desperate to join the allies, that is all I remember before

I was found, severely injured, left to die, in a mountain hut, they told me much later. They, the enemy, saved my life, transported me to a hospital. They thought that I was a German soldier, because I was dressed in one of their uniforms. I was unconscious for many weeks. Because of the trauma to my head, I had to learn to speak, walk again, like a baby, even to feed myself. My memory is still fragmented. The doctors were good to me, even when they suspected I was not who my papers said I was – a Lieutenant Karl Schmidt. There, that name will shock you as it did me, I know that. Yet, it must be a common name. Why should it be *him*?

Many of my compatriots made their way to Britain, later, some escaped via Sweden. If I could, I would, but it was too hard for me. When I recovered enough, I was allowed to work in the area as an interpreter and there I stayed until the liberation. My status is now cleared. I am allowed back in Oslo. See my new address. My old home is gone.

Dear Phoebe, I hope that you were not too touched by the war, and are well? I hope to hear from you soon. I would like to come to visit you, but my health, you see is still uncertain, like my past and now, my future.

With affectionate regard, Nils (Norland)

Phoebe looked up from the letter to Jube. His expression was hard to read.

'Now, at least you know,' he said finally.

'Know that Nils is alive, yes, but that's not all, is it? I have to accept that Karl did try to kill him, I believe he thought he *had*. To leave him like that, to adopt his identity, to lie to me as he did, I will *never* forgive him for that!'

'It seems he is past forgiveness.' Please God, he thought, that *I* am not . . .

'I hope he is dead!' she cried out.

'I'm sure he is,' Jube said quietly. It really was too late now to confess what he knew. 'You should tell Lawrence about the letter, I think,' he added.

Aubrey was coming home for Christmas. Nell and Georgia were so excited at the prospect, but a little apprehensive too. Five years was a long time. So much had happened since they last saw him.

Kenny gave Nell a lift to the station. 'He'll have a lot to carry,' she said gratefully. The young soldier was indeed loaded with bags, but he had a big beam on his face.

'Mum! You look just the same!'

'Not exactly I don't, and nor do you, but I'd know you anywhere!'

Georgia was waiting impatiently at the cottage gate and for a moment Aubrey looked at her uncertainly, because she was as tall as their mum. 'Cor, you're much better looking!' he said frankly, before he gave her a great hug. 'How old are you now?'

'Seventeen,' she said proudly.

'Well, I never! Where's the old dog?'

'Lives next door,' Nell told him. 'Doesn't bark much. He must be thirteen.'

'Well, ain't you going to invite me inside the family pile?'

'Approve do you?' Nell could see that he did.

'Just wish,' he began, 'dear old Dad was here.' He didn't mention Eunice.

'So do we,' Nell agreed. 'Have a nice time with Martin and Lizzie?'

'Certainly did! She's a smashing girl. Wouldn't mind one like her myself.'

Was that bravado, Nell wondered? 'I hope you'll be lucky like that, one day.'

'I want to get back to where I come from, Mum. I couldn't live anywhere but London. I don't want to follow Dad on the river; I want to get some proper qualifications. They say they'll help us service types do that, and then I'll get a good job, find a good girl to marry and maybe provide you with a few grandchildren, eh?'

'I'd love that,' Nell said. 'But let's have a wonderful Christmas first.'

'Just you wait till you see what I got for you gals – and here's Kenny with my bags. Thanks!' He winked at Georgia. 'See the young man off the premises, eh?'

'Mum might have invited you in for a bit, after all you've done,' Georgia said, walking with Kenny to the motorcycle combination, parked outside in the lane.

'I didn't expect it. You enjoying working life, Georgia?' He swung into the saddle.

'Not really,' she said frankly. 'Like you and May, I'm often frustrated.'

'You can take that two ways,' he grinned. He'd filled out, was broad like his dad. He was a handsome young man, what Mum called a 'catch', she realised.

'You know what I mean! Kenny, I don't see much of either of you nowadays.'

'Well, you did give us both the brush-off, when you made new friends.'

'They're just people I work with; we've nothing much in common.' This was true, particularly of Mal. His landlady was welcome to him, as Monica said.

'You know where we are . . . Cheerio!' He revved up the bike, was gone.

She thought, I never realised he'd grown up too. It just took him longer than me. May's a lucky girl. *I've* lost my chance with him, and it hurts.

Nell and Aubrey sat up for a while after Georgia had gone to bed. Nell guessed he wanted to say something to her alone. 'Well, boy? You've gone very thoughtful.'

'We haven't talked about Eunice, Mum. I haven't forgotten her, you know.'

'Of course you haven't.' She looked at him thoughtfully, waiting for more.

'I guessed the things you didn't – couldn't say at the time. How can it be a proper marriage when you're far apart? I realise it wasn't easy for you –'

'I tried, for your sake, Aubrey.'

'She had a will of her own. But she helped me, during that short time, to pull myself together, after Dunkirk. She made a man of me.'

'Mrs P – remember her? – once said about Eunice, "you're only young once". Maybe she had a feeling she hadn't got long to enjoy life.'

'That's how I see it, too. I felt like that myself, Mum, often, and –'

'You don't have to tell me; I understand. I'm so lucky to have you back.'

'You're quite a girl, Mum, and Georgia's just like you,' he said fondly.

TWENTY-THREE

'Mum, guess what?' Georgia said disconsolately, on an April evening in 1946. 'The supercilious old remote relative pinned up the holiday list on the noticeboard today. I've been allocated the dates the men don't want, the last week in May and the first in June. Monica's got the other end – first two weeks of September. It's not fair!'

'*Holiday*'s the important word,' Nell observed, stabbing the sausages in the frying pan. 'The butcher said these were all pork – fat, more like, the way they spit. I was talking to Mona in the shop, about having a break, and she said she'd never had a holiday away from home since she and Bob got married. I told her about our trips to Brighton, and got all nostalgic, then I said why didn't we get away for a week.'

'You and her, you mean?'

'Me and you, and her and the little girls. We could ask May to come, too.'

'Well, if you hadn't added that, I might have turned you down. I don't fancy being nursemaid for a week. What about Kenny?' she asked, rather too casually.

'I'm afraid he'll be needed in the shop with Bob. He's off to do his national service in the autumn. Mona said this could be her last chance to get away.'

'Where are you thinking of going?' Georgia had definitely cheered up.

'Mona looked in the local paper, spotted an ad for Bungalow Town near Clacton. Essex, that is. I know we've got lovely country round us here, and the sea's not far away, but that sounds a bit more like Brighton, or Southend, plenty of amusements and jellied eels and that! Everything's starting up again now, after being closed for the duration: the bungalows are cheap and cheerful; there's even one of them new holiday camps in Clacton itself, but I don't want to be regimented, do you?'

'No. A bungalow sounds all right. How many could we fit in? We could ask Helga as well, and what about Phoebe?'

'Helga and Phoebe will want to be around for Eva's baby, that's due around then. Anyway, the bungalows sleep six maximum. You ask May if she can take her break then from the post office, and I'll write and book us up. It'll be cheap rates then!'

'May and me can pay our whack, that'll help, won't it? Now I've got something to look forward to, on days when I feel like scribbling all over those darn ledgers!'

They travelled to Clacton by train, and Georgia was reminded of her younger self as she jumped up to haul

Nettie or Dinah, rising six and seven years old, from leaning perilously out of the window. She'd said she wouldn't
play nursemaid, but Mona allowed those two tykes to do
what they liked, she thought, with a wry grin. Still, they'd
voted Mum leader of the expedition! Someone had to take
charge.

They stood on the busy station platform, heavy cases at
their feet, for they were lugging along bed linen, towels and
tea towels, too. It was hot and humid for the time of year.

'The details said you can walk a couple of miles along
the lovely sands to Bungalow Town, but we're not doing
that this afternoon in this bleedin' heat! *Taxi!*' Nell yelled
at the waiting line of shabby black vehicles.

Bungalow Town lived up to its nickname. A great
sprawling development begun in the twenties with a modest row of beach huts; followed by now ramshackle holiday
homes built without planning permission; and, later, row
upon row of wooden or pebble-dashed bungalows, built
on spec by get-rich-quick builders, along often unmade
up roads, which were more sandy tracks. Assuming that
holiday-makers would be interested only in spending all
day on the beach or trekking to town, mod cons were not
high on the list of priorities.

Ocean View – a misnomer because it was among a strag-
gle of shacks right at the end of Bungalow Town, meaning
that there was a long walk even to smell the sea – backed
onto a forlorn stretch of scrubby grass.

'Oh look, we can play cricket there after tea, and it's somewhere for the girls to let off steam,' Nell said, seeing the long faces at first sight of their holiday home. She flourished the key, as the taxi departed in a cloud of dust.

Inside, the floorboards were ill-fitting, with gaps; there were two bedrooms, and a creaking settee in the living-room to double up as a bed for Georgia and May. The kitchen had a stove (on which sat a tin kettle without a whistle-cap on the spout), a pull-down ironing board, a sink (no hot tap), a cupboard with two saucepans and a frying pan, assorted, chipped crocks, a cardboard box of rock-like soda, an empty drum of salt, a bucket with a mop and a dustpan and brush.

A table and mismatch of chairs were in the living-room. The table drawer contained six knives, forks and spoons, a bread knife, a carving knife and fork, four cork table mats and, pounced upon by the little girls, a greasy pack of playing cards. Another prized find was the linings of the chests in the bedrooms – old comic papers.

It would take too long to go back to the Bungalow Town shop, 'sells everything', for milk for that longed-for cup of tea; so they drank it black with plenty of sugar, and were grateful to Mona for the carrier bag of basic provisions for their first day.

'Won't need my special bath cubes,' Georgia sighed. She and Nell were used to a bathroom now, as this facility had been installed in both cottages, replacing the scullery and privy. Here, it was a return to chamber-pots under the beds.

'But you can open these French doors, see, and sit out on the veranda at the back,' May discovered. 'Even if there are only three deckchairs.'

Georgia promptly bagged one, and there was an ominous tearing sound. 'We'll have to bring the chairs from inside, out!' Then she screamed. Nell came running.

'Whatever is it?'

'I saw a lizard! It darted indoors.'

'Gone under the floorboards I 'spect. Help me make the beds, you two.'

Kenny came down for the day on Sunday, arriving on his motor bike around seven, hoping for breakfast. Mona answered his knock, still in her pyjamas.

'Lucky we brought bacon and eggs with us,' Mona said, cracking two in the pan.

'Wake up!' Kenny said, prodding the two recumbent forms on the settee.

'Cor, what a night,' Georgia groaned. 'Broken springs whichever way you turn, and *itching* . . .' She sat up, scratching her bare arms. 'I'm all flea-bitten!'

'You should wear something decent then,' Nell reproved her. 'Especially since we've got an unexpected visitor. Turn the other way, Kenny, while she gets dressed.'

'What about washing?' Georgia asked, whipping off her nightdress and reaching for her clothes. She nudged May to hook up what her mother called her 'brazeer'.

'We're on holiday, gal. Lick and a promise'll do.'

Kenny hummed a snatch of a familiar song. 'It's only a shanty in old shanty town.'

'Shanty's right,' Georgia said with feeling. 'You can look round now, Kenny.'

'No, he can't!' May squealed. 'Let me out of the room first! Then he can help you collapse the bed.'

'Not quite the way I'd have put it,' Mona said. 'Here, Son, breakfast for one.'

Later, Georgia, May and Kenny, with the two little girls in tow, trekked to the Bungalow Town stores for a Sunday paper and bottles of milk. The 'stores' was a flimsy affair with a tin roof; a colourful place with its piled buckets, wooden spades, beach balls, shrimping nets and other seaside paraphernalia, though these were not allowed to be sold on the Sabbath. Next door, closed for the day, were the penny-in-the-slot amusements, and a jukebox – something the young people had not seen before. *All the latest records!* a notice proclaimed.

'Sixpence a go,' May reminded Georgia, noting her excited expression. 'You can get two Sno-fruits for that.'

'I'd rather listen to music than lick ice-cream!'

They spent the morning on the beach, amusing the children. Nell and Mona joined them later with a picnic lunch, wrapped in greasy paper. The gulls swooped to snatch crumbs and crusts, and the fish-paste sandwiches were soon gritty with sand.

'Now, off you go, enjoy yourselves, you three, you've done your bit,' Nell said.

'Be back by six for supper,' Mona added. 'Kenny'll have to leave at seven.'

They took more than an hour to walk the sandy trail to town: diverted by the donkeys, with Georgia sighing, 'If only I wasn't too big to have a ride!' and splashing about in the shallows to cool their feet. Georgia was glad she was wearing shorts; May's skirts were soon damp and clinging. They had both caught the sun, being fair.

They enjoyed window-shopping, but the big attraction was still some distance away: the new holiday-camp. They had heard music and announcements over loud-speakers while they were on the beach.

They followed the notices stuck on lamp-posts: VISITORS WELCOME TO THE HOLIDAY CAMP FUN FAIR! HALF-PRICE RIDES FOR THE UNDER-FOURTEENS.

'D'you think I could pass for that?' Georgia asked Kenny.

'Brainpower or body?' he teased.

'It's all right for you,' May said. 'I can't slide down the helter-skelter in a skirt.'

High above the stalls, merry-go-rounds, ghost train, bumper cars and boat-swings, was the big wheel, which even looked down on the perilous big dipper. It was still early afternoon and the wheel was motionless. The attendant stood beside it, calling out hopefully to those passing by. 'Thrill a minute! See for miles around!'

'My treat,' Kenny said gallantly.

'I haven't got a head for heights,' May told him. 'You two go. I'll watch.'

Kenny and Georgia climbed into the seat at ground level; a bar held them secure.

'I'm not sure ...' Georgia began doubtfully, even as the wheel gathered momentum and they were swung to the very top. There they stayed, while they waited for the other seats to be filled and the ride proper to begin.

Georgia was trembling, she couldn't help it. 'Oh, Kenny, can't you ask the man to take us down again, I want to get off!' She closed her eyes in real fear.

A comforting arm went round her back, held her tight. 'You'll be all right with me, Georgia. See, May's waving at us.'

She opened her eyes, looked down at the tiny figure below, then buried her face against his shoulder. 'I feel sick.'

'No you don't,' he said. 'This gives me the chance to tell you how I feel about you. You're beautiful, Georgia Smith, and –'

'I'm not! I was a very unprepossessing child, Kenny, you know that.'

'You've grown up. I love you, I suppose I always have.'

'No, you don't! You and May –'

'*You and me.* You can't deny it, can you?'

'We can't hurt her. I shall never forgive you, if you say anything to her, Kenny.'

There was a sudden jerk, music began, they were on the move again.

She looked up at Kenny, blinking away tears. His gaze was tender.

'I'll be going into the army soon. You'll have time to think things over, then.'

Her confidence returned; with Kenny holding on to her, how could she fall?

May greeted them with three, dripping ice-cream cones. 'Here, eat them quick.'

Georgia held back when the others went out to wave Kenny goodbye. He saluted. It was hard to read his expression in goggles and with a scarf round his mouth.

Nell looked at her daughter keenly. 'Shame he can't stay, eh?'

'Well, he's got to go and that's that,' Georgia said flatly.

'Cheer up, for May's sake, dearie.' Nell advised.

'I will, Mum, I promise.'

Then Nell hugged her daughter and whispered, 'I know how you feel . . .'

Georgia played the jukebox every day. She always selected the same record. They didn't watch it spin, because they were only a few steps from the beach, and she and May lay on their towels in the sun, dreamily listening to 'Jealousy'.

She learned to swim that holiday, with May's help. Maybe it was just as well that Kenny was not there to compare them in their bathing costumes. Georgia's was a new, white towelling two-piece; May wore her old, navy-blue wool one.

She heeded her mother's wise words. The girls went roller-skating where they were shyly approached by a couple of youthful admirers; to a concert on the pier; even to a decorous tea-dance, which didn't seem right on a sultry afternoon. They giggled at the silliest things, like trying on clip-on shell earrings and pink lipstick.

'It's been the most wonderful holiday ever,' May said, as they boarded the train for home. 'I can't wait to tell Kenny all about it! I'll never forget it, will you?'

'I certainly won't,' Georgia agreed. 'I'll even miss dear old Ocean View.'

'And your favourite tune?' May asked slyly.

'Oh, I played that once too often, I think.'

'Will we come here next year?'

'Trouble is, things are never as perfect a second time,' Georgia said.

There was another period of change ahead. They arrived home to discover that Eva had given birth to a little son, named for Lawrence's grandfather, Bernard. Just a few weeks previously, they had married quietly in a register office, with Phoebe and Jube as witnesses. Eva would take up her new post after the school holiday. It all fitted in very nicely. Helga was happy to take on the new baby.

Eva had been busy in other ways, too: she'd written to her old college on May's behalf. The principal had agreed to interview May and, if all went well, which it did, to offer her a place in September. She went with Helga's blessing.

So it was to be a parting of ways for the three friends, with Kenny off to do his two years' national service and then hoping to go to college himself.

Mona confided in Nell that she thought it was a good thing, because she and Bob thought that Kenny and May were becoming too serious, at too young an age.

Georgia wished she had a chance to spread her wings too, to leave Goodbody's Bank, but Nell advised her to get a good grounding there, first.

And in the spring of 1947 there was some exciting news: Phoebe and Jube were expecting their first baby. Phoebe had to take care, because she was just on forty, and it would prove to be a difficult pregnancy.

TWENTY-FOUR

Georgia had now been with Goodbody's Bank for eighteen months, and was still the junior. The lowly members of the staff were not informed of any imminent changes, so one Monday morning in March, she and Monica arrived to find an unfamiliar male clerk in Mal's place.

'Mal might have said goodbye, and how mean of them not to promote you, Monica!' Georgia whispered, loud enough to make the young man look up from sorting out his desk. He grinned. That was an encouraging sign.

'I was junior for five years before you came, remember; senior positions are usually filled from the other branches.' There were three more Goodbody's banks within the area; local farmers, in particular, trusted the name and reputation.

'I can't see *me* lasting five years,' Georgia told Monica, with a sigh.

'You won't be eligible for the marriage gratuity, if you don't.'

'Two hundred pounds, is that what keeps you here?'

'Down payment on a house; if only I can find me a man, Georgia.'

Not until the tea break did they get a chance to speak to the new clerk. When Georgia put down his cup and saucer and offered him the plate of biscuits, he boldly took two before she could say they were only allowed one, and asked, 'Any sugar?'

She shook her head. 'I'm afraid not. Sorry.'

'Thank you for the tea, anyway. Looks a decent brew. You are?'

'Georgia Smith.'

'I'm Bill Brown, originally from London Town, like you.'

'Oh, I've been living here so long, I didn't think anyone could tell.'

'Well, I can. Introduce me to your friend, eh?'

Monica heard; came over, with a lump of sugar concealed in a scrap of paper.

'This is Monica, Miss Wood – Monica, Mr Brown.'

'What did you call my predecessor?' he asked, dropping the sugar in his tea.

'Malcolm, well, Mal,' Georgia said.

'Then I'm William, well, Bill,' he said, 'except when the senior clerks are around.'

Later, as they braved the dismal cloakroom, their excited whispering resumed.

'He's even better-looking than Mal,' Monica sighed happily.

'Where's he living, I wonder? Not with the man-eating Mrs Grant, I hope.'

'We don't want to fall out again, Georgia, like we did over Mal till we realised we girls should stick together, but bear in mind I'm nearly twenty-five and getting desperate, while you've already got a steady.'

She means it, even though she appears to be joking, Georgia thought. She's referring to Kenny, whom I haven't seen or heard from for months, although he writes to May at college . . . but then, *I* don't write to him, because of *her*.

'And I'm getting on for nineteen – my mum was married at my age,' she said.

When they emerged from the closet, the remote relative was waiting.

'One at a time, is the rule,' he reproved them. He looked at his fob watch. 'You have precisely thirty minutes left to extract Mr Brown's life story from him and to eat your lunch, young ladies.'

'Cor,' Georgia said, as they scuttled away. 'He's human after all!'

Bill Brown, they learned, still lived at home with his parents, in another market-town where they had moved during the war. It was a half-hour bus ride away. He was twenty-six, had been turned down for active service because he had

had polio as a child. This had left him with a limp which they had not noticed while he was sitting down. He used a stick outside, which with a duffel coat made him appear rakish rather than disabled. He had dark curly hair, and a cheerful disposition. Even the senior clerks smiled at his banter, because it was soon evident that he was very good indeed at his job. It was rumoured he might well break the ten-year barrier to become a cashier. *Life at Goodbody's is looking up!* Georgia wrote to May in Sussex.

'Mona's expecting Kenny home this weekend,' Nell mentioned on Friday evening.

'Shame that May won't be here, then,' Georgia said.

Her mother looked at her keenly. 'D'you really mean that? It'll give you a chance to see him on his own. He's going overseas, Mona says.'

'Mum, I can't break a promise,' Georgia began.

'A promise you made to May, or to yourself?'

'Well, to myself, I suppose. They're alike in lots of ways, Kenny and May; they're both very determined, but both easily hurt, too. May worries because she told Helga she'd never leave her, and now she has, going off to college.'

'Oh, dear Helga understood, and she's been busy with Eva's baby, which is a blessing. I don't want you to say you'll stick by *me* forever, either, Georgia Smith. You've got your own life to lead.'

'Would you stay here, if I did go, Mum?' It was important to her to know that.

'Right now my answer is "yes". Phoebe's been warned by the hospital to rest as much as she can. I haven't said anything to her and Jube yet, but I'm considering giving in my notice at the shop and helping out on the smallholding; that's if they want me to, of course. They've done so much for you, for us, and I'd like to do it.'

'Mum, you're a brick,' Georgia told her. 'Any chance of supper?'

'Can't talk with your mouth full?' Mum grinned. 'But think about what I said . . .'

Nell was working that Saturday afternoon in the shop, so it was Georgia, just back from work herself, who answered the knock on the door. For a moment, seeing the lofty young man in the khaki uniform, she didn't take in that it was Kenny.

'You've grown some more!' she blurted out. He was now well over six-feet-tall.

'Aren't you going to ask me in? Dad met me at the station, but I asked him to drop me off at the lane, so I could see you before I went home. I may not get another chance. Mum's pretty upset I'm being drafted.'

'What about you?' she asked, ushering him into the sitting-room.

'What d'you think? I'm excited. I feel like a real soldier now. And a *visitor*,' he added. 'What's wrong with sitting in the kitchen? We usually do.'

'Oh, sit down on the sofa and shut up!' she said, with the old familiarity.

'Only if you sit beside me,' Kenny said. There was no mistaking his meaning.

'I ought to get changed,' she faltered, as she still wore her bank clothes.

'Go on then, but don't take too long about it.'

Old slacks and a rather shrunken jumper, no dressing up, she thought, but she unpinned the prim roll of hair and gave her curly locks a swift brush through.

He was smoking when she returned, but he immediately stubbed out the cigarette. 'Now you look like you, Georgia.'

Oh dear, she realised, seeing his expression: is this tight jumper provocative?

He didn't waste any time. She was locked in his arms, and it was not at all like the last time he'd kissed her, rather experimentally, but full of passion and purpose.

She struggled free. 'Kenny,' she protested breathlessly.

'You can't say you didn't want that to happen, I know you did.'

'I'm not stupid, I'm fully aware what it can lead to.'

'Well, it *won't* today, with me going away, and not being allowed to divulge where until it's a fact. Still, what you're hinting at definitely *will* happen, in the future.'

She had to say it. 'What about May?'

'She must suspect how we feel.'

'You wrote to her all these months,' she reproached him, 'but not once to me.'

'As I've said before, May and I have always been close, but never like *this*.'

She relaxed against him. 'I trust you Kenny, remember?'

His hands tightened round her slim waist. 'Who'd have thought,' he whispered, 'that straight-up-and-down little Georgia Smith would grow up to be so desirable?'

They parted reluctantly when they heard the dogs barking.

'Mum! It must be,' Georgia exclaimed. 'You'd better go.'

'I love you, don't forget that,' he told her. 'I'll be away eighteen months and two or three years after that at college, *then* we can –'

She put her hand over his mouth. 'Meanwhile, we won't upset May, eh? Let her finish her course, first. Write to us both, but don't give her false hopes, please.'

Nell tapped on the door, opened it. 'Your mum's getting fidgety, Kenny.'

'I know. I'm sorry,' he said, making a move.

'You didn't –' Nell began warily, when Kenny had gone.

'Get carried away? No, Mum. But, is it awful of me to wish we had?' Then Georgia was sobbing in Nell's arms. 'Why is life always so complicated?'

'I can't answer that one. All I want is for you to be happy, dearie,' Nell said.

'Georgia, give me a chance with Bill,' Monica said. 'I've seen how he looks at you.'

'I haven't encouraged him, honestly, Monica; I like him, but I'm sort of spoken for. He's not a charmer like Mal was, but he's a nice chap. Why don't you ask him out?'

'What would he think, if I did?'

Georgia opened the morning post, making separate piles of correspondence and envelopes. They seized a chance to gossip, while the men collected the ledgers.

'I don't think he'd mind at all. He likes football, doesn't he, even if he can't play. Ask him to go with you to watch your favourite team.'

'Haven't got one.'

'What about Ipswich? You could catch the bus directly after work on Saturday.'

'Shush! Here he comes. I'll think about it . . .'

'Don't think, do it!' Georgia advised.

She'd arrived at her desk that morning before Monica. There was a note on her blotter. *Fancy coming out for a drink after work?* It was signed 'B'. She'd looked over at Bill, shook her head, mouthed, 'Sorry!' Then she screwed up the paper and aimed it at the waste-paper basket. It was an unkind thing to do, she knew that, but she didn't want Monica to suspect that Bill had asked her out first.

It's going to be a long time waiting around for Kenny, Georgia thought wistfully. Maybe I need a change of scene, too. She'd talk to Mum about it soon.

Phoebe was resting on the couch, with her feet propped up on a cushion. She was pleased to see Nell on Wednesday afternoon, when the shop was closed.

'How are you, dearie?' Nell asked, pulling up a chair.

Phoebe doesn't show much, she thought; she's only a couple of months gone.

'Sick,' Phoebe said with feeling. 'I can't keep anything down. Jube worrying doesn't help – I have to remind him, someone has to do the work.'

'I wanted to speak to you about that. I'm ready and willing to help him, Phoebe.'

'You've got your job at Buttons.'

'I only went there temporary, remember? It's cheaper for them to employ a youngster in my place. I'm leaving there this Friday, and you don't want to see me unemployed, do you?'

Phoebe managed a smile. 'Well, if you put it like that, Nell, it'd be a godsend to have you, I must admit.'

'Now, what can I do for you this afternoon, or would it help just to talk?'

Phoebe reached out to take Nell's hand. 'I'm scared, Nell, I really am.'

'About the birth? Things have improved since my day, you know.'

'I never believed I could get pregnant. Oh, I couldn't bring myself to tell Jube that, because I knew how much he wanted us to have a baby before it was too late.'

'This is a little miracle, then?'

'I suppose it is. Please don't think I don't want the baby as much as he does, because I do. I couldn't help feeling sad when I held Eva and Lawrence's little boy for the first time, thinking it would never happen for us.'

'But now you've been warned that it won't be easy, eh?'

'Yes. It'll be hard on Jube in other ways. No normal married relations, the specialist advises. We were both celibate for so long, but now, well, that side of our life has been a joy. We've, well, made up for lost time, you see, Nell.'

'I still miss all that,' Nell said, almost inaudibly. 'But at least you'll be close at nights, you can take comfort from that. He'll understand. Jube's a very special person.'

'Yes he is. And so are you,' Phoebe told her friend.

May came home at Easter. Georgia and Helga pushed young Bernard along to the station to meet her. As the baby was now sitting up, they could balance May's case across the end of the pram.

May looked different, with an attractive gamine hairstyle and coral lipstick. 'I wondered if Kenny would be on leave, if he'd meet me, take my luggage in the sidecar,' May said, then, intercepting the glance they exchanged, 'What's up?'

'I thought you would have heard; he's serving overseas now,' Helga told her.

'No, he hasn't written lately.' May looked directly at Georgia.

'I only knew because he came to see his family before he went.'

'I'm sure you'll hear from him soon,' Helga assured her.

Georgia left them at their house, promising to join them later to catch up on all the news. She wheeled the baby back to the gatehouse. His parents, of course, looked after the children themselves at weekends and in the school holidays.

She didn't hurry back to Helga's, wanting to prepare for unexpected questions.

'Living with all those females!' May told them. 'Still, I was brought up to community life, you could say. It has its advantages, of course. One of the girls was a hairdresser before she decided she wanted to train as a teacher. She cuts all our hair and only charges a bob! We borrow books from each other, and clothes if we've got a date. Not that I go out on the town very often. The last time was when Kenny turned up unexpectedly and we went to the pub. Have I shocked you, Helga?'

'Please don't go in a place like that on your own, will you,' she cautioned her.

May's much more confident, talkative, Georgia thought. She's independent now, while I'm not.

She said aloud, 'Your friend did a good job on your hair, May.'

'She cut off all the wisps! I don't need to curl it at nights now, that's a relief.'

'Met any interesting men?' Georgia asked casually.

'Some. But it wouldn't be fair to Kenny if I encouraged them.'

'I'd better go. Mum will be dishing up supper,' Georgia said.

It was time to talk things over with her mother, after the stew and dumplings.

'You wipe, Mum; I'll wash. Your poor old hands look red and chapped after a day working outside! I'll buy you some glycerine and rosewater, to sooth 'em, in town tomorrow, eh?'

'Out with it,' Nell said in her forthright way. 'Get it off your chest.'

The words came out in a rush. 'Mum, I'm getting nowhere in the bank. What would you say if I wanted to leave?'

'Where are you thinking of going?' Nell dried the plates carefully.

'Oh, Mum – it's really mean of me to say this, after you coming to live here for my sake and all, but, well, seeing May all grown-up today, and fulfilling her ambitions, it's made me wonder if it's time I left home, too . . . I'd come home if it didn't work out, honest. You asked "where", didn't you. Now Aubrey's got a two-bedroomed flat in south London, maybe he could do with a lodger. It'd be a start.'

'You can't assume he'd want the responsibility of a young sister.'

'I wouldn't! But *responsible*'s what I intend to be. Can I go with your blessing?'

' 'Course you can,' Nell said. She concentrated on stacking the crockery. We were apart so long, she thought, and now she wants to leave me. 'I won't come back to London myself,' she added. 'I'm needed here, you see.'

TWENTY-FIVE

Georgia was disappointed to discover that Aubrey's flat was on the second floor of a decaying apartment house, with dark poky rooms and a kitchen in an alcove, curtained off from the living-room. The shared bathroom was down a flight of echoing stone steps, and Aubrey advised Georgia to wash in the sink in the mornings.

'I'm not here much,' he said cheerfully. 'Made an exception for you, today! I leave for poly first thing: catch the bus to the city as it's cheaper than the train and eat my main meal of the day in the canteen. I work four evening shifts as a barman in a small hotel. I'm allowed a sandwich and half-a-pint in my break. I have to work, Georgia, to pay the rent and buy college books, because my gratuity is almost gone.'

'I'll soon be helping with that,' she said with more confidence than she felt.

'You'll have to find a job first. There's not much on offer locally. Most shops and small businesses that weren't bombed put the shutters up and moved away for good. You don't get to know everyone like we did in the East End. My girlfriend –'

'I didn't know you had a girlfriend! You kept that very quiet.'

'Well, I'm treading cautiously in that respect. Janey lives in the flat downstairs, with the bathroom. She keeps it nice and clean. Janey works for Coralie Glass, an employment agency in Holborn. That might be a good opportunity for you.'

'I could try for a position there, you mean?' she asked hopefully.

'Oh, they're fully staffed, just Janey and her boss. Janey's coming round tonight to meet you. I'll ask her if she'll take you to the agency on Monday.'

Janey supplied their dinner: meat pies and chips, for which she'd queued for more than half an hour. 'They'd run out of fish, were cagey about what's in the pies, but at least it's all piping hot. Nice to meet you, Georgia – can you wash some plates, then we can eat. Aubrey's not very domesticated, I'm afraid.'

'He hasn't changed then,' Georgia smiled. She took to Janey right away. Mum would approve of her too, she thought.

Janey was small and energetic, blue-eyed with prematurely white hair. Catching Georgia's interested glance, she explained airily, 'The shock of being bombed out did that for me. My hair came out in handfuls, then grew again like this. I always say it's preferable to being mousy, like before! And in case you're wondering, I'll be twenty-one in two weeks' time. I keep dropping hints to Aubrey . . .'

'Oh, you're not much older than *me*!' Georgia exclaimed, pleased.

'Between us we'll be able to keep your ancient brother in order, eh? Tell me, has he made your bed up for you, yet?'

'I thought I'd leave that to you, Janey,' Aubrey grinned, 'as you're in charge!'

Coralie Glass was a startlingly attractive mature lady, with an intriguing accent. When Janey introduced Georgia, she gripped her hand and pronounced, 'I shall look after Miss Smith myself. Come into my sanctum. Janey can take care of the front desk.'

As she followed Miss Glass into her office, Georgia noticed that she was wearing a gold snake anklet, which matched the bracelets on her bare upper arm.

'Get's hot in London in July,' Miss Glass said, switching on a whirring fan. 'People here don't dress for it; where I come from the ladies wear simple loose garments in fine cotton with little underneath. I see we are in accord, Miss Smith.'

'Oh . . .' Georgia murmured. She hadn't worn her formal office clothes today, because they needed pressing and Aubrey didn't possess an iron. She needn't have worried,

Miss Glass obviously approved of her light daisy-patterned summer frock.

Miss Glass flicked through a box-file of cards. 'These are current positions on offer. My efficient assistant made it clear, I'm sure, that it is the employer who pays for my services, not the applicant. Now, can I ask you fill in this form please. Use my pen. Apart from personal details, you need only tick the relevant answer.'

Janey has an efficient boss, too, Georgia thought, ticking away.

Studying a sheaf of cards, Miss Glass began the rejection process. 'Counter clerk, modern city bank?' she queried.

'It would be mechanised, of course; Goodbody's was a manual branch, way behind the times. I never got behind the counter.'

'Insurance? You must be good at figures. Free lunches, good conditions.'

'I'd like to escape accounts.'

'Comptometer operator?'

'Whatever's that?'

Another card discarded. The job situation was not looking rosy for Georgia.

'It would be to your advantage, of course, if you were proficient in shorthand and typing. We always have plenty of secretarial posts.'

'Sorry, can't do either,' Georgia admitted.

'Tell me, what do you really expect from a job?'

'Enjoying my work, meeting people, being involved, stimulated: not willing away the hours until it's time to go home. When I was interviewed by the bank manager I was told that enjoyment was equated with frivolity, and that would never do. I'd like to try something completely different from my last job.'

Miss Glass rang a bell. After a few minutes, Janey appeared with two steaming cups of coffee. 'Any luck?' she asked.

Georgia shook her head. 'I haven't got the right qualifications,' she said.

'I think we're looking in the wrong box,' Miss Glass decided. 'You came to London hoping for a complete change, didn't you? Let me make a phone call . . .'

Georgia emerged from the sanctum to find Janey just bidding goodbye to a satisfied client.

'I've got an interview, Janey! If only I can find the place within twenty minutes.'

'A–Z, that's what you need.' Janey handed her a dog-eared copy. 'Don't lose it! What's the job?'

'It's at a new art gallery. *Avant-garde*, your boss says. I'd be general dogsbody, but I'd get to meet interesting people, and talk a lot!'

'That must be her friend's gallery. Not too far from here. Miss Elsom and Miss Glass came over here together as refugees before the war. What's the pay?'

'Less than I was getting at Goodbody's; nothing like the banks pay in London, but I hope I strike lucky.'

'You will. Sit down and take a deep breath, work out your route, then go! Call back here for me at five if you like, and we'll catch the bus home together. I'll keep you company until that brother of yours gets back about eleven, eh?'

The art gallery was above a restaurant. More stone steps to climb, Georgia discovered. She entered a world of light and bright colours through a perfectly ordinary door. She was in Dorita's Gallery, and Dorita, obviously a free spirit like her friend, came hurrying to greet her.

Dorita was of indeterminate age, with long raven hair kept back off her face with a childish Alice band. She didn't have an anklet, but Georgia could glimpse thick fishnet stockings, probably hand crocheted, beneath her swirling skirts. She was very thin, with an angular face dominated by a splendid nose.

'Let me look at you, darling! Come over by the window. I adore red hair, especially when it's *wild* like yours.'

'Oh dear,' Georgia said, 'I should have combed it. I got hot and sticky hunting round for the gallery, although I found the street all right.'

'Darling! We are so new here! When can you start? Today?'

'But, you haven't interviewed me yet, I might not be right for the job.'

'Of course you are! My friend Coralie tells me you don't care for figures of the numerical kind and I said, "If she doesn't mind the painted sort, I like what I hear." I am an artist myself, promoting other artists, you know. Allow me to show you around.'

Some of the pictures were modern art and rather puzzling; others were striking, some even beautiful. Georgia genuinely admired them all.

'And these are mine,' Dorita said. 'You will see that I like to paint from life. Perhaps you will model for me one day.'

'As long as it's only head and shoulders!' Georgia felt she should say, for most of the subjects of Dorita's bold oil paintings were completely naked.

'Ah, I make a quick sketch or two, then a simple clay figure, I paint from those. I could change the face, but not the hair. I shall ask again, when I know you better! Now, will you take lunch with me? Then I will put you to work. We open at two this afternoon.'

A week after Georgia joined the art gallery, she received a letter (the second from her mother) in a large, flat envelope. She was intrigued, but she didn't get a chance to open it until she and Janey were on the bus en route to work that morning.

A friend of yours, Bill Brown brought this round.
I hope you don't mind, I gave him your address.
I said I would post this off to you, as I was going to
write anyway . . .

The photograph was mounted on stiff card.

'All the staff at Goodbody's Bank!' Georgia exclaimed.
'It's such a surprise, because they didn't do anything like
this when Mal, one of the clerks, left, but the remote
relative – that's what we called the chief clerk, I'll explain
that another time – lined us all up outside the bank when
it closed and got his wife to take the picture. Quite good,
even though you can only see Mr Ledward's arm at the
end. That's the manager, Mr Puddefoot, next to me. I bet
he felt embarrassed! That's Monica.'

'And who's this on your other side?' Janey pointed. 'The
only good-looking bloke in the picture.'

'That's Bill Brown, it was his camera, and I suspect the
photo was his idea.'

'What else did your mum say?'

'Give me a chance, and a bit more elbow room to read
it! She says Bill told her he used to live in Streatham and
still has relatives there. She says he intends to pop in and
see me when he next visits them.'

'Hope I get to meet him then. He sounds smitten with
you. But you're spoken for, aren't you?'

Georgia carefully inserted the photograph back in the envelope, put Mum's letter in her bag. There was more news to read later, about Phoebe.

'Kenny? That's rather complicated. He's out in Malaya, and will be for at least another year. I've only had one letter in the last six months . . .' She could repeat that word for word she thought, but she wouldn't. *I've been thinking, I can't expect you to hang around all that time. It's not fair to either you or May.*

'Forget him then,' Janey advised. 'I repeat, Bill Brown's keen, I can tell!'

Georgia retired tactfully to her room soon after Aubrey came home. Oh dear! She thought, thin walls again.

'I've missed you,' she heard Janey say. Then there was a lengthy silence.

Janey's voice again. 'I must go . . .'

'No, please stay. You can leave before Georgia gets up in the morning.'

'I don't like this secrecy. Commit yourself, Aubrey Smith – marry me.'

'I'm seriously considering your proposal, Janey Roberts.'

'My birthday, the day after tomorrow –'

'Is it really?' he teased.

'Oh, *you!*'

The talking ceased abruptly. Georgia turned over, thumped her pillow. The silly chap can't do any better than little Janey, she thought. I'll tell him so, when I get a chance. And as soon as I'm earning, I'll have to look for a bed-sit on my own.

'Your turn at the sink,' Aubrey called at 6.30 next morning. 'I'm just going in my room to get dressed. The kettle's on. Save a drop for tea, eh?'

Mum would be upset, Georgia thought, if she knew we don't have breakfast. No wonder I'm always starving by mid-morning, and Dorita says I look pale. She feeds me homemade rock-cakes without currants, and stirs sugar in my coffee. She clucks round me like a mother hen. Would Mum approve of that?

Georgia and Aubrey sat at the kitchen table sipping their tea. Aubrey had made it – he hadn't reboiled the kettle, but she had other things on her mind.

'Aubrey, are you going to ask Janey to marry you?' she asked.

'What's this, matchmaking, old girl?'

'Why not? You should think yourself lucky she's picked an old boy like you.'

'I've got nothing to offer her until I'm qualified,' he reminded her.

'Of course you have! Why do couples always have to wait so long?'

'I didn't, first time around,' he reminded her. 'That was a mistake.'

'Look, Janey told me how she lost her parents when their house was bombed during the war, how she's had to more-or-less fend for herself ever since; no wonder her hair turned white almost overnight. She deserves to be part of a family once more, don't you think?'

'I ought to tell you off, interfering in my affairs, but I won't. You've got a lot of sense for your age, Georgia. What about you? Mum hinted about the young chap, Kenny, wasn't it, who met me at the station that time.'

'I think that was *my* mistake,' she said quietly. 'I hope I get another chance, like you.'

Two days later, Janey was proudly displaying a modest engagement ring. 'We're getting married as soon as we can afford the wedding licence! I'll go on working, of course, and we'll put off having a family until Aubrey has a proper job.'

Mum wrote:

Delighted! Make it before September because then I'll be rushed off my feet when Phoebe has her baby.

TWENTY-SIX

Phoebe, resting on her couch, heard voices outside. Jube had pulled the curtains across the window to darken the room before he returned to work after lunch. He'd insisted she must have a nap. She had done too much this morning, hanging the washing on the line while he and Nell were busy picking runner beans and fruit for the market tomorrow. Nell ran a stall for them there, now. It was proving a financial success. Nell helped Jube with the by-products of the bee-keeping, too: candles and beeswax polish, which had been Phoebe's special project. But rest was even more imperative since the doctors had discovered she had developed an erratic heartbeat.

There was tapping on the window now. She called out, 'Come in.'

It was Eva and the children. She was losing track of time, Phoebe thought. Of course, school was out. It would be August bank holiday this weekend.

'Pull the curtains, Eva, and I'll get us some lemonade. Phew, it's hot!'

'You stay where you are,' Eva told her. 'Talk to the children. I'll do it.'

Seven-year-old Win held onto her brother's hand. He was wobbly on his feet.

The children stared at her, solemn-faced. Phoebe thought, I must look like a beached whale, struggling to sit up. I feel like it too, in this ugly smock dress.

Eva said from the kitchen, 'Toys and books in the bag. Rag ones for Bernie.'

Phoebe winced, but thought it was inevitable the baby's name would be shortened. Bernard was rather a mouthful for a little chap in a romper suit. She wondered if her baby would look like his cousin. Strange that young Win resembled her stepfather rather than her mystery father. Adopted children often did. Georgia and I, she thought, grew alike in ways, if not looks, when we were together.

'Try not to spill your lemonade,' Eva told her two. 'Now, I'll sit down beside you Phoebe, so I can keep a watchful eye on them. Drink up.'

While the children played with their toys, Eva asked, 'Come on, what's up?'

'I hate being pregnant. I hate being huge. It's too hot to have a baby.'

'Mine were both born in the summer, remember. I know the feeling.'

'But you were able to work, Eva, almost to the day you gave birth.'

'I appreciate that it must be frustrating for you. Not long to go now.'

'I've got to go into hospital as you know. I may have to have a caesarian.'

'Grumble all you like to me, better than having a go at Jube, eh?'

Phoebe gave an involuntary gasp. 'Ow, that hurt!'

'Twinges? Common at this stage . . .' Eva's voice betrayed her anxiety.

'I stretched up to the washing line; Jube was cross with me.'

'So he should be! Where is he right now, Phoebe? I ought to call him, I think.'

Phoebe was leaning back, her face ashen, breathing shallowly. 'Ring the bell . . .'

Eva looked round desperately. 'Where?' It was Win who answered.

'On the kitchen windowsill, Mummy. A big bell. I saw it when we came in.'

Thank goodness, Eva thought: children notice everything.

'Hang on,' she told Phoebe, 'I'll keep ringing it, till he comes.'

Jube was soon there, followed by Nell, who almost fell over the dogs dashing in after him. He took one look at Phoebe and cried, 'Thank God for the phone!'

'Take the children outside in the garden,' Nell said quietly to Eva. 'I don't like the look of her. Jube's ringing the hospital; I'll stay with her. It's good you were here.'

'I have space for you here, and it will be to my benefit,' Dorita said immediately, when Georgia told her about her brother and Janey. 'You don't want to be a goosegog, is that what they say?'

'Almost!' Georgia smiled. 'Are you sure?'

'Darling, I didn't like to tell you yet. This is not really a nine to five job – the gallery opens some evenings, and bank holiday times. Also, there is the royal wedding to come, and London will be thronged with visitors. I won't charge much for the room, because I cannot afford to pay you for the extra hours. Does that suit you?'

'It does. Especially as you haven't known me long –'

'Darling, I am a good judge of people, like Coralie. You were the first one *she* approved to assist in the gallery. It took three weeks to find you. If you move in here tomorrow, I needn't worry that you have a bus to catch over the next busy weekend.'

Like Phoebe, Dorita was good at adapting clothes: although her stitching was not as trustworthy, for she plied a flying needle and whatever thread came to hand.

So, on Bank Holiday Monday Georgia wore a wrap-over skirt, which she safety-pinned at a strategic point so that modesty was preserved. The brief, matching top crossed at the front and tied at the back. Far too much cleavage, Georgia thought.

Dorita opened a box. 'Here, all paste jewellery, but it glitters – you choose.'

Glass beads encircled Georgia's neck; gilt charms jangled on her wrist.

'You need your hair up,' Dorita considered, 'and lots of lipstick.'

Georgia submitted to the transformation. She could always blot her lips later.

The gallery was crowded. Georgia went round with the tiny glasses of wine, making sure the visitors were all happy. Dorita had sold three pictures already.

Georgia felt a touch on her bare arm. She turned to see a familiar face.

'*Bill*! Whatever are you doing here?' she asked in amazement.

'Officially, spending a week with the relatives; unofficially, I wanted to see you.'

'I thought –' She realised she was glad to see him.

'You thought you'd fixed me up with Monica, eh? Now is not the football season! I missed my fellow joker: you, Georgia. Goodbody's is tedious without you.'

'But how did you find me? Mum didn't give you this address.'

'I called at your brother's flat. His fiancée lent me her *A–Z*!'

'Have a glass of wine,' she offered. 'Then I'll introduce you to my boss . . .'

The gallery closed at ten. Bill was still there. Dorita beamed. All had gone well.

'You will join us at our meal, Bill? We haven't stopped to eat all day.'

'Offer accepted,' Bill said. 'And if you're about to say how will I get back to Streatham, well, don't. A walk will do me good.'

Dorita gave a swift glance at his stick. 'You can telephone your aunt, I suppose? Stay tonight. If you don't mind the couch in my workroom. The pictures will keep you company. Especially the beautiful ladies, I think.'

Georgia didn't need to blush on Bill's behalf; she was flushed from the wine.

'Thank you again,' Bill said. 'As long as Georgia doesn't mind.'

'Why should I mind?'

'Only if you have misinterpreted my intentions.' He turned to Dorita. 'I should explain that we are friends of recent standing, Dorita.'

'Friends, of course you are! But in tune, as they say.'

'Yes, we're definitely in tune,' Georgia smiled. 'It's good to see Bill again.' There wasn't the intensity she felt when Kenny was around. She could relax.

They entertained Dorita with outrageous tales of Goodbody's Bank, which amused her greatly. It was rather late for a hot vegetable curry, but they enjoyed it.

'Goodnight, Bill,' Georgia said, after giving him a blanket and pillow. Then she added ingenuously, as they were on their own, 'I thought you might expect a kiss.'

'I don't expect anything, Georgia, honestly. Unless you want me to . . .'

'D'you know,' she giggled, 'after three glasses of wine, I believe I do.'

'Come here then.'

She could feel the heat of his hands through her flimsy top. It was a satisfying kiss. He gave her a little push. 'Now leave me to the painted ladies.'

'Georgia!' Dorita called, as she passed her door. 'Come in for a moment.'

Georgia hadn't realised that the long black hair was a wig. It now adorned a plaster head with blank features. Without it, Dorita looked older, frailer.

'You did very well today, darling. Take tomorrow off. Spend it with Bill.'

'Are you sure?'

'I like your friend. You deserve a break.'

Phoebe's baby had been delivered by caesarian section. Everything had happened so fast after her arrival at the hospital. There was no time to lose.

She lay in a bed in a secluded side-room in the cottage hospital, which had been endowed by her grandfather. The Bliss family still had a certain standing in the area. The National Health Service was yet to come.

Jube was grateful for the privacy. He was there at her bedside, as he had been the last four days. Lawrence had come earlier, but she couldn't respond through the haze of drugs. Eva and Nell had looked in, too. Visiting was strictly restricted.

At last, the whispered words she had struggled to say, 'Jube, is the baby –?'

'The baby is all right. Six weeks early, but breathing by itself.'

'Don't call him, it,' she reproved him gently.

He was sobbing, but why? If the baby was alive, that was surely good.

'The baby is a girl, Phoebe. But that doesn't matter, does it?' he appealed.

'I thought . . . we'll love her anyway, Jube.' Phoebe's eyes closed.

She didn't wake again from what seemed to be a peaceful sleep.

An eternity later, he was gently escorted from the room. Nell was waiting; she had already been told. She enfolded him in her motherly embrace, comforted him as best she could, then they were driven home by Bob Button in his new van.

'I'll stay with you, until you tell me to go away,' she told Jube.

Nell coped valiantly with everything at work. Jube had the support of Lawrence and Eva with the necessary arrangements to be made. Nell had the painful task of letting Georgia know what had happened. A telegram would be too terse; a telephone call too upsetting. The day before the funeral she wrote a long letter to her daughter. It would be too late for her to come here – she thought that was best, remembering the bewildered little girl at the service for her own father. She should remember Phoebe as she was, she thought.

The church was packed, as it had been on Phoebe and Jube's wedding day. It was a moving occasion. Prayers were said for the tiny daughter who would never know her mother. As yet, the baby had no name. Jube had not been able to bring himself to visit her in the hospital. She was doing well and would be coming home in two weeks' time, arrangements would have to be made.

After Lawrence and Eva had gone home, Nell washed up, tidied the room. Jube sat there quietly, head in his hands.

'The cow needs to be milked,' Nell said at last. 'Would you like me –?'

'I'll do it,' he said heavily. He went out, the dogs at his heels.

He was gone a long time. Nell tried not to feel anxious. She guessed that he wanted to be alone with his thoughts.

When he returned he said, 'I think I'll go up to bed, if you don't mind, Nell.'

'It's been a long day,' she agreed. Then, 'Jube, what will you name your baby?'

'Phoebe wanted Stephen, for a boy, after her father. We hadn't decided on a girl's name. *You* pick something.'

'I can't do that! Jube, what about her mother's name, or your mother's?'

'Her mother couldn't even bring herself to come to her daughter's funeral.'

'We don't know the full story, do we? It doesn't mean she didn't care.'

'My mother was Flora. She actually had *me* when she was forty-five.'

'That's a good name. I think Phoebe would have approved of that, don't you?'

He nodded. 'Goodnight, Nell, and . . . thank you for everything.'

'I'll bring you up a cup of tea,' she said. She'd add a dash of whisky to it.

He was lying there with the lamp turned low, and Nell guessed he was crying.

'Let the tears flow, Jube, it's the only way. It's been such a shock, you see.'

'Stay with me, Nell. I . . . don't want to be alone tonight . . .'

'Drink your tea, I'll be back, I promise,' she said. She went into the other bedroom, where she had been sleeping, to collect her own thoughts, and to undress.

It can't be wrong, she thought. He just needs me to be there.

She slipped into bed beside him, put her arms round him, held him tight. The realisation came then. It was something she'd not acknowledged when Phoebe was there. *I love him. I can't tell him, of course. But I can care for Jube and for Flora.*

'She has been crying on and off all day, ever since she received her mother's letter,' Dorita told Bill, when he arrived at the gallery on Thursday evening.

The gallery had closed at six. Bill had hoped to take Georgia out for a meal, and perhaps to a show. His holiday was drawing to a close; he would leave on Sunday.

She was in the workroom, curled up on the couch.

'Georgia, what is it?' he asked gently.

'Phoebe, my foster mother all through the war, she died last weekend. I think I told you she was expecting a baby, well . . . everything went wrong. It was the funeral today, but Mum didn't let me know in time. Oh, Bill, I should have been there!'

He sat down beside her, stroked her hair. She clung to him, dampening his shirt with her tears.

After a while, she said, 'Phoebe had a baby girl. Jube will be devastated.'

'You should go home, I think,' Bill said gently. 'I'd travel with you.'

'I can't ask Dorita to let me have time off, Bill, I've only been here five minutes.'

'Of course you can, and of course I will,' Dorita said from the doorway.

'You heard, Dorita?'

'I didn't mean to, but I could not interrupt. Bill should go back to his aunt's now and pack his things. Then come back for you tomorrow, eh?'

'I'll see Aubrey and Janey while I'm about it, keep them informed,' Bill said.

When he had gone, Dorita observed, 'He really cares for you, your Bill.'

'I hardly know him, Dorita. I do like him very much, though, he's so kind.'

'On happier days, you laugh a lot together – give him a chance, Georgia.'

'There's someone else. We grew up together . . .'

'Sometimes it happens that you grow apart. Where is this someone else?'

'He's not here, and you see, *he* has someone else, too . . .'

TWENTY-SEVEN

'I'm coming with you all the way; I promised, didn't I?' Bill said, when they stepped down from the train. 'Taxi!' he hailed the solitary vehicle waiting in the station yard.

'No one at home,' Georgia bit her lip. 'Mum must be at work.'

The gate between the two gardens swung open, and there was Nell, looking as if she could not believe her eyes. 'Georgia, dearie!'

'Mum! You *are* here, after all. Bill came with me, he's been wonderful.'

'Thank you for looking after her,' Nell told Bill. 'Come next door both of you; Jube's just seeing to his bees. I've been staying here since . . .'

'Where shall I leave my things?' Georgia asked.

'Bring them with you. Unless you want to stay our side by yourself.'

Bill picked up the case, deciding for Georgia. 'Best to be with your mum.'

Nell was determinedly cheerful. 'You'll stay for supper, Bill, won't you?'

'The taxi's waiting. I'd better go home and surprise my own parents, eh?'

'Will I see you tomorrow?' Georgia asked, as she saw him off.

'D'you want to?' He was always direct.

'Yes, I do.' On an impulse, she gave him a swift hug and a kiss on the cheek.

'I've got a lot to talk over with my mum and dad. They've been overprotective since I was so ill as a child. I can understand that. But I want to move on from Goodbody's Bank and get a job in the City,' Bill told her.

'London, you mean?'

'Yes, because *you* are there. Cheerio!' he said, as the taxi sounded its horn.

Georgia went upstairs to the spare bedroom, painted blue for the baby. There was only a single bed. 'Can we both fit on that?' she asked Nell.

Nell hesitated. 'No. Jube, well he needs me with him at nights.'

'Mum!' Georgia was scandalised. 'How *could* you!'

Nell took hold of her shoulders as if she was a child, and gave her a shake.

'It's *not* what you think! I couldn't do that to Phoebe's memory, nor could he. He's lost without her, Georgia, like I was when your dad died. Please understand.'

'It doesn't seem right. Are you sure –?'

'I don't have to ask your permission, do I?' Nell's voice rose. She was angry.

Then Jube was calling from the kitchen, 'Who's here, Nell?'

'I'm sorry, Mum,' Georgia whispered. 'It was a shock, you see.'

'Come down and see Jube, and don't you dare upset him.'

Georgia didn't sleep much that night. She stuffed her ears with cotton wool so that she would not eavesdrop. There was such a lot on her mind. She would miss Phoebe terribly, for she really had been a second mother to her. Then came the realisation that she was falling for Bill. Would Kenny be jealous, if he knew?

'Nell, are you awake?' Jube said, after a long silence, when the light was out.

'Yes, dearie, what d'you want?' Nell was worried about arguing with Georgia.

'There was something I *had* to keep from Phoebe; Lawrence advised me to. I'm . . . not sure how she would have taken it, if I had . . . confessed.'

'You make it sound as if you'd done something awful, Jube. Will you tell *me*?'

'I badly need to tell someone, Nell.'

'I won't betray your secret, Jube, I promise.' She held him tightly in her arms. She'd try to make up with Georgia tomorrow, before that nice Bill Brown came.

Flora looked very tiny in her Moses basket. Despite the warm weather, she wore a knitted coat and leggings and a little bonnet, which concealed her thatch of black hair. Her eyes were closed, but the nurse who had cared for her in hospital said they were slatey-blue, which meant they would probably turn brown like her mother's.

Jube had been determined to bring her home himself, despite Bob offering to do so. Naturally Nell went along to hold the baby while Jube drove.

Flora's cradle, loaned by Eva, was by the big bed; the basket was for carrying her around, or for laying her in, downstairs. There was a folding pram in a corner of the kitchen, bought second-hand because nursery equipment was still in short supply. They couldn't take her out in this for another week or two, the hospital decreed.

Jube sat by the basket in its swinging frame, gazing at his daughter. Nell bustled about. Time for afternoon tea. They'd worked hard all morning, starting at dawn, to get ahead of themselves, as Jube said, though the second milking couldn't be changed. There had been an offer of help, while Nell was caring for the baby, from an unexpected quarter.

Lawrence had said, 'I'll do my best, just bear with me . . .'

'I'll move into the small bedroom.' Jube sipped his tea. 'You stay with Flora.'

Nell didn't look at him as she said, 'Good idea. You need your sleep.'

'I want to play my part,' he insisted. 'You've to call me if necessary, Nell.'

'I will. When you're here, *you* pick her up when she cries, eh?'

As if on cue, there was a little mewing cry from the baby.

'Go on, then,' Nell said. 'I'll see to her bottle. Nurse gave me the instructions.'

She needn't remind him to be careful, she thought. Despite his huge hands, he had a gentle touch, especially with his animals. Flora would have a good father.

Nell tested the heat of the milk on the back of her hand. Some things you never forgot, she thought. She held the bottle out to him: 'It's ready.'

'You take her, Nell. She needs a woman's touch, I believe.'

She cradled the baby against her bosom and coaxed Flora to take the bottle. This procedure would have to be repeated every couple of hours, because Flora could only manage a very small amount at a time. Nell was aware that Jube was carefully easing a cushion behind her back to give her extra support.

'You haven't lost your touch,' he said quietly, when the feeding was done.

'It's almost nineteen years since Georgia was a baby. It's instinctive, Jube.'

'I couldn't manage without you.'

'I couldn't have managed, either, without Phoebe taking on my girl in the war.'

'I know Helga offered to look after Flora, and I was very grateful because she's got her hands full with young Bernard and the other children she has there, but –'

'You've chosen *me*, and I'm honoured, I really am,' Nell said.

'Letter for you from Georgia,' Jube said, when he returned from the early chores.

'I'll read it over breakfast,' Nell replied, passing him his full plate.

Dear Mum,

I am happy that you have forgiven me for jumping to conclusions. Even if I had been right, it is still none of my business, as you told me. Thank you for your lovely letter. The baby, I do like her name! sounds sweet. Yes, it is sad she will never know her real mum, but we will all keep Phoebe's memory alive for Flora, won't we? I still can't believe Phoebe has left us. Maybe it's because I am not at home, and picture her as she was. That helps. Bill was in London one day last week. He had an interview with one of the big banks! Luckily he is 'mechanised', I told him! (He did the course.) Dorita, Coralie Glass and Janey all think he is the one for me!! What's your opinion? Aubrey won't be drawn on the subject, he's too occupied with thoughts of his own marriage! He understands that you won't be able to come, but Martin and Lizzie intend to be there. Only a month to go. I'm to be bridesmaid again, but alas, the blue dress no longer fits! Dorita insists she will make me a dress that will make Bill's eyes pop out! So long as I don't pop out of it, eh?

Oh, Mum, is it awful of me to joke when we are all so sad about Phoebe? But she was full of fun. Give Flora a kiss from me. Tell dear Jube I am thinking of him. Love to Eva and Helga when you see them. I haven't heard from May for ages, but this is her final year at college, and I imagine she is studying very hard.

All my love always, from Georgia xxx

PS. Perhaps I shouldn't say this, but if in the future you and Jube, well, you know . . . you will have my blessing.

'What does she say? Can I read it?' Jube asked. 'Phoebe always let me.'

Nell hesitated for a brief moment. Perhaps he should see the letter, she thought. After all, they really had nothing to hide, especially now they slept apart at nights.

'I didn't know Georgia was upset,' he said. 'You should have told me, Nell.'

'We sorted it out, as you can see.'

'It's made me think, what she said at the end. In time, Nell, if you agree, we could get married, though I mustn't presume that you're thinking of bringing up Flora like one of your own. You've been so kind to us both; we get on well together. Folk could say that I looked after myself perfectly well all those years as a bachelor, but I would have wed Phoebe long before, if she would have had me. If you say "yes", well I expect the village will gossip about that. But they'll talk, anyway, if we live together like this. Nell, I wouldn't expect more of you than being a mother to Flora, you know.'

'You don't think I'm too old for that? I'm forty-eight, Jube.'

'That's not much more than my mum was when she had me.'

'In time, as you say, Jube, when you feel right about it, we could marry . . .'

The rest would follow, she was sure. She reached out to clasp his hand.

Georgia was reclining on the couch, hoping the gallery doors were locked. It wasn't as bad as she had imagined it would be, posing for Dorita. She'd finally agreed when Dorita had repeated her promise to alter the face, if not her hair. The preliminary sketches were done; now Dorita slapped wet clay on a board and moulded, pinched it into shape. It was a small figure, but detailed.

'You are not too cold, darling? This will only take a few hours.'

'I feel hot all over!' Georgia replied with feeling.

'You will tell Bill I'm sure that you are having your *portrait* painted?'

'Don't tease, Dorita! I shall keep this experience – um –'

'Under your hat?' Dorita was fashioning a curved part of Georgia's anatomy.

'Well, a hat is just what I could do with now, and not on my head!' Georgia said.

Up for the wedding, Bill spent the night before with the painted ladies, noting, 'The new one is *very* good. I don't recognise the face, but the *hair* . . .'

'You say any more at your peril!' Georgia said firmly, but she had to smile.

She wished he had found a more inspiring job, like hers, but Bill said the bank paid well, he could afford a nice flat, and to take his young lady out and about.

The wedding reception was being held in the gallery, courtesy of Dorita. 'From two until five, darlings, on Saturday, then we clear up quick, to open at seven!'

It was a simple ceremony in the local church. It had been bomb-blasted in the war, no stained glass remained.

The service was moving, as always. Janey wore a pink dress; the bridegroom his demob suit; and the bridesmaid crossed her fingers, hoping for the best in purple satin stitched by Dorita.

Bill sneaked Georgia into the workroom for a quick embrace before the meal.

'When will it be our turn?' he asked.

'Bill, we haven't known each other a year yet!' Georgia protested.

'Does it matter? *I knew*, the moment I saw you at Goodbody's, Georgia Smith.'

'I'm enjoying myself at Dorita's –'

'Of course you are! I'm not asking you to leave. Work as long as you like.'

'Let's wait until Christmas. Ask Mum's permission then, eh?'

'How about us getting engaged on your birthday?' he suggested.

'If you can get a ring with a stone to match this dress!'

Then Aubrey looked in on them and said, 'Come on you two. Grubs up!' Then he whispered in his sister's ear, 'This time it's for keeps.'

I must write to May, Georgia thought; she'll be happy for me, and for herself, because I've relinquished Kenny at last. *I'm in love with Bill and it's wonderful.*

*

'It's a lovely ring,' Nell said, admiring the amethyst set in silver.

'It's second-hand, Mum. But it's just what I wanted. Goes with my dress.'

'Purple goes with your hair, but I wouldn't have thought it would, dearie.'

'Mum I'm not expecting the usual Christmas celebration, you know. It wouldn't be very tactful, would it? I'll sleep next door, and Bill'll come over on Christmas Day, if that's all right – and can he stay the night? No hanky-panky, I promise.'

'Announcement to make?' Nell was jigging the baby in her arms.

'How did you guess?'

'Don't be surprised if Jube has something to say, too,' Nell said, mysteriously.

'I think I can guess, Mum. If I'm right, then I'm sure it's the right thing, for both of you. Flora needs you, and it'll take time to get used to not being an only daughter, but it's what Phoebe would want.'

'I've got something else to tell you now, Georgia. Lawrence and Eva had another offer for the gatehouse. They've discussed it with Jube, and they'd like to sell it and buy our cottage, when it all goes through. That's really what has made us come to a decision, sooner than we might have. It would be nice to have them so close; Lawrence is helping

Jube with the work until Flora is strong enough to take out in the fields with us – next spring, I suppose. She'll grow up with other children, too.' Nell looked at Georgia. 'What about Kenny? You ought to tell Mona and Bob.'

'He'll be all right! He's got his life mapped out for the next three years. May will be a certificated teacher by then. I'm sure May and Kenny will eventually get back together.'

'I'm not so sure as you are about that . . .' Nell said, but she wouldn't be drawn.

TWENTY-EIGHT

Georgia and Bill were out in a paddle-boat on the lake at Wandle Park. It was May, 1948, and they were to be married in Suffolk in June. Georgia worked the paddles, and Bill idly splashed her with water to cool her down as it was a scorching day.

'It's rather like being on the dodgems at a funfair,' she said, as they narrowly avoided a collision with another boat, then had to push off again from the side.

'No hoopla stalls or big wheel here,' Bill said unwittingly.

Georgia hadn't thought of Kenny in ages; now she recalled the thrills of that day when they sat high above the fairground below and were very aware of each other.

'You're getting sunburned,' Bill observed. He leaned forward to fan her face.

'Watch out!' she squealed. 'Or we'll end up in the water!'

'You can swim, can't you? You'd have to save me: I can't.'

'You're only making an excuse for me to clasp you to me, Bill Brown!'

'All the time in the world for that next month,' he said lightly. 'How are the arrangements going? How is Nell managing all that with the baby to see to?'

'Mum's the most efficient person I know. She believes in delegation.'

'Friends are helping out, you mean?'

'Of course they are. Mona Button always takes charge of refreshments.' She was suddenly serious. 'I wish we could have been at Mum and Jube's wedding.'

'They wanted a very private affair. Now Nell's going to town for *us*!' He added, 'You haven't told me yet what you'll be wearing – *not* the purple dress?'

'It came apart at the seams, remember, when we danced in the gallery.'

'You slapped me because I poked my fingers in the gaps and enlarged 'em.'

'I do love you, Bill, you know that, but you deserved it for being cheeky.'

They strolled round the park, found a seat in the shade of a tree.

'I heard from my friend May,' Georgia said, taking a sandwich from their packed lunch. 'She'll have finished her exams, and will leave college in June. She says she's delighted to be my bridesmaid. She and Janey will make a good pair.'

'What colour will they wear? You avoided telling me your own choice.'

'Yellow for them. I'll be wearing Mum's original, ivory wedding dress.'

'I like the sound of that,' he said softly. 'I really do.'

It was the Thursday night before the wedding. Georgia, with Janey, was due to arrive on Friday afternoon. The rehearsal was booked in the church for that evening. Jube had already retired upstairs, but at midnight Nell was carefully pressing the precious ivory dress with her electric iron.

Her own marriage had been three months ago; although she and Jube shared a bed once more, it was still, she thought, a union of friends, of convenience. She knew Eva had guessed for, recently, her new neighbour had said, when they were alone, 'I made the first move with Lawrence, Nell. You may have to with Jube.'

How can I? She thought. *Unless . . . Phoebe did exactly the same.*

She climbed wearily into bed; Jube turned over, moved toward her.

'Is Flora asleep?' Flora was crawling and into everything, now. Life was hectic.

'Mmm,' she murmured. 'Goodnight, Jube.'

'I wanted to say thank you, Nell, for asking me to give Georgia away.'

'She's always been very fond of you, you know.' Nell yawned.

'That's how I feel about her – and you. *You've* been my salvation, Nell. I don't expect you remember how or why it happened, but you kissed me the day I wed Phoebe. I had to give myself a little shake to clear my head and told myself off . . .'

'We *need* each other, don't we?' she whispered, as Jube drew her close. I'm so lucky, she thought. I've got another fine man in my life to love.

They didn't dress up for the wedding rehearsal. To amuse Bill, Georgia asked Nell to machine the side-seams of the purple dress, quickly, so she could wear that. Those attending were the bride and groom, the bridesmaids, the best man, the stepfather of the bride, her mother and the groom's parents. Flora was with Eva; Aubrey was coming on the wedding morning; Helga was helping Mona with the baking.

'It's lovely to see you again!' Georgia hugged May. 'Tried your frock on yet?'

'I have. It fits perfectly. Helga says it's my colour. Your mum looks very happy.'

'I should think so! She says Bill is perfect for me.'

'Mother knows best, as they say . . .'

'Are you talking about me?' Bill asked, slipping an arm round Georgia's waist.

May was self-assured these days. 'Wouldn't you like to know!' she said.

'Heard from Kenny lately?' Georgia asked casually. Bill's grip tightened.

'Not for a while, but I wrote to tell him about your wedding, and my new job.'

'Oh, what's that?' Georgia asked.

'I'm going to teach the infants here, at the school. Helga is thrilled about it.'

'Sorry to interrupt, but the vicar is signalling for the rehearsal to start,' Bill said.

They were all up early on the wedding morning. Janey had slept on the camp-bed beside Georgia, in the spare room. They'd shared a delicious secret last night.

'I'm expecting a baby next January, Georgia! It wasn't planned, but I'll have my own family again, isn't it wonderful? Aubrey's already applied for a proper job.'

'I'm thrilled for you both. I know Mum will be, when you tell her.'

'Well, I won't say anything to her until after your big day, eh?'

'Roses from the garden: Jube grows the best,' Georgia had stipulated earlier.

When she drifted downstairs in her dressing gown, she found Nell and Jube at the kitchen table, snipping stalks, trimming leaves and fashioning her bouquet.

'Funny old eggs and bacon,' Georgia said. 'No smell of cooking.'

'First things first,' Nell told her. 'You can help with the buttonholes.'

'Flora's awake, rattling the bars of her cot,' Janey said. 'Would you like me to make her breakfast and look after her while you're busy?'

Nell looked at her keenly, smiled. 'It'll be good practice, I reckon!'

'White roses for the buttonholes,' Jube told Georgia, 'I'll go and pick some more asparagus fern. The red roses are all for you.'

Georgia hugged them in turn. 'Thank you for everything, both of you!'

Later, Eva whisked Flora away next door to bath and dress her. Georgia was glad to see Nell and Jube had such good support. Lawrence even did the early milking. He had arranged for the wedding car, as he had for his sister almost three years ago.

Then she and Janey were on their own upstairs, for May would meet them at the church. Jube waited at the gate for the car. The others had gone ahead.

Georgia dabbed sudden tears from her eyes. Janey looked at her with concern.

'You're wishing your dad was here, aren't you?'

Georgia nodded. 'Yes. And Phoebe, of course.'

She walked up the aisle on Jube's arm, aware of all the familiar faces; particularly of her family in the front row, her mum with Martin and Lizzie, who had arrived just in time. Red roses for love; Mum's silk gown, a perfect fit; a borrowed veil; and Bill turning to greet her, managing without his stick, but glad to hold onto her hand. The best man, Aubrey, gave an encouraging smile. Georgia passed May her bouquet to hold, along with May's own posy of garden flowers.

The organ, played by Lawrence, swelled. The congregation rose to sing.

They made their solemn vows without a hitch; Bill kissed his bride. It was as if they were part of a happy dream. They walked back along the aisle, the bells pealed again, then they were blinking in the sunshine and being showered with confetti. Lawrence took the photographs, stopping when they'd all had enough. Then they walked in procession to the hut where the feast was spread.

Janey and Aubrey were staying the night at Helga's with May; Martin and Lizzie would manage in the single room at Nell and Jube's. But the family would all meet up this evening at the cottage, to continue the reunion and celebration.

Georgia changed into her going-away outfit in the room at the back of the stage. It hadn't changed much; it was as dusty as it had been on VE Day. Nell was with her. She refolded the silk dress and packed it carefully in the case.

'All right, dearie?' she asked.

'Of course I am!' Georgia replied. 'Mum, you're all right, too, aren't you?'

'Does it show? Yes I am, Georgia. I'm starting all over again, with Flora.'

Time to throw the bouquet. Georgia aimed it at May. The others didn't need it, she thought: all our family are married now. May fielded it smartly. When Georgia gave her a goodbye hug, she murmured, 'You'll be next – I know it! When Kenny –'

'When Kenny comes home, he'll be too busy for all this. I don't mind.'

'He'll be a fool if he doesn't realise what he'll be missing. Good luck.'

Bob Button drove them to the station. They were going to London to stay in a hotel tonight, kindly arranged by Bill's parents, and travelling to Dorset the next day.

'I had a bath this morning, but I feel like taking another one,' Georgia told Bill. It had been a long day, and the hotel, despite an imposing address, was not very plush. The decor was old-fashioned: dark paint, flowery wallpaper, ugly furnishings.

'I'll run the water for you,' he offered. At least they had their own bathroom. He was turning off the taps, realising that the water was now luke-warm, when Georgia came in, wound round with a towel.

'I'll leave you to it then,' he said, as she threw down the towel and literally jumped in, splashing him all over as he stood there, transfixed.

'You can wash my back,' Georgia said demurely.

Later, when they were in bed and had forgotten their initial reaction to the scratchy sheets, Georgia kissed him and asked dreamily, 'Aren't you glad we saved ourselves for tonight?'

'With difficulty, on my side,' he sighed.

'I thought it was best to get it over quickly you know, my revealing all, but I hope it was a pleasant surprise?'

'Not exactly. Why are you squirming? I didn't know you were ticklish.'

She giggled. 'Well I am. What d'you mean, you weren't surprised?'

'Dorita gave me a little present, a while ago. A clay figure. Left nothing to the imagination. She said I could get anything I wanted from you, if I showed you that.'

'She *didn't*! But I can tell she *did*! I wondered where it had gone. Where is it?'

'I smuggled it in my case, in case you were feeling coy.'

'Have you ever known me be that?'

'No. I have to tell you that clay is cold and clammy, which you certainly aren't.'

'Nor are you. I love you, love you, *love you*! I'll prove to you just how much . . .'

May and Helga were sharing a room. The visitors had not yet returned.

'May,' Helga said, 'you said you had guessed who your father was.'

'Why bring it up now? Lawrence Bliss, isn't it? It all ties in with music lessons.'

'It may seem like that to you. The poor man certainly got blamed for my plight.'

'Who was it then? Someone I know?'

'Bob Button, May.'

'But – I know you worked in the shop, but wasn't Mona expecting Kenny?'

'She was. I couldn't help myself, May, I really couldn't. Mona was so shocked when she found out. They pleaded with me to keep quiet about it. They wanted to save their marriage. I was so fond of them both. I was the one to blame.'

'I don't believe that! He took advantage of you. I'll never forgive him!'

'As you grew up, he changed his mind. He wanted to acknowledge you.'

'I suppose that's why he always saw me home, looked out for me,' May said, furiously. 'And what about Kenny, does he know?'

'Not yet. None of us realised that you would become fond of each other, what it might lead to. I'm so sorry, May, you can't marry Kenny: he's your half-brother.'

'It's just as well he isn't here then, isn't it? I hope he doesn't come back.'

'May! You mustn't think like that – he's fighting for his country right now.'

'Of course I didn't mean . . . His mum and dad must tell him. I can't!'

May was crying as if her heart was broken and all Helga could do was to rock her in her arms as she had when May was a baby, but couldn't say she was her own.

I caught Georgia's wedding roses, May thought. But *my* dreams are ashes.

Nell couldn't get to sleep. 'I thought you were tired,' Jube said, concerned.

'I was. I am. I keep thinking about Georgia. She's not twenty yet. So young.'

'He's that bit older. He'll look after her.'

'Oh, I know he will. But she was so keen on Kenny at one time, you see.'

'Kenny's still got some more growing up to do. The army will see to that.'

'She's a good girl, Jube. She told me she – waited, you know, for today.'

'You didn't have to tell me that. She might not like it.'

'I won't have any secrets from you. I never did with Albie. You're alike in lots of ways. Good, decent men. I have to tell you, I've grown to love you, Jube.'

'That means a lot to me, I'm truly touched,' he said quietly. 'Georgia has a great deal of love to give, like her mum. Bill's a lucky bloke, like me. Off to sleep now, Nell dear. Your other little daughter will be awake again before you know it.'

Epilogue

September, 1949

'You really don't mind, d'you darling?' Georgia asked Bill. 'I'll only be away for two days, Dorita can't spare me longer in the busy season, but it'll be a sort of *pilgrimage* for me, you see, leaving London for Suffolk on the same date as I did in 1939.'

'You've got butter on my shirt front,' he said mildly. 'Breakfast is not a good time to spring surprises. No, of course I don't mind. What did your mum say exactly?'

'She phoned to tell me that the Button family are emigrating to Australia. They've sold the shop – it's been in the family for years. Kenny's going with them, he's home sorting out his stuff. He'd like to say goodbye to May and me.'

'Is he aware that May confided in you, Georgia? Has he been told, himself?'

'Don't you think that's why the family is leaving the village?'

339

'Seems rather drastic. The locals will have guessed their secret long ago.'

'I don't understand either. You must go to work, Bill, and I must get dressed.'

'Give me one of your big hugs, one to last me till you get back,' he said.

'I *will* come back, I promise . . .' she assured him.

'Look, I'm coming to see you off, don't protest – just be ready in five minutes!'

Liverpool Street was swarming with commuters: men in pin-striped suits buying newspapers; women in costumes nipped in at the waist, and hats and gloves.

They had to wait for the Ipswich-bound train. Bill stood there in his bank clothes, with his briefcase in one hand, her weekend bag in the other. He was very quiet.

'I forgot my gas-mask,' she joked, remembering that other August day. She felt rather conspicuous for a week-day: in casual slacks, a sleeveless blouse, and pumps.

She climbed aboard. She thought, Bill looks so solemn; *why* am I doing this?

Kenny met her at Stillbrook station. Mum had arranged that. She felt her heart race despite her good intentions. He looked like a man now, not a boy. He'd grown his hair longer, after leaving the army. He greeted her with a friendly hand-shake.

'I'm glad you could come, Georgia. We're walking, it'll give us a chance to talk.'

She came straight to the point. 'I know about you and May, Kenny. I'm sorry.'

'I suppose we were naive. Mum and Dad were more to blame than Helga.'

She had to hurry to keep up with his long strides. She held onto his arm.

'Is that why you're going away?' There was a cloudless sky, she thought. Like there was ten years ago, when she walked beside Miss Stedman, bundled up in a winter coat. She was much more comfortably clothed today.

He paused. Looked down at her from his superior height. 'No, you know why.'

'Away from temptation? Poor May, she loved you, in her innocence.'

'I couldn't say it to her, it would be too cruel, but I didn't have such strong feelings for her. We were good friends, the three of us. Then we grew up, and I knew *you* were the one for me. You felt the same way, didn't you? I thought you'd wait.'

'If I'd really loved you, Kenny, don't you think I would have hung on for you?'

'I found it hard to believe when May wrote that you were married.'

'One year, two months ago,' she told him. 'Bill and I, we're right together.'

'Don't you ever think of that day we said goodbye before? How we found it hard to let go? What might have happened? *We* were right together, you and I, then.'

'First love is usually painful, Kenny. It wasn't meant to be, I believe.'

He looked around. There was not a soul about. He put down her bag, and propelled her backwards towards the hedge. He kissed her, long and hard. She pummelled on his chest with her fists. 'Stop it!' she tried to say.

He released her abruptly. 'You won't forget that, Georgia, nor will I!'

She snatched at her bag. 'Goodbye, Kenny. I still wish you good luck. I'll walk on to May's on my own.' She marched resolutely away. He didn't try to stop her.

May opened the door immediately, as if she had been looking out for her.

'Georgia! Where's Kenny?'

'We said our goodbyes. There was no point in him hanging around.'

'Helga's making tea, you must be hot and tired. Do come in!'

May sounds all right, Georgia thought, she's quite composed.

'Your arms are all scratched!' Helga exclaimed, concerned.

'I couldn't resist the blackberries; I forgot about the brambles.'

'You look very bonny,' Helga approved. 'You've got a look about you –'

'I know Mum'll pick up on that, too!' Georgia said sheepishly. She was feeling more relaxed by the minute. It was good to see these friends again. 'Yes, I'm pregnant, I think – not that I've told my dear Bill yet! It seems to be catching in our family. Janey and Aubrey had a little boy last Christmas; Lizzie and Martin have been lucky at last; and Mum and Jube have got Flora, of course!'

'I hope I can be called Auntie May!'

'Of course you can. But you'll have a family of your own one day.'

May smiled. 'Perhaps. Maybe I'll be like Miss Worley and have lots of children, the sort you can send home at the end of the school day, eh? I'm not sure I need all these complications in my life, Georgia. Helga and I are happy as we are.'

'I'm glad. I really am,' Georgia said. 'Now I ought to get on, or Mum and Jube will be wondering where I am, and I want to see how Flora's grown. Mum says she's the image of Phoebe. Eva's two will be rushing round to see me, too.'

She thought, Bill will be ringing to see if I arrived safely. He won't ask what happened when I saw Kenny. I'll tell Bill how much I love him. And I'll save the best bit of news for when we're together again.

DISCOVER THE WORLD OF

Sheila Newberry

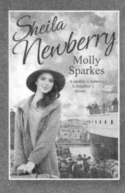

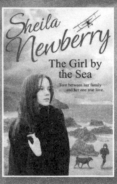

Available in ebook now

Z